The World of Mercury

The World of Mercury

by
Chevalier de Béthune

translated, annotated and introduced by
Brian Stableford

A Black Coat Press Book

ISBN 978-1-61227-410-2. First Printing. July 2015. Published by Black Coat Press, an imprint of Hollywood Comics.com, LLC, P.O. Box 17270, Encino, CA 91416. All rights reserved. Except for review purposes, no part of this book may be reproduced or transmitted in any form or by any means, electronic or mechanical, including photocopying, recording, or by any information storage and retrieval system, without permission in writing from the publisher. The stories and characters depicted in this novel are entirely fictional. Printed in the United States of America.

Introduction

Relation du monde de Mercure by the Chevalier de Béthune, here translated as *The World of Mercury*, was originally published in Geneva by Barilot et fils in 1750. The text was reprinted in Charles Garnier's classic set of *Voyages imaginaires, songes, visions et romans cabalistiques* (1787-1789), when it undoubtedly reached a larger audience than it did on its initial publication. There it was slotted into the final category of "cabalistic romances," by virtue of its frequent references to alchemy and its deployment of Rosicrucianism and other varieties of allegorical mysticism, although all of them are obviously ironic.

The Bibliothèque Nationale catalog does not attribute any dates to the author, and previous writers citing the work, including Charles Garnier, have not been able to say anything at all about him. The resources of the world wide web provide considerable detail regarding the various branches of the prolific Béthune family, but none of the members cited in the various guides to the French aristocracy who used the title "Chevalier de Béthune" was alive in 1750. The most likely candidate to be the author of the text, if the author does appear in the genealogical lists, was one of the sons of Henri de Béthune, Comte de Selles, Marie-Henri de Béthune, who died in Paris on 3 May 1744 at the age of 78.

It is, of course, possible that a family member who used a different title in everyday life—most of the family members had several, the majority being Comtes, Marquises or Ducs—employed a minor one for a signature, just as it is possible that someone who had no connection with the family simply borrowed their name as a pseudonym, but it seems much more likely after examination of the text, that the publication was posthumous—which would not be unusual for a book of such a sensitive nature that it had to be published in Geneva, although its author was clearly a resident of Paris.

At any rate, none of the references in the text suggest a date of composition later than 1715, the year in which Louis XIV died. There are numerous references to individuals active at Louis XIV's court, and the latter's reputation as the Sun King certainly seems to be wryly reflected in the text's celebrations of the Court of Mercury's Solar Emperor, so it does not seem at all implausible that the text might have been the work of a man born in 1666 into a family prominent at the Court of Versailles.

There is also a hint of nostalgia about some of the references, which suggests that the text might have been finished after 1715, whenever it was begun, but probably not long after. The book was first published after Voltaire's first few *contes philosophiques*, but before *Micromégas* (1752) or *Candide* (1759), and its publication also closely antedates the more extravagant works of Charles-François Tiphaigne de la Roche, *Amilec* (1753; augmented 1754) and *Giphantie* (1760)[1], but considering the text as if it were actually nearly contemporary with those works would probably be mistaken. *Relation du monde de Mercure* does have some resemblance to Tiphaigne's work, in terms of its imaginative scope and, in particular, its eventual supplementation of a fanciful, satirical, Rabelaisian and quasi-allegorical narrative with an earnest exposition of a pseudoscientific thesis that was obviously dear to the author's heart, and it is certainly possible that Tiphaigne took some influence from it, but in philosophical and literary terms, Béthune's text is evidently the product of an earlier era.

The patchwork nature of the work is not unusual for the time, but might well indicate a cobbling together of materials that had never been properly gathered and organized for publication by their author. If that had been done as a kind of memorial by another member of the family, one might have ex-

---

[1] Both translated. in *Amilec and Other Satirical Fantasies*, Black Coat Press, ISBN 978-1-61227-033-3.

pected a preliminary note of some kind to be attached to it, but the sensitive nature of some of the ideas expressed in the work, especially those relating to marriage and religion—like Voltaire, the author is a deist who has no sympathy at all with the dogmas of the Catholic Church—might have counseled discretion even in that regard. Whoever wrote the book, though, and however belatedly it worked its way into print, it is a spectacularly ground-breaking work, which took interplanetary satire to an entirely new level of hectic flamboyance.

The author acknowledges in his text the influence of Bernard le Bovier de Fontenelle's *Entretiens sur la pluralité des mondes* (1686; tr. as *Conversations on the Plurality of Worlds*), and one of the narrative's many functions is to extend the long-running argument relating to the plurality of worlds on to a much vaster stage than Fontenelle's, or the one depicted by Christiaan Huygens in *Kosmotheoros* (1698). To the notion that God would not have made a universe full of stars and planets without populating all of them, Béthune adds an elaborate system of linkage involving a complex and highly ordered system of cosmic palingenesis, long before Charles Bonnet's *Palingénésie philosophique* [Philosophical Palingenesis] (1769) repeated the notion of a soul's possible serial reincarnation on different worlds, much more tentatively, in the interests of a gradual ascent of a scale of moral perfection, in a more earnest framework. Béthune's work was published more than a hundred years ahead of Camille Flammarion's repopularization of the notion in the classic *Lumen* (1866-69; in *Récits de l'infini* 1872; separate publication 1887; expanded 1906; tr. as *Lumen*), on which it probably had some influence, Flammarion having had access to Garnier's *Voyages imaginaires, songes, visions et romans cabalistiques*.

Although Béthune's work cannot compete with Flammarion's, understandably, for the sophistication of its thinking with regard to the relativity of space and time and the ecology of adaptation to alien environments, it does have an edge in terms of the inordinate complexity of its palingenetic schema. Because it is innocent of any but the most rudimentary evolu-

7

tionary thinking, and its notions of chemistry and physics are primitive and vague, even by the standards of its time of publication, it is nevertheless possessed of an insistent sarcastic skepticism, which makes it one of the few "Creationist fantasies" entirely unhampered by any kind of religious dogma.

In developing the elaborate secondary creation of his world of Mercury, Béthune sets out to shape the kind of world that God might have built had he been somewhat more kindly inclined toward humans than the existential situation of Earthly humans suggests. His description of Mercury is very much a tongue-in-cheek exercise, with many elements of pure comedy, and his account of life there is far closer in spirit to the land of Cockayne than to any kind of political Utopia, but that certainly does not rob the thinking behind it of any ingenuity or zest—quite the contrary, in fact.

Seen as a whole, the work is certainly disorganized and rudderless, but the fact that it seems to have been written in fits and bursts, probably over a long period of time, in response to a series of disparate whims, with sections ranging in kind from lewd anecdote to ponderous allegory, undoubtedly encouraged the author to let his fancy fly freer that it could ever have done if he had attempted a more focused narrative with something vaguely resembling a plot or a story-line.

Because we now know that the author's pet medical theory is pure nonsense (as were all medical theories in the 18th century) the concluding section of the text is bound to seem a trifle tedious to modern readers, although its negative component, attacking the then-conventional treatment of bleeding, is equally bound to attract sympathy—but that section at least has the merit of being left until last, and the lavish compensation provided in advance is more than adequate in terms of its originality, its adventurousness and, especially, its sheer bizarrerie. In particular, the description of the aerial conflict between the defenders of Mercury's Great Mountain and the monstrous invaders from the "crust" expelled from the Sun is triumphantly eccentric, a match in its colorful extravagance for any space battle featured in the great tradition of 20th century space opera.

Whoever he really was, if he was not, in fact, the late Marie-Henri de Béthune, the Chevalier de Béthune could not begin to compete with Voltaire as a literary stylist, and must be reckoned inferior to Tiphaigne de la Roche in terms of his narrative coherency, but his text was a significant precursor of the new kind of *conte philosophique* that they developed, and he had the edge on both of them in terms of the reach of his imagination; his scheme of cosmic palingenesis remains the ultimate model in terms of its organizational planning and sheer bravado. The book would be remarkable for that alone, but there are many other delightful nuggets tucked away in the untidy folds of its sprawling patchwork.

As "utopian novels" go, *Relation du monde de Mercure* is a long way from the serious end of the spectrum, and it would be difficult to find many works less earnest in their descriptions of a supposedly ideal society. If it really were the case, however, that immortal human souls could eventually live, not only on all the worlds of our "Vortex" (the Cartesian term for what would now be called the Solar System), but all the worlds of any other Vortex that they eventually decided to visit, it is difficult to believe that they could ever find a world where the living was easier and more fun than Béthune's Mercury. For that reason, the book is certainly entitled to be considered a classic of sorts.

This translation was made from the copy of the Barilot et fils edition reproduced on the Bibliothèque Nationale's *gallica* website.

Brian Stableford

THE WORLD OF MERCURY

PART ONE

Advertisement

Everyone knows that the surest means of instruction is to disguise the counsels of reason beneath the veil of allegory.

Rome was on the brink of doom by virtue of a popular revolt against the Senate when the apologue of the limbs that refused their ministry to the stomach snatched the weapons from the hands of the frenzied populace and averted the storm in a trice.

The Athenians, intoxicated by prosperity and neglectful of their own security, seemed to be holding out their hands to Philip's chain when Demosthenes awakened them by means of a children's tale. That innocent artifice, having rendered the people attentive, produced the salutary decrees that would save the Republic.

Aesop, who knew the power of Fables, made use of them to form the mores of humans, having speech addressed to them by animals and insensible things; they would not have listened to Socrates, but they heeded the lessons of the Hare and the Crow.

It is with the same intention that Comedy was invented, and the counsels of Epictetus never corrected as much ridiculousness as the Theater of Molière has reformed for us.

The Account of Mercury is nothing but a Fable, in which an attempt has been made to combine ideas amusing by virtue of their novelty with a few useful observations. The opinion that leads us to believe that the planets are inhabited is so familiar to us, since we have seen the ingenious description of

11

the Worlds by Monsieur de Fontenelle, that there is no reason to fear that the Account of Mercury will pass for an absurd idea; since it seems, on the contrary, that one would be far more embarrassed seriously to deny the plurality of inhabited worlds than to sustain it in a very probable manner.

In fact, our Earth, which is swarming with inhabitants, cannot be anything but a Planet, since it fulfills all the functions of one, which are those of rotating about its center and circling around the Sun, being opaque, reflecting light and, finally, of always having one of its halves illuminated and the other in darkness. All that one can say about the Planets one can say about our Earth. If one saw it from afar, as one sees the Planets, one would find a perfect resemblance to them, and would admit that one could not imagine why the Sovereign Architect would have wanted to populate one rather than another; since there is not one of the Planets that does not merit being inhabited as much or more than our Earth, either by virtue of its far superior grandeur, by its more advantageous situation relative to the Sun, or by virtue of the more attentive care that the Author of Nature appears to have taken of the apparatus that accompanies them.

If the Planets are uninhabited, what is the point of the Sun rising and setting so regularly for them? What is the purpose of the light that is communicated to them if no one enjoys it, and why do the seasons follow one another on those Globes with the same regularity as on our Earth? Is it possible that God has made with such artistry such a great number of useless things? Is it imaginable that in forming those prodigious masses of matter, He only deigned to create immense deserts and frightful solitudes?

It is, therefore, generally suspected that all the Globes that turn around the Sun are inhabited, no longer excepting any but the Sun itself—which is doubtless a great pity, for, Suns being distributed innumerably throughout the space of the Universe, that is a great deal of wasted space; since every individual Sun is infinitely greater in itself than all the heavenly bodies that are enclosed in its Vortex.

But what appearance is there, it is said, that the Sun, which is nothing but a liquid Globe of light and flame, can be inhabited? What body could subsist for a moment in that fiery Vortex, since light that is merely reflected burns and devours everything on our Earth, in spite of the enormous distance of several millions of leagues that separates us from it? Let us remain in repose in that regard and leave the Omnipotent be; He would have no difficulty creating beings to whom fire would be as necessary for the conservation of their life as water is to fish or air to the inhabitants of our land.

Nothing, therefore, prevents the Sun being inhabited like the other Planets; it appears, on the contrary, more worthy of that distinction than they are, by virtue of the place that it occupies at the center of the Vortex and its prodigious grandeur; for Astronomers make it a million times larger than the Earth we inhabit. What a loss it would be for the Universe if such a vast terrain, so well placed to see the symmetry of the Universe, were absolutely useless?

In any case, if one supposes our Sun to be inhabited, as well as all the other Suns that swarm in the space of the World whose limits are unknown to us, what would be the number of their inhabitants, since those bodies are themselves innumerable and they are enormous in their grandeur! The imagination is veritably confounded here, losing itself in an endless calculation; but the further that calculation is beyond our comprehension, because it approaches infinity, the more worthy we ought to find it of the unlimited power of God.

The Author of the World of Mercury has not contented himself with rendering his fiction amusing, he has also had the design of making a light sketch and a kind of Essay of the variety that Nature is capable of distributing in all the Globes that he supposes might be habited.

He describes other rational Creatures, other Birds, other Fish, and often other ideas, in order to show that if a man has been able to imagine these varieties in a world he describes as pure fantasy, the Divinity ought not to have any difficulty in finding millions of others, all simpler and more reasonable, since they are founded on His infinite knowledge and a power that knows no bounds.

Preface

Mercury is so close to the Sun that it is almost swallowed up in its light, and escapes the attention of astronomers most of the time.

One morning, when I was observing the countryside a few moments before daybreak and was lamenting the sight of that little planet, almost effaced by the nascent light, I was surprised to hear footsteps nearby. I turned round with some anxiety and perceived an individual of respectable appearance, who was holding a little telescope in his hand.

"Monsieur," he said to me, "According to every appearance, the approach of daylight is interrupting your observation, but if you would like to continue it with this optical device, it will give you all the leisure that you need, and I hope that you will not be disappointed."

In spite of the scant reason I found in gazing at the stars with an instrument that seemed to me ill-fitted to that purpose, at a time when the Sun was about to appear, the attitude of the individual who was speaking to me imposed itself upon me in such a way that I did not disdain trying the experiment. I was very astonished, however, to see that instead of Mercury, for which I was searching, I encountered in my telescope an inhabited world, on which I could easily distinguish the beauties of the landscape and the movement of people and animals.

I thought at first that some unknown artifice contained in the telescope was presenting images to me, and, with that idea in mind, I was about to take it apart, in order to discover the case of such an agreeable illusion.

"Stop," said the owner of the instrument. "What you see is a philosophical microscope, in which you will only find glass and nothing more, but it is constructed with such artistry that it renders the most distant objects as visible as the nearest ones, the darkest as visible as the brightest. It is not yet perfect; I was just trying it out when I met you and I intend to finish it during the day. If you would like to test it tomorrow, not only will it enable you to see the stars and their inhabitants, but you will also discover by its means the elementary peoples, the Atoms of Epicurus, and even the movements of the soul and human intentions."

At this speech, I fell to my knees; I adored the individual who was speaking to me almost as a God, and I begged him in the most affectionate manner in the world not to permit the fortunate hazard that had put him in my path to be entirely useless to me.

"Celestial spirit," I said to him, "do not disdain to instruct a wretched and ignorant man, who only seeks to enlighten his reason by knowledge, and correct his mores by the study of the truth."

He reflected for a few moments before replying to me, and suddenly assumed a graver and more majestic attitude.

"My Son," he said to me, "for the supreme intelligence that inspires you tells me that you are not unworthy of that adoption, I am a Rosicrucian, whom my antiquity has set me almost at the head of that Order. Are you capable of entering a Society about which you have heard so many extravagant fables told?"

"Yes, my Father," I exclaimed, delightedly, "And I would give my life, if it were necessary to acquire such a rare joy."

"Nothing is impossible," replied the Sage. "Some of those who compose our Society are ready to quit it, to become Citizens of the Eternal Fatherland. That is what dying is called in our society. It only depends on me whether you will receive the first vacant place. It is merely a matter of knowing whether you have the necessary qualities. But it is dangerous to test that; your life is at stake; decide whether you want to run such a great risk."

"Yes, undoubtedly," I replied to him.

Then he told me to take a powder that he was carrying in a crystal phial. I obeyed, and I sneezed several times; although it was without violence, I sensed my soul separate from my body.

In fact, it remained in the arms of my Rosicrucian, who carefully laid it gently on the ground. As for my soul, it entered into a Myrtle[2] flower that was only two steps away.

What astonished me then was that the new organism did not prevent me from thinking, reasoning and even seeing objects as usual and judging them in the same way that I had done a few moments before.

While I was making these reflections a very bright flame emerged from the ground, consumed the bush on which I was, fortified my spirit and, running through my entire body, purified it in such a way that it was instantly rejuvenated, acquired an extreme lightness, became almost inalterable, and able to take on all possible forms, even the transparency of air or subtle matter.

Scarcely was it in that new state than my soul, which had emerged from it without wanting to, reentered it without thinking about it, by virtue of a kind of magnetic force.

"You have just made a perilous experiment," said my Rosicrucian, "and you have been great strengthened by it; but know now that if your soul had chosen any other plant than the Myrtle for incorporation, you would have died without resource. The choice it made of that tree consecrated to love marks the nobility of its nature; our souls sympathize with all plants in accordance with their inclinations, and always combine with them for a time before reentering the immense mass of intelligences.

"As soon as the bonds that attach them to their bodies are broken, that of a sad and severe man favors the cypress; a drunkard seeks the vine; a poltroon the sensitive plant or the

---

[2] It might be relevant that the French name of the myrtle (clearly the intended reference, give the subsequent mention of its symbolization of love), which would normally be rendered *myrte*, is given as *Mirthe* in the original, and that the English word "mirth" was occasionally spelled "mirthe" in old texts.

truffle; a light, weak and inconstant character attaches itself to a reed, an effeminate one to a jasmine, a presumptuous one to a pumpkin; a flatterer to a melon; a perfidious one to a rose-bush, etc. Souls of all those tempers are unsuited to our mysteries. Those whose faults we know are abandoned in the proof that you have just undergone; their bodies destroy themselves and they remain attached to the plants that are sympathetic to them, until hazard separates them in the destruction of the plants.

"That is how the fables of Dryads, Fauns and the prophetic oaks of Dodona came into the world. That is what I wanted to teach you, because there are secrets unknown on this earth where you live. Furthermore, these verities are the elements if the veritable Philosophy.

"Now I have to ask you two questions: are you in love and do you know Arabic?"

"Yes and no," I replied.

"I understand," he said. "You have more sentiment than doctrine; so much the better, for it will also be necessary to forget everything that you have learned without our help. Any human science whatever is always imperfect, but we provide in a moment all sorts of knowledge and the habitude of all the arts; it is only the sensibility of the soul, which we regard as the foremost of virtues, that we are unable to give. But in order not to leave you with dry instructions and without experience of our power, I shall teach you Arabic instantaneously. Pass your thumb between the first two fingers of your right hand and place the little finger of the same hand on your forehead, turning toward the four parts of the world."

My turn was scarcely complete when the Philosopher began speaking Arabic to me, and I understood it like my natural language. I threw myself at his feet for a second time.

"Get up," he said, "and if you are content, begin your novitiate. There is one law from which no one can be exempt. It is necessary for everyone, before being received among us, to have done something for the good or the pleasure of the humans that he is about to quit. That task is at the discretion of the person who is our sponsor; I am yours, and I shall only order you to translate into your language an Account that I shall make in ours of the World of Mercury. You know that the language of the Sages is Arabic; the attention with which I have seen you observing the planet whose History you will transcribe assures me that the work will not be disagreeable to you, and I hope that it will be of some utility in society."

At that moment, I took the manuscript that he gave me, and went to shut myself in my home. I then began the translation that follows.

CHAPTER I
A Description of Mercury

Mercury, which we regard as a planet, like all the heavenly bodies we perceive, is a world like our Earth, except that it is considerably smaller and, being much closer to the Sun, the Nature of which the latter is the parent seems to have taken pleasure in enriching it with all her gifts and in embellishing it with more cheerful and more numerous varieties than those with which she adorns the rest of the Universe.

Because Mercury is smaller than the Earth, the land, the mountains, the seas, the trees, the plants the animals and the people are also smaller than they are here. There are few rivers deeper than our shallow springs. The highest mountains do not much exceed our hills, but some of them nonetheless have in that modest height the lofty air of the Alps and the Pyrenees. The highest trees are similar to our potted orange-trees, and there are few flowers which rise higher above the ground than the jonquil and the narcissus.

The entire globe in strewn with little mountains that spread in the valleys they leave between them a shade that is infinitely necessary in that burning world. Those mountains are almost always covered in trees, which are laden with flowers at all times. They perfume the air, and those flowers, which do not produce any fruits, are eternal, for in the world of Mercury, the subsistence of the inhabitants is not cultivated as it is here; benevolent Nature furnishes it herself, and hides the places that serve as storehouses, in order only to leave within the range of people objects that are always cheerful and solely appropriate to pleasure.

CHAPTER II
The Inhabitants of Mercury

They are all shorter than humans of the smallest stature, as tall at the most as a five-year-old child. With regard to facial features and the form of the body they resemble the charming ideas we have of zephyrs and genii. Their beauty only fades after several centuries; youth, health and delicacy seem inalterable there. If it happens, however, that by some error of Nature someone is not content with their face, there are means, as we shall see in due course, of correcting the faults that are reproached.

All of those small people have wings, of which they make use with a marvelous grace and agility; and although the ardor of the Sun prevents them from flying high enough to emerge from the shade of their mountains, they nevertheless fly from one place to another very easily. In truth, they prefer to walk, and only to make use of their wings for the sake of grace.

The women have wings too, which they take off and put on again at will, as the women of our world do with their gloves and fans. They attach them with ribbons, and make use of them with as much facility as if they were natural. Although they dread difficulty, they almost never go out without them, whether to satisfy some new taste, to seek some new pleasure, or for other reasons that we shall see in due course.

CHAPTER III
On the Emperor and the Government

The title of Emperor is given to the unique Sovereign of Mercury. It is not that the planet is not divided into numerous kingdoms, but they are all governed by Viceroys dependent on the Emperor, who can allow them to continue their government or recall them at will.

Once, in a time that is barely remembered, there were several states there—which is to say, several Monarchies, and a few Republics. I shall not say anything about those remote centuries, the extreme distance of which renders history susceptible to an infinity of fables, restricting myself to talking about the reign of the Emperors, the history of which is very faithfully conserved.

One day, so the story goes, when the air was very pure and the sky very serene, a dense could was seen descending, as if from the limits of the Universe, and arriving over the planet. That cloud was separate from any other exhalation and floated alone in the air currents. As it drew closer, brilliant streaks of fire and light were distinguished, which caused the people of Mercury, unaccustomed to meteors, to fear some frightful ravage, or, at least, that they were about to witness an unprecedented spectacle.

It was, in fact, new to them; the cloud came very close to the ground, in order to be seen without difficulty, and everyone then remarked that there were luminous characters in different parts of the cloud, which distinctly formed these words: *Adore the divine power that destines a new Master for you, the only one worthy to command you, and submit to his Laws.*

The cloud remained in the same place for some time and allowed the planet to rotate beneath it in order to be seen by all the peoples. Then, suddenly sinking down, and extending ever further, it fused with the ground. By virtue of a marvel that could not be admired too much, a large and superb city stood in the place where the cloud had dissipated. All the people of the surrounding areas saw with an admiration that had no limit the surprising marvel that had just burst forth before their eyes.

That enchanted abode was entered by a hundred open gates; a hundred streets led to the square of the Emperor's Palace. It was huge and magnificently ornamented, but the house that occupied the middle of the square was so magnificent and pleasant to behold that it is easier to imagine than to describe. I shall nevertheless give a plan of it one day, based on the memory of a Salamander—you will discover in due course what the Salamanders are—who knows it as well as my own, which he has done me the honor of entering at least once a week for a thousand years.

The Emperor was in his palace, surrounded by an innumerable crowd of his friends, who had accompanied him in order to install him on his new throne—or, rather to see him for longer; for, to tell the truth, their help was quite unnecessary, the will of the one who sent him to govern Mercury being sufficient guarantee that he would be well-received.

The Emperor's retinue, and the Emperor himself, as I think you will be impatient to know, were inhabitants of the Sun, whom the Supreme Intelligence had destined to govern the planet Mercury.

The inhabitants of the Sun have no bodies, or at least, none sensible to our eyes, and if those Intelligences are linked to some portion of matter, it is so subtle that they alone are capable of perceiving it; but when it pleases them to render themselves visible, they build a body as they please, which is very easy for them because matter is obedient to their will.

The first Emperor of Mercury and all those who have succeeded him made a body similar to those of the people they had come to govern. In truth, it is more perfect than theirs, and nothing that could be imagined or painted could approach the graces of the one who had just established in the will of his people an empire as full of charm as of equity.

Some of those who had accompanied the Emperor spread out in a short time throughout the Planet, and recounted to all the inhabitants of distant places the marvel that had only been seen in one place. The neighbors of the Imperial City flocked there in crowds, attracted by the novelty of the spectacle; they could not weary of admiring it.

The Emperor soon knew, on his own account and by the reports of the friends that had followed him, the merit and capacity of all his subjects; for although I have said that there are no people more accomplished than those of Mercury, that does not exclude the inequality of merit, talents and virtues. There is only the Sun where everything is uniform and perfect, inasmuch as any creature of Being can be.

The Emperor having been thus informed of the personal qualities of all individuals, he called to his Court those he judged it appropriate to place under his orders at the head of affairs, and sent some of them to install themselves in the various States that had been formed on the Planet by the ordinary ideas of the people.

In a matter of days the entire Empire was submissive to him, and if the Tyrants and Chiefs of Republics had tried to resist, they would only have made futile attempts, belied by the general revolt of peoples who submitted to their new Master more by inclination than necessity.

After having applied himself to his first duty, the Emperor thought about making new Laws, but only did so after having assembled delegates of all his Subjects and having permitted them to represent their needs or explain their desires, regarding it as a crime to render the people happy against their will.

He reserved the unique right to show them their veritable interests, in cases where they presented requests to him that were contrary to them; at the same time he swore an authentic oath to prefer the ideas of his Subjects to the Regulations that he wanted to make and his own views, except to abrogate their consent with regard to decrees whose danger and inconvenience was recognized subsequently.

CHAPTER IV
Fundamental and Imperial Laws
The Form of the Oath that
the Emperor Pronounced

1. I swear to leave to the peoples who have sworn an oath of fidelity the full enjoyment of their liberty, their property, their tastes, their speech and their actions, provided that the general good does not suffer therefrom.

2. As I only accept the Empire for love of my Subjects, it will be permitted to them to assemble to request a new Master from the Sun as soon as they cease to be content with me or my successors.

3. I oblige myself to be accessible at all times to all my Subjects and never to put off until tomorrow opportunities to render them justice or accord them graces.

4. Nothing of importance shall be done in the State without the advice of Delegates of every Order having been sought, to whom I ordain to that effect a continual residence at Court.

5. It is forbidden under the most rigorous penalties to anyone whatsoever to spend more than thirty-three hours—which are three Mercurian days—in a situation disagreeable to body, spirit or fortune without taking steps to inform His Imperial Majesty, who will attend to it without delay.

That small quantity of essential articles sworn by the Emperor and rendered public was avidly welcomed by the people. He then made a few police regulations, which are too long to report here, but which will be cited later when I talk about the mores and customs of the people,

Ordinarily, an Emperor only reigns on Mercury for a hundred years. When that term expires he returns to the Sun, leaving his petrified body on Mercury in the attitude it most commonly adopted. The body, thus rendered incorruptible, loses none of the attributes with which he had animated it except speech and movement; all the rest is conserved: color, youth, the brilliance of the eyes, and the sheen of the complexion.

Such a precious statue is conserved in a Palace destined for that sole purpose. Each Emperor has left his portrait in that fashion, and it is called by a name which becomes that of the Imperial Cenotaph.

The Inhabitant of the Sun who replaces the defunct Emperor places himself on the Throne without pomp and ceremony, except that he convenes an Assembly, the most general possible, in order to swear in public the observation of the laws and to make known to everyone the form in which he has made himself visible. For although the Emperors have all taken a body similar to those of the people of Mercury, as I have said, they can take the form of a animal, a plant or any being they please.

Their infinite intelligence has the power to organize all kinds of forms and to render them capable of human functions, so the Emperor is able to metamorphose in any manner and as often as he wishes. That talent, which he is able to communicate in perpetuity or for a fixed time to any of his subjects, is one of the finest rights of the Crown, and the one with which he is the most economical. If I have time, I shall relate a few singular adventures the occurred by the use of those transformations, for which I think you might be grateful.

CHAPTER V
On Life, Temperament and the most common Maladies on Mercury

The temperament of those people is firmer than those in the rest of the Vortex; all of nature contributes to that. The ardor of the Sun dissipates harmful vapors that might form in the air. and the earth, always penetrated by the first trays of light, only exhales a benevolent dew. Nourishment there is always healthy and succulent, and the taxing endeavors that it is necessary to undertake in our world to acquire useful and delicious things are banished from this Planet.

In addition, the people of Mercury are the absolute masters of the movements that take place within their bodies. They regulate the circulation of their blood in accordance with what they intend to do; they maintain their stomach by the use of certain delicious elixirs, the effect of which is unfailing, and they are also sure of a perfect digestion, as we are of having clean hands, after washing them well.

All the mechanisms that so often refuse to obey us are submissive their will; it is only the movements of the soul, which we call sentiments, that they cannot regulate by choice. Thus, they are the sources of all their maladies, and sometimes of their death. But those who are fortunate enough not to have overly keen passions have almost nothing to fear and they can enjoy an almost eternal youth.

It is true nevertheless that age imprints its sad character, as it does elsewhere, but it is scarcely sensible. It only blackens one plume of their wings in half a century, and it is always the smallest and most hidden ones that tarnish first; thus, it requires a prodigious number of years for the accusing feathers to have any consequence, and they still only harm opinion, for all the graces of youth and all the strength of maturity are perpetuated in spite of the blackening of the plumage.

Thus, one sees every day pretty women with black plumes disputing conquests with rosy-tinted wings, who can acquit themselves by never wearing their own. In the long run, however, those bold enterprises are not entirely successful; hidden wings often give rise to suspicions more injurious than the truth, which means that women rarely make use of the liberty they have to leave them in their wardrobes. For men, as theirs are inseparable, their birth certificate is written, much as it is in our world, where it can be read in the face.

The inhabitants of Mercury never sleep; the proximity of the Sun maintains a perpetual movement on the Planet, which can only be slowed down by major accidents, when all those who fall into inaction find themselves in manifest peril. That is why one of the greatest tortures to which criminals are condemned is that of sleeping for a few days. There are soporific poisons of which the Sovereign Council is the custodian; it prescribes them to guilty parties in proportion to their faults, and only an enormous crime can be punished by a week-long sleep. The torpor of the soul, and what are known in our world as idleness and nonchalance, are very considerable maladies among these people; anything that can cause such accidents is regarded as very contagious.

Boredom, for example, is harmful to the highest degree, and everything that can cause it is reputed to be dangerous and unhealthy: leaden conversation, a relation by a distracted person, cold music, passable verses, the absence of a loved one, the presence of someone annoying, etc., can all bring plague on Mercury. People therefore take great care to avoid bad moods, and even encountering those who are in them; that is why the Police maintain order by obliging people afflicted by those infirmities, under the threat of heavy penalties, to wear masks that everyone recognizes.

Thus, someone who goes out with someone boring has to keep a fan in hand in order to chase away the contagion; and furthermore, it is forbidden for him to go into an honest house for twenty-four hours thereafter. It is said that certain glutinous substances remain after such a visit, capable of infecting the most vivid imagination and stifling all the forces of the soul.

Encountering a fool, a pedant, a devotee or an affected woman—for they are also found on Mercury—obliges the person who has done so to carry a whip garnished with little bells, as if to drive away those infections and to warn anyone who happen to find themselves in his path.

There are a few other maladies, the symptoms of which are manifest spontaneously. A presumptuous individual, for instance, swells up like our hydropics; the extremely ignorant contract a sort of paralysis; anyone who talks about himself loses as many feathers from his wings as he has given himself items of praise, true or false; misers melt away visibly and are finally annihilated; flatterers die by force of laughter; traitors and liars, only forming a single class, become as transparent and as brittle as crystal, so that they usually die shattered into a thousand pieces.

To avoid all these evils, it is only necessary to follow the counsels of reason and the intentions of Nature—which is to say, to refresh oneself in the pleasures that she inspires and permits, and to yield in moderation to the tastes that she distributes to people with prodigious abundance and variety.

By following this facile regime one can live forever on Mercury, or at least as long as one desires, In fact, there are some among the inhabitants of the Planet who have been there for as long as it has been circling the Sun. In truth, the majority weary of such a long life and are eventually tempted to reunite with the great principle—which is to say, to go to populate the Sun; for the certain knowledge they have of their condition after death, founded on the indubitable word of the Emperor, enables them to have no dread.

CHAPTER VI
On Death

This is what they do in that circumstance. When someone want to quit the Planet, he assembles his friends and distributes his talents to them. For, in order that you should know, the gifts of the soul and its acquired qualities are reckoned to be movable effects on Mercury, and one can leave the usufruct to anyone one desires, after which one returns to the common mass, as you shall see from what follows.

So, the voyager, as the dying individual is called, asks five or six witnesses whether anyone has need of any of his favors, which he only holds by courtesy of Nature.

In order to understand the voyager's discourse, it is necessary to know that in all the Planet there can only by a certain portion of beauty, of pleasure, of strength and skill; but by virtue of a particular favor that the Emperor is able to accord the globe he governs, all the corporeal talents left vacant by the death of an inhabitant of Mercury have to be divided between the survivors in accordance with their choice. Thus, those who are content with their faces, which make up the greater number, make no claim on that part of the succession, but the others have the right to request part of the voyager's residue.

By virtue of that right, a hunchback can inherit in an instant a beautiful stature; an awkward person an easy manner; a base physiognomy a fine face; a cripple one or two sound limbs. If one were bald, one could suddenly gain by that stock-transfer an admirable natural hairpiece. In sum everyone can request what they imagine will suit them most, and can obtain it. As soon as the voyager has quit the Planet, the exchange is made in an imperceptible manner.

As often occurs on the departure of a beautiful person, if several people find themselves in competition for the advantage, the aspirants regulate their pretentions with three dice, by means of the highest point-score, but as there is something impolite about disputing the future residues of the voyager in that manner, the losers are condemned to do before everyone that which is expressed by our proverb *Qui a perdu gratte*, etc.[3] As for those who have won, or with whom no one competes, they all leave the house of the dying person as soon as their requests have been noted.

His most intimate friends stay with him, and they hold a communal celebration, after which the voyager is read a detailed list of the benefits that await him and a description of the world to which he is going. That relation, which is always known by heart and which is long, bores him and puts him to sleep; at that moment his body is divided and in next to no time is reduced to a fine powder which resembles gold. That is the ultimate reduction of the body on Mercury, and what might be called the ashes of the dead. Then the perfections that he possessed pass on to those who desired them, and nothing remains of him but that pinch of powder, which is soon devoured in its turn by the elements.

---

[3] Actually, this "proverb" does not seem to exist anywhere else but in the present text. It signifies, roughly "Who has lost, scrapes."

CHAPTER VII
On Talents in General

There are two kinds: those which are solely due to the liberalities of nature and those that one can acquire by art and study.

The former cannot be alienated except by dying, as you have seen. All the others, on Mercury, can be conserved, communicated, sold and bartered like jewels and clothes.

Over and above the institution of Nature, a Painter, a Geometer or a Musician is free to pass on acquired talents by sale or exchange and transmit them to anyone who wishes, by paying, to acquire them without difficulty. As soon as the agreed price has been paid, the purchaser enjoys the talent that he has bought and the vendor is deprived of it. All the liberal and mechanical Arts are amenable to that species of commerce.

In truth, those who surrender the precious property lose esteem to the same degree as those who acquire it gain esteem, for in this world, in which intelligence is regarded as a treasure, anything that enhances it, extends its knowledge and ennobles it seems priceless. That is why there are many more potential buyers than sellers of talents. There are, however, some, and on Mercury, as on our world, those favored by fortune can find anything that they desire.

It is perhaps that custom of buying talents on Mercury that gave rise to our proverb which says that people of quality know everything without learning anything. It is not impossible that some of the sages who travel incessantly between the Planets have said on our world that talents and the ornaments of intelligence can be acquired on Mercury at a monetary price. By virtue of that, our rich individuals, who think themselves very great, are able to imagine that by paying their Masters dearly, they can do likewise, and that a talent for which a high enough price is paid can be sufficiently acquired.

Unfortunately, that privilege, particular to the world of Mercury, has not reached our Planet, and whatever price it costs the Proselytes of Science and the Arts, they can only acquire without study and effort a few specious terms and phrases, appropriate at the most to impress a vulgar imbecile.

Another way of obtaining talents is to become a pupil of someone who possesses them; in that case the master and the person who can be regarded as the apprentice agree on certain terms of service, which the proselyte must fulfill, and, depending on whether he acquits himself to his master's liking, the Art or the Science is lodged in his intelligence and the appropriate organ.

Thus, someone who serves an Orator carefully and in an agreeable manner will acquire perfect eloquence; his voice will become sonorous, extended, harmonious; the decorum of gesture will take possession of his arms and hands, and the pathos that works in favor of an Orator will spread throughout his entire personality, while his mind will be furnished with all the necessary knowledge and Art that informed Aristotle, Longinus and Cicero.

But if it is the case that a negligent or surly student is insufficiently industrious to make his services agreeable, he will find himself no further advanced at the end of his apprenticeship than on the first day, for Nature is so attentive to the wellbeing of the people of this Planet that she only recompenses in some the benefits that they provide to others.

It is not sufficient for the good of society that people mutually render one another real services; it is also necessary that the price of cares of services be augmented by the attention to render them agreeable to the recipients; a friend, a relative or a domestic will be poorly recompensed on Mercury if they undertake to procure someone real benefits that are unwanted. That habit of our world is proscribed on Mercury; the zealous but importunate amity of someone who tries to render another happy against his will is considered there to be hatred.

CHAPTER VIII
Aliments

On this Planet there are no cooks, restaurateurs, confectioners or any of those Officers to whom the delicacy—or, rather, the falsity—of our taste gives so much employment on our world. Nature takes care herself of preparing and seasoning in an exquisite manner the meals of the fortunate inhabitants. It does not cost the lives of any animals, as in our world; on the contrary, they are the concern of human nourishment. This is how it works.

I have said that, the country being extremely hot by virtue of its proximity to the Sun, ever-wise Nature has distributed an infinity of small mountains, which are covered at all times to a certain height by trees, flowers, grass and an extremely fresh and brilliant moss. The summits of these hills are steep and seem arid, like our most impracticable rocks; it is in these seemingly sterile places that Nature lavishes the most precious treasures. The rocks in question terminate in a kind of platform, on which delicious foodstuffs grow and are conserved at all times.

All the tastes that are distributed in other worlds obtain their origin from the Sun and, stopping first on Mercury, those influences, instead of spreading out over the entire terrain, are concentrated on these hills; there they produce fruits of all the species we know and an infinity of others of which we do not have the slightest idea.

These fruits—for it is necessary to give them a name—enclose all possible favors. One pumpkin, for example, speckled in a certain manner, will have the taste of an excellent bisque, another will be an Amiens pâté, a calabash, a Meccan ham, etc. An excellent broth can be found in a cassia stalk and ready-roasted ortolans can be picked in pods like our broad beans; a Rambour apple is a partridge, the stem of a cabbage is a white sausage, and little bushes similar to our gooseberries bear English oysters in shells the color of fire. It is in that fortunate world, and no other, that turnips are sweet.

Beverages are found ready-made and totally refreshing in crystal carafes, which it is only necessary to take back to where one obtained them for them to be refilled. All the wines that we know and all those that are drunk on Mars, Jupiter and Saturn are found there; the source is inexhaustible, since it comes from the influences of the Sun.

It only remains to describe the manner of going to find on these steep mountains the fruits and liquors that one desires. One might imagine at first that it is difficult, but we can depend on the supreme intelligence not to lack expedients to render its favorite people happy.

Large birds of an agreeable forms, painted in all the colors and more affectionate to people than our dogs, are the Planet's purveyors.

These birds are very common and extremely familiar. There is no one on Mercury who does not have several in their service, without buying them or taking them treacherously, for it is sufficient to call them. On Mercury there is a general language, which everyone knows, which is called the language of animals. They all understand it, and it is almost as extensive as the human language. They know it by nature and possess it from birth; in truth, they cannot speak it, because they lack vocal organs, but they nevertheless make good use of it for they understand it marvelously.

These birds, which are strong and very rapid in flight, are ever ready to be commanded. As soon as one has said what one wishes and has furnished them with a basket appropriate to its transportation, they depart diligently.

They always work in pairs; one chooses whatever has been requested and arranges it in the basket with its feet and beak, and its comrade brings it back. If the carrier is unable to acquit its commission because of some accident, such as dying *en route*, the one that is free takes its place and returns promptly to serve its master.

When several inhabitants of Mercury eat together, which is quite usual, each sends his own purveyors and the meal is served almost as soon as it is commanded, so alert and careful are the marvelous birds.

CHAPTER IX
Domestics

In addition to the winged domestics, which are principally destined carry out errands over some distance, there are others for inside the house and for ordinary service. They are not slaves, but people who are reduced by their own fault to that unfortunate condition, such as those who, for want of cultivating their talents, have allowed them to be lost, and no longer have any but that of serving others, and also those ruined by the dementia of excessive passions, of whatever kind.

Domestic servants are also taken from people who have fallen in status. That misfortune happens to the third member of a family of father and son, who is found to be devoid of merit and intelligence and useless to the State, and to those who are dishonored in public Charges by ill intention or incapacity. On Mercury anyone who fails in his duty by virtues of stupidity is punished, like those who prevaricate deliberately—because the Public suffers equally—and anyone guilty of having applied for an employment that he does not know how to fulfill adequately, as if they had betrayed the State.

It is futile to say, to excuse someone who had taken an employment without the required capability that self-esteem blinds all men, that everyone adjudges in good faith that he has more merits than he veritably has, and that one can be mistaken without being criminal. The excuse is accepted when the Public does not suffer, but in Employments it is frivolous, the inhabitants of Mercury say, for the means of knowing oneself are innumerable, if we will only pay attention to that which regards us.

A hundred times a day, they add, we appreciate that which surrounds us, and our intrinsic value is what shows itself to us most often, with the result that a week of attention, at the most, can enable to most limited imbecile to know what everyone thinks of him.

The eyes and the countenance of those who listen to us reveal to us without difficulty their disposition in our regard. The yawns of a man of intelligence, or his distraction, are marks of our failure to please; his hasty, sharp or disdainful interruptions mark the insufficiency of our reasoning. A bitter smile on his part shows the indignation that the incapacity of the speaker causes him, whom he nevertheless does not want to interrupt out of regard for politeness; and if he shrugs his shoulders, the absurdity must have reached its peak.

On noticing some of these things, therefore, when one encounters people who are generally esteemed, one cannot doubt their opinion of us, and in consequence that which everyone will have.

Another reliable indication of our worth is the haste or indifference that those same people show for our commerce, for it cannot be imagined that a conceited fop, an imbecile or a man devoid of merit would ever be sought out by anyone, if not for some wretched reason of interest, or human respect compelling an honest man—but in that case, his constraint reveals his sentiment.

It is, therefore, with reason that having a false opinion of oneself is punished on Mercury, since, in order to have a true one, it is only necessary to open one's eyes and ears.

A third species of domestics, who might be called pupils, consists of people who, not having sufficient wealth to buy talents or qualities of the soul attach themselves to those who possess them in order to acquire them by habitude or imitation. In fact, in the commerce of those who are superior to us in knowledge, taste or talent, the soul is cleaned, instructed, stripped of prejudices, acquires enlightenment, obtains a taste for the Arts, and becomes accustomed to making use of its own rationality—which ought to be regarded as the most sublime of all the sciences.

One man becomes fond of geometry in the home of a Geometer; another studies nature in serving a Physician; a third man acquires the graces of eloquence in the familiarity of a Salamander; a woman gains politeness and social graces in the home of a Courtesan; a pretty girl sometimes makes use of another less so than her, but more knowledgeable in the art of self-presentation, wittier, more refined and, in consequence, more capable of instructing her in delicate coquetry, so necessary to anyone wishing to please for a long time.

An infinite number of other reasons, which are easily imaginable, attract pupils. One often finds more than one wants, and there are even some that one rejects; they are the ones that one suspects of only wanting to acquire talents in order to sell them, or to make a kind of traffic of them, which is considered dishonest.

Those people are regarded as, in our world, we regard women who make a commerce of their beauty for money; that kind of negotiation is not forbidden, but the people who carry it out are scorned, because it goes directly against the intentions of nature to traffic in the precious gifts that we obtain from her, and which she gives us *gratis*, with the design that we should do likewise. Thus, that species of simony turns to dishonor, and the brokerage of qualities of the soul or talents of the mind is reputed on Mercury as a shameful stain.

CHAPTER X
Animals in General, and their Language

The Animals of Mercury are proportionate to the size of their planet, and are consequently much smaller than ours, but they are not very different with regard to species and form. Furthermore, their brains being much better composed than those of the brutes of our world, they are, generally speaking, more intelligent than them. They are also different in their natural inclinations, in the education they receive from humans and the employments to which they are destined.

In truth, those whose nature renders them less sociable are still gross and ferocious, as among us; the Lions and Tigers of Mercury do not engage in a commerce as mild as that of sheep and dogs, even though they understand the general language. For those we call domestic, however, it is amazing how docile they are and how desirous they are of making themselves useful to people.

As I have said, they cannot speak, but instead of the voice that Nature has refused them, she has endowed them with a mute language composed of expressions, actions and different postures, which are scarcely less intelligible than speech, and the people of Mercury understand them better than the inhabitants of a Seraglio understand the mutes, whose language is perfectly clear to those who are accustomed to it.

It is in that language that they testify to humans that they understand them and that they take account of the commissions with which they are charged. They even make use of it for conversation, and one can sometimes communicate with a nightingale in a wood as reasonably as with a sensitive person.

It is true that in those species one affects only to talk about matters appropriate to the animal one is with. For example, a conversation with a nightingale does not treat morality or politics, but the beauty of the day and the pleasant nature of the landscape; one talks about trees, flowers, plants, one's mistress, amour, one's comrades, or one's adventures. All these bagatelles, treated with artistry, are a sufficiently abundant resource, although they seem at first to be quite simple. It even happens that in conversing thus, one is instructed as to a thousand properties of plants, the singularity of places, and finds the opportunity to notice many things that reveal Nature, and educate us more fully than a more serious study could.

What I say about a nightingale applies equally to a wolf, a snake or a hare, provided that the prudence of humans leads them to choose subjects of conversation proportionate to the range of each species. One can easily appreciate that a leopard does not reason like a leveret, a turkey like a fox, or at tiger like a rabbit, but natural politeness demands that one is sociable, and only talks to others about matters suitable to them.

The animals on Mercury do not eat one another, but one sees nonetheless between various species the antipathies that we see among those of our world. The difference there is between the animals of that Planet and ours is that instead of setting ambushes for one another and employing cunning to destroy one another, as it were, stealthily, they make open warfare between nations, until one of the parties, weary or weaker, cedes the terrain to the victor and sues for peace. They sometimes make it the negotiation of the two parties, sometimes by the mediation of a neutral species, often via the intermediary of humans, who act as guarantors of treaties; in that case they are very solid, both sides fearing equally to break them.

It is not that humans ever amuse themselves by getting actively mixed up in these quarrels, nor that they take action against the breakers of treaties, but they counsel the injured parties and inform them of means to render themselves superior to their enemies, so such conventions are very rarely violated. All the animals of the Planet respect them and even the most indocile of its inhabitants, the lion, thinks twice before declaring war on the red deer or the roe deer when they make a collective peace via the mediation of our species. That is what ensures that, in spite of their antipathy, one sees them living together with sufficient familiarity, greeting one another when they meet, chatting gaily, inviting one another to meals and making alliances and marriages, which seems rather disproportionate but are authorized and rendered viable by political interests.

That is why one is not really surprised on Mercury to see a tiger making love to a pretty hind or a wolf flirting with a goat. People very worthy of faith have assured me that they have seen foxes highly reputed among their own kind attach themselves to fluffy young chickens and defend them against eagles or hawks at the peril of their own lives. Such alliances are no more shocking on Mercury than those of our world appear strange to us. Are we surprised here to see serious men of decrepit age marrying young coquettes? Do not the greatest Lords seek alliances with uncouth individuals who enrich themselves by the most garish concussions? Everyone knows that it is not without example for a Magistrate to marry an actress.

CHAPTER XI
On the Nourishment of Animals

The land furnishes all animals with the nourishment appropriate to them, and although they do not graze pasture, and browse neither flowers or bushes, they have an abundance of all the aliments necessary and appropriate to their nature. The pebbles furnish them; all stones emit a kind of universal sap, which humans find insipid, but of which all the animals that suck it are exceedingly fond; everyone knows by virtue of the commerce they have with the animals that it tastes admirable to them.

The carnivorous beasts sense the taste of meat therein; the animals that browse compare it to fruits and vegetables; the birds think they are eating bread soaked in milk and cakes baked with eggs. In sum, each species is content with the aliments destined for it, using them deliciously and without difficulty, finding what is necessary to them everywhere and in all seasons.

Thus, the animals of Mercury enjoy the most perfect liberty that there is in nature, for they only recognize the empire of humans to the extent that they love them, and are not enslaved by any force or law or by violence—for the inhabitants of Mercury are too opposed to tyranny to put animals in chains, to keep birds in cages and to force them to serve by constraint.

Nature has established between humans and animals a much gentler kind of subordination; amity is its only bond. Animals attach themselves to humans by a sympathetic inclination that nothing can destroy, and by the force of that instinct they are always disposed to render them all possible services, each according to its small talents. The better they are treated and welcomed, the more committed they are, for the politeness of superiors is one of the strongest bonds of that species of commerce.

I will give a few examples of the service ordinarily obtained from animals.

If a man wants to compete in a public race, and courts the amity of extremely fast stags and horses, they come of their own accord to be hitched to his carriage, and without any need for a coachman, because they understand the universal language, they make every effort to vanquish the speed of the opposing party.

Is it a matter of having excellent Marionettes? Parrots learn by heart speeches of an astonishing length, and are directed by signs to make admirable gibes at a Polichinelle who is usually an old fox. Apes dance on tightropes and perform perfect pantomime tricks of their own accord; kittens catch mice there and play with them without hurting them, with the naïve grace particular to them, and canaries sing tremulous tunes in the intermission that would put Descoteaux[4] to shame.

Does someone want to build a house? Foxes, rabbits and moles will excavate the foundations; beavers will cut down big trees and fashion them; donkeys will carry the large pieces of fashioned wood on their backs, if one wants to make use of them; bears will take charge of the materials that it is necessary to carry up the scaffolding by means of ladders to the top of the building, and elephants will use their trunks and cranes to lift the heavier burdens. Thus, the workmen only have to put them to work, and only have to pay the zealous animals in politeness.

They do even better; when the edifice is finished and it is necessary to decorate the interior, the elephants will furnish ivory *gratis*, the tortoise will donate its shell and the fish that lives in nacre will furnish pearls and precious shells, with which the prettiest grottos in the world can be made. Silk-

---

[4] René Pignon Descoteaux (1645-1732) was a flute-player who was a member of Louis XIV's "Grande Écurie" until the king's death. If the author of the present text really was Marie-Henri de Béthune, he would certainly have heard Descoteaux play in his younger days.

worms are no more miserly with their labor; it is not only that the moths, which mutate four times a year, offer their cast-off clothing with pleasure; the admirable colors with which their wings are painted never fade, and I remember having seen studies furnished with fabrics to which they have applied and bound themselves artfully, which created a brilliant and very varied spectacle.

It is not necessary to kill geese or swans to obtain their quills; they carefully pick up all those that they shed, and make a present of them to those they love, as if by way of a kind of homage.

All the birds sing pleasantly, and do not make a racket, as ours do, but sing in concert, which they have the art of varying infinitely. What is admirable about it is that they compose it as they go along, and never repeat the same thing without ornamenting it with new decorations.

The fish on Mercury are no less useful, nor less agreeable in communication; like other animals, they understand the general language. The fish all have little feet; they can live for some time out of water, and attempt excursions of four or five paces without dying; in truth, their gait is rather awkward, and befits them less than swimming, but they nevertheless take advantage of it when the occasion warrants. Their skin is not sticky, as on our world, but granular like that of lobsters, and painted in bright colors that gold, silver and precious stones would have difficulty imitating.

The only thing that spoils their appearance is their contracted form and their stupid physiognomy, but although they do not look very intelligent their actions give the lie to the prejudice that is held against them, and when one gets to know them one soon perceives that, although they do not have much to say, they nevertheless think a good deal. It is a pleasure to watch them searching the bottom of a pond into which one has dropped something; they bring it back more rapidly than our Spaniards, and never refuse to obey the command of a human being, however unfamiliar he might be in the vicinity of the river or pond in which they live.

When one walks along the water's edge, they assemble in troops, making a thousand turns and somersaults in order to divert the company. Sometimes one sees them divide up into platoons and perform innocent combats on the surface of the water, races of surprising rapidity and dances as varied as ours. Different species form quadrilles distinguished by form and color, and those kinds of games are played with so much art and intelligence that, even without the aid of speech, one nevertheless understands the sequence of events. They are really mute dramatic poems, such as were once played in Rome, when a single actor represented, by dancing wordlessly, the abduction of Helen, the joy of Paris, the horns of Menelaus and the burning of Troy.

Fish render humans another service as well as entertainment; they guide little boats made of malleable crystal, of which people make use to travel on water. Long cords are attached to them, which the fish never fail to catch in their teeth, and as soon as they are informed of the route that it is necessary to take, they follow it, working in shifts, until they reach the destination. If, by mischance, a man falls into the water, they support him, carry him to the bank, and infallibly save him.

When one wants to bathe, they retire, for fear of being indiscreet, and only come when they are called; only one remains on watch in order to alert the others in case of an accident, for they are extremely attentive to making sure that nothing untoward happens to a human who does them the honor of inhabiting their element for a time. In addition, it is easy for them to find themselves within range to amuse him, to the extent that they are capable. Unfortunately, it is not with their songs, like the birds—for the poor fish are mute everywhere— but as they understand the general language they can make their replies in writing, using their little feet to trace characters on flat stones, of which the rivers are full, and certain plants, so that it is not astonishing to see honest people sometimes amusing themselves for hours on end, and laughing uproariously while conversing with a tench or a green oyster.

The animals that do not have the talent of writing have often complained to the Emperor that the fish enjoy that right to their unjust exclusion; they have always received the response that, the abode of Fish being rather melancholy by nature and very restricted, they would die of boredom if they did not have that resource. Thus, they write, and even read, in spite of the envy, and the rivers are all replete with libraries for their usage, where all of them can amuse themselves as they please.

No one is entirely sure what their books are about, but it is presumed that there is a great deal of moral reflection and political reasoning therein, which demand less imagination than solidity, for no one is unaware that Fish have something cold and heavy about their mentality, which adapts quite well to sciences of that sort.

CHAPTER XII
On Clothing

Clothes do not serve to defend their wearers from the rigor of the seasons, as on our world, since an eternal serenity reigns in the atmosphere and cold is utterly unknown on the Planet. Nature has nevertheless given the people an instinct that leads them to dress themselves, doubtless because a certain appearance of modesty only renders the most perfect beauty more piquant.

There is no question of general fashion on the Planet; everyone imagines fanciful clothing, somewhat in the vein of our masquerades, and everything seems appropriate, provided that skill and genius are manifest in one's costume. Fabrics are not purchased on Mercury; Nature furnishes them liberally, and it is the Emperor who distributes them. The storehouses are always open, and everyone can go to choose, provided that they present a prescription to the steward commissioned to that employment. Those who want more than their entitlement according to the regular tariff need an order from the Emperor, which is difficult to obtain. That does not prevent the most magnificent and various wardrobes in the Universe from being found on Mercury.

The manufactory of those fabrics contains the whole extent of a great lake located in the Emperor's Gardens. That vast basin is always filled with a liquid that Philosophers call Universal Spirit, the Mercury Principle, or Solar Sulfur. A very ardent fire sets the liquid in question ablaze, in which an infinity of Salamanders swim incessantly, as in a delightful bath. They mix that flaming matter with certain doses of Projection Powder, and it is that mixture, worked by a secret art, that composes the fabrics.

The Salamanders that I mentioned are not the monstrous animals of which Painting offers us such vile portraits, nor the chimerical inhabitants of the Sphere of Fire known to the mistaken faith of Gabalis.[5] They are young inhabitant of the Sun obliged to voyage to all the Planets in order to form their minds, and to stay there to work for a time for the wellbeing and pleasure of the inhabitants.

When they are on our Earth they fertilize the fields, populate the gardens, produce fruits and create, so to speak, metals and precious stones in the bosom of the earth; they ripen the vines of Tokay and Champagne, distribute beauty, talents, graces, genius, tastes and sentiments, and preside over agreeable dreams.

On Mercury they are artisans of fabrics, jewels and an infinity of curiosities, which they manufacture from the same raw material as the fabrics, for it is equally appropriate to making the lightest gauzes, the heaviest stones and the most solid metals; it is merely a matter of the cooking.

The edges of the lake where all these masterpieces are made are surrounded at a certain distance by superb storehouses, in which the Salamanders transport and store their work, which they distribute *gratis* to the choice of anyone who wishes, provided that they have an order from the Emperor or a ticket from the steward, as I have already said.

In addition to the fabrics, one finds in these storage depots all the devices appropriate to the adornment of men and women, except for gold and precious stones, which are not used for ornamentation. It is considered that the excessively vivid gleam of gems harms beauty rather than enhancing it, and with regard to metals, their uniform color does nothing but dazzle, without saying anything to the intelligence.

---

[5] The ostensibly-Rosicrucian mystical text *Le Comte de Gabalis* (1670) describes Salamanders, fire elementals as "Children of the Sun." The present author might well have modelled aspects of his text on that book—his prologue is somewhat reminiscent of the earlier text's account of the meeting of the Student with the Comte—but the details of his cosmic schema are very different.

These ingenious and delicate people are only impressed by the industrious mixtures of nature and productions of art, so all the magnificence of their fabrics consists in their fine texture, the brightness of their colors and the variety of designs. It is in the last respect, especially, that the Salamanders excel; they represent in their works not merely flowers, fruits, animals and grotesques but more; as they know everything that happens on Mercury and the other Planets they make little enigmatic tableaux, with the consequence that one sometimes sees on the same garment anecdotal adventures of five or six Planets, painted like the miniatures on our most beautiful snuff-boxes.

When one chooses one of these pieces of satirical cloth—that is what they are called—the Salamander that has fabricated it gives you the little strip of manuscript that serves to interpret the tableaux. Everyone can make a mystery of the explanation if they wish, or show it to their friends, and even make it public.

That might make one imagine that people on Mercury are not very charitable, and they would agree, offering as an excuse that everything ridiculous and humorous that arrives on their world belongs to all those who can understand it, and that one acquires at birth the universal right to laugh to anything that merits it. They add that since they are compassionate, and weep visibly at the narration of harrowing adventures, it is only just that they should laugh at the narration of comical events.

CHAPTER XIII
On Money

Money is not composed of any metal, and if I subsequently refer to it as if it were, it is only out of habit, or in order not to distance myself too far from a manner of speaking that is familiar to us.[6]

The money, therefore, which is neither metal nor fabricated by human hands, is simply found on the platform of a very high tower situated in the Emperor's gardens. The vapors of the Planet, which rise up to the level of that tower, condense there into little tones as hard as metal, and as pliable, similar in shape to our large pastilles, but not as thick.

These pieces of money are imprinted in relief with the forms the Planet that was dominant at the time of their formation. For example, those of Saturn represent the planet and its great characteristic ring; they are the color of sapphires. Those of Jupiter are imprinted with a globe surrounded by its satellites, and their material is similar to diamond. Those of Mars resemble rubies and the money of Venus has the color of emeralds.

The pieces of the most distant Planets from the sun are of less value than those of the nearer ones; thus, ten Saturn pieces are only worth one Jupiter, and ten Jupiter pieces one Mars, etc.

What are known on our worlds as Talismans and starry stones[7] are nothing but Mercurian money, but they only ac-

---

[6] This is problematic in French because *argent* means both silver and money; the problem disappears in translation.

[7] The linking of these two terms is reminiscent of a passage in Molière's *L'amour médecin* (1665) in which a physician claims to cure by means of "words, sounds, letters, talismans and starry rings." The terms *anneau constellé* [starry ring] and *pierre constellée* [starry stone] are linked together in 18th cen-

quire the marvelous virtues familiar to us by passing from that plant to others, which sometimes happens in a manner that will be described.

When the Emperor sends a few young Salamanders to our planet, he gives them a few of those starry stones, for use on occasions when their strength and their industry are insufficient to get them out of difficulty. Then the Emperor distributes to these stones the different virtues that he judges necessary to the Follets—as they are called on our world—that he sends to travel between the Planets, and they make use of them when the occasion rises to produce meteors, excite storms, calm seas, render them invisible, change shape, and, in sum, to work an infinity of prodigies, or I don't know how many petty mischiefs that all nurses know by heart.

When the voyage of these young goblins is concluded, or they go from one planet to another, they ordinarily leave a number of those Talismans behind, as if to compensate the people for the little tricks they have played on them. It is a lucky man who encounters those treasures! Hazard has sometimes given several of them to the same person, and it is by virtue of those fortunate incidents that men have been seen to do so many things beyond nature, such as walking in the air, rendering themselves invulnerable, handling fire without being burned, walking in the rain without getting wet, predicting the future, curing with words and making all women fall in love with them.

---

tury French dictionaries as subsidiaries of *constellé*, there defined as "manufactured under a certain constellation" (astrologically speaking).

CHAPTER XIV
The Distribution of Money and its Usage

The Commissioners of the Public Treasury, who are responsible for distributing the wealth committed to their care, apply themselves to that employment incessantly, and everyone can go on an appointed day to receive their due, in accordance with a rule fixed in all the dependencies of the Empire.

As the land furnishes nourishment *gratis* and the Emperor provides clothes and furniture, money is merely for luxury purchases, gambling and, as one might say, dealing in secondhand goods, which is much more common on Mercury than any other Planet, for everything can be sold: adornments, jewels, and even—which does not happen elsewhere—complexions, characters, qualities of the soul, talents, and, in sum, everything that might tempt human curiosity.

It is true that the qualities of mind, the complexions and characters are not sold purely and simply; it is necessary that some exchange enters into the bargain. For example, if a severe and taciturn man has a desire to become lively and good-humored, it will be necessary for him to trade his Saturnine character for the one whose turn of mind pleases him, apart from a transfer of money to equalize the bargain. If a coquette is tempted by curiosity to become faithful and tender, it is necessary for a heroine of Romance to adapt to coquetry and cede the plaintive tone to her. Those two examples should suffice.

The acquisition of talents is simpler, one can become at a stroke a Painter, a Geometer, a Musician, a Poet or an Actor, but the person who sells the talent loses it without return, and the buyer possesses it in its entirety from the first moment, as was said previously.

This is the usage that is made of wealth and money on Mercury. The Emperor distributes them with sage economy, which is not opposed to magnificence, and which has no trace of avarice, since he does not take from his subjects and does not levy any subsidy.

O Noble Son of the Sun, respectable image of Divinity! cries the Author of the story at this point, the people who live under your laws might well be called, veritably, the most fortunate in the universe. Invincible Father of Believers, he adds, redoubtable Sophi,[8] your mildness and your equity are not far removed from the sublime character of the great Emperor of Mercury. It is true that the misery of our Earth and the needs of your State oblige you to demand a few tributes from your Subjects, but they are light, they are easy to pay. Alas, may it please the holy Envoy that they pass directly from their affectionate hands into our sacred Treasury.

But, magnificent Sultan, you do not know how many of those who raise the whip impose it unjustly! Their will serves as their law, and influenced by personal interest, or by the solicitations of those who are in credit at your Sublime Gate, they exempt a part of your Subjects, or only impose of them a tiny part of what they could pay, while others are overcharged and buckle under the burden. Two injustices result from this pernicious usage against which the divine Prophet never ceases to cry out: one that all the Subjects of the Empire do not contribute equally, although they all enjoy equity under your laws and the protection of your invincible armies; the other that the weak are oppressed and the weight of their misery even prevents them from raising their eyes to the redoubtable steps of your Highness' Throne.

Every day, your unfortunate Subjects whom the tyranny of the Pachas oppresses see everything snatched away, including the bed on which they sleep; all they possess of instruments or beasts appropriate to labor is sold at a vile price; the

---

[8] Strictly speaking, Sophi [Sages, in Latin] is a plural and should not be used as a singular, but it often is, especially in its Arabic derivative, Sufi.

roofs of their houses are removed and thy remain, with their families, prey to the insults of the seasons, which run their health and cause their children to perish.

If they acquit themselves promptly to avoid these vexations, an imposition heavier than the first causes them to repent of that exactitude. What am I saying? The fear of being mistaken for rich obliges them to hide even the bread that they eat. It is in silence, and banishing innocent joy from their meals, that they sometimes dare to hazard one less frugal, a unique resource in their misery; then they fear once again that an envious neighbor, by publish that appearance of ease, might cause the next tax to be doubled.

Who would believe, magnificent Emperor, that such a tyranny was exercised under the reign of the most just and most humane of all Princes?

After that long digression by our Philosopher, he returns to his story.

CHAPTER XV
Marriages

The usages that are observed on Mercury on the subject of marriages will perhaps appear bizarre and extravagant to the inhabitants of our world, so I would dispense with making mention of them if the quality of exact and faithful translator did not oblige me to report them.

The taste that humans have for variety being so universally distributed among us, says the Manuscript, the people of Mercury had refrained from rendering marriages durable and indissoluble.

It is necessary to regard our penchant for variety as an insatiable curiosity natural to humans and which makes them to desire incessantly to acquire new acquaintances, new ideas and new talents. If that natural curiosity were not very extensive, we would remain in a kind of ignorance and stupidity similar to that of animals that only apply themselves to things absolutely necessary to their needs, which are not very numerous, and only to experiences that are indispensable, and only acquire very limited knowledge in consequence.

The Author of Nature, having placed us at a level far superior to that of animals, wanted our souls to acquire knowledge of all kinds and almost infinite enlightenment regarding all sorts of objects; with that in view He has given us the ability to reflect, the art of planning and the faculty of judging similarities and differences.

To facilitate the usage of these intellectual faculties He has given us the voice that serves to make other people hear us and put us in a condition to give one another mutual aid, very necessary to perfect our knowledge. He has also formed us perfectly convenient hands with which to make experiments, to trace signs and characters appropriate to represent our ideas, and prevent them by that means from being confused with others by virtue of their extreme variety.

But all these presents of His bounty would be almost useless to us, and the intention of the Creator would remain without effect, if He had not imprinted in our souls an immense depth of curiosity, which does not permit us to attach ourselves to the knowledge of a small number of objects but draws us continually to the pursuit of those less familiar to us, for they are the only ones of which it is important for us to acquire the knowledge.

With regard to those of which we have a clear and distinct idea, they remain in our memory, and as they have brought to our mind all the enlightenment with which they are capable of furnishing it, we no longer have any need to occupy ourselves in their research, and they no longer inspire curiosity in us, so it is to new objects that we attach ourselves.

From that, undoubtedly, comes our insurmountable appetite for diversity: that desire to know everything and incessantly to enjoy new objects drives us with so much force and rapidity that nothing is capable of pleasing us by uniformity alone, that or mind goes to sleep and that distaste never fails to march in the wake of that numbness of the soul.

The Emperor, given this reasoning, has regarded the uniformity that soon slips into the best matched marriages as an almost inevitable source of ennui, and as that infirmity of the soul is mortal in the Planet that it governs, he thought to ward off that inconvenience by limiting the durations of marriages to a few years.

The first propositions are made in this fashion: as soon as two people conceive a taste for one another, they agree to ask their parents for the Chamber of the Sphinx. That is the name given to an apartment in all houses were there are marriageable daughters; it is normally the most magnificent and ornate place in the house. It is destined to show the future couple to one another, which takes place as follows.

When the Chamber of the Sphinx, which is hardly ever refused, is granted, the young man, conducted by his father, goes to salute ceremoniously the father of the young woman, who, after the customary politenesses, has him taken by his servants into a little apartment adjacent to the Chamber of the Sphinx, in which he finds a bath prepared with all imaginable elegance and propriety. The future bride goes with her chambermaids into another bathroom opposite to that one, and they bathe separately.

The customary cleansing having been concluded on both parts, the two Lovers, clad in colored robes of a crystal that is as pliable on that Planet as our taffetas, are each introduced by an opposite door into the Chamber of the Sphinx. An invisible Salamander has taken care to prepare a delicious light meal so that anyone who wishes might eat. There are only two chairs in the room but in compensation, it is abundantly furnished with sofas, settees and divans, in addition to the nuptial bed, which is magnificent and furnished with curtains impenetrable to light.

The two Lovers are obliged to remain in that place for two days and two nights, without going any further than the bathrooms, in which it has been made certain that nothing is lacking.

The name of the apartment derives from the fact that it is where one discovers the enigmas of adornment, the disguises of clothing, and where one unmasks at liberty sentiments, tastes and character, which are more difficult to hide in an intimacy of forty-eight hours than in the embarrassment and dissipation of the wider society.

On emergence from the apartment, if the future spouses have not changed their minds, the contract is drawn up, but if one of the two refuses, nothing is done. That refusal, which is fairly common, does not prejudice one or the other; one simply says "We do not suit one another yet," and as it often happens that those who are refused are often taken back subsequently, no one is offended by a first refusal, for they have had the pleasure of stating all the reasons in the Chamber of the Sphinx, and it is always there that these matters are agreed.

The contracts are always composed of very few articles. The first concerns the clothes, jewels and furniture that are being placed in common; it also regulates the advantages that each is giving to the other, and what each will withdraw from the community and the expiry of the term.

The second establishes an Arbiter, a man or woman agreeable to both parties, to whom all domestic disputes and marital quarrels are to be taken; that Arbiter will make a sovereign judgment, and impose a fine or some customary penalty on the one who appears to be in the wrong.

The third regulates the number of petty conjugal deviations and real infidelities that each is obliged to let pass on the part of the other, in order to conserve peace in the household. That is of no great importance during the early months; it is more by precaution than necessity that it is mentioned in the contract, but afterwards, each of them uses the right, and the Ladies especially, even if, they say, it is only to reserve a privilege that they regard as the most beautiful ornament in their crown.

Beyond those authorized faults, many more escape in the course of a two year marriage of which the contract makes no mention, but ordinarily, no more attention is paid to them than to spelling mistakes.

On that basis, from the day after the wedding, a woman can make eyes at someone, put on airs, tease someone, go out alone, come back late, have herself brought back and even sleep elsewhere in case of need, provided that she gives plausible reasons for her absence—as for example that she was very distracted and amusement retained her, or that pleasure carried her away. All of that is ordinarily well-received, but when a husband is peevish, the Lady gets away with it by adopting a sulky expression and saying: "Oh, that's how you are; one can never do anything that doesn't put you in a bad mood; to content you it would be necessary to bury oneself in a room and never see anyone in one's entire life." One is rarely obliged to go that far, but at the worst, the domestic spat goes no further.

The fourth Article exhorts the couple never to be neglectful of one another, even in bed, extreme undress being, it is said, susceptible to a suitable adornment and a few simple ornaments in good taste.

When the term of the contract—which is to say, the two years of marriage—is about to expire, the two families assemble, accompanied by a Justice of the Peace. That public official is present to give the two parties the reciprocal liberty to commence a new lease or to separate; that is usually what happens. Then, in order to give a material form to the dissolution of the contract, he presents the husband and wife with a straw and instructs them to break it in order to mark their desire to separate. It is apparently from that custom the Molière derived the proverb: "A broken straw renders an arrangement between two men of honor concluded."[9]

---

[9] The quotation is from *Le Dépit amoureux* (1656).

CHAPTER XVI
On the Empress

By virtue of the superiority of his nature, the Emperor is stronger and more powerful on his own than all the people of the Planet. He is perfectly beautiful, since his beauty depends on him, and he can always render himself amiable to the woman he marries. He enjoys all the talents, has all the graces of intelligence, boundless power and inexhaustible wealth.

With all those advantages, would one not think that the greatest joy would be to spend one's life with him? People think very differently on the Planet Mercury. Love consists so strongly in equality of rank, sentiments and tastes that it can almost never arise in people so disproportionate. The Emperor can approach humanity by virtue of the familiarity and gentleness that are natural to him, but beautiful women, although grateful for his politeness, are nevertheless repelled by that superiority.

Accustomed to empire and adoration, the thought that someone merits it as much as them irritates them, and without the grace that the Emperor can make to the Empress, and almost never refuses, he would perhaps find it difficult to marry. That grace is to grant her the privilege of Metamorphoses from the moment that he marries her, and to assure her of it for a certain time after the expiry of the contract.

That right, the most desired of all the wealth of the Planet, is the facility of taking on any form, even those of plants and inanimate things.

With the aid of that secret, one can inform oneself of almost all those of nature, by animating any body, and borrowing all the tastes and all the ideas of different created species.

As one conserves reason in whatever form one adopts, and only acquires more, the different ways of thought appropriate to the beings that one assumes as garments, one can carry out an infinity of experiments, each more interesting than the others. The Emperor, the only one who can grant that privilege, is very sparing with it, with the consequence that there are never more than fifty individuals who employ it simultaneously in the whole of the Planet—but he always accords it to the Empress; it is, so to speak, his wedding present.

Women, who are naturally very curious, and whom that disguise is by no means useless, have a very keen appetite for that kind of masquerade, and the hope of enjoying it is the cause of the fact that not one refuses to takes part in "Assemblies of Beauty"—which is the name given to the fêtes given in the Emperor's Palace when he wants to marry. All the women in the Empire who are invited to them never fail to go. It is easy to imagine that all kinds of pleasures are encountered in such assemblies, which men are free to enter, and where all the beautiful women on the Planet are gathered.

In order to form an idea of the charms of the Court at those times, one only has to remember that it is taking place in the most beautiful place in the Universe, that it is composed of the everything that is most pleasant, and that the people of Mercury are the richest, the most cheerful, the freest and the most gallant of all the peoples in the Universe.

At these assemblies people occupy themselves with an infinite number of games, and everything imaginable that is appropriate to amuse such a brilliant Court is there with an abundance and a variety that leaves nothing to be desired.

The Emperor is to be encountered at any moment in the midst of the assembly. The charms of his person, his humor, his intelligence and his familiarity, which could not be greater, spread no small pleasure in that spectacle, where everything is marvelous.

The last Emperor, who married several times without love, more to follow custom than by inclination, had sought nothing in that pleasure but the pleasure itself; his heart had not experienced the slightest emotion or the slightest stir in the Assemblies of Beauty, his temperament alone guiding him therein.

One day, when he found himself in the placid distraction that was usual to him, he was struck by the beauty of a person who was offered to his eyes. It was a young woman who was extremely pretty, but who did not make any effort to be beautiful, who did not have the vanity to put on any pretence, and was content to see the Emperor that she loved passionately without even daring to imagine the slightest return on his part.

Soon, the Emperor was no longer occupied with anyone but her, and as love never enters into a kind heart without delicacy, he learned that the possession of what one loves is not the most sensible of pleasures, and that without being master of the heart, it is futile to be master of the person.

With that idea, which our Ladies call Romantic, the Emperor, who simply followed the appetite of nature, had an extreme impatience to know the heart and the sentiments of Zenis. He went past her several times, affecting not even to notice her; he perceived that she blushed, and took that as a good omen. He mentioned it to one of his confidants, changed that day into a Canary, who was playing in his hair and chatting in a low voice into his master' ear, when he saw the lovely Zenis leave with an anxious expression, in which was painted the chagrin of not even having been noticed.

The Emperor, who was still extracting flattering conjectures from her action, told the Canary he was entertaining to follow her; the other obeyed, and did not lose sight of her.

She went through the garden rapidly, passed over a fairly broad meadow and plunged into a little wood of jasmines and orange trees, somber and solitary. After she had walked for some time, without knowing where she was going, she sat down with the same distraction, got up to walk around several times, and finally lay down, vanquished by lassitude.

The Canary perched in a jasmine close by, entertained her with a charming song, singing her tunes from Lambert,[10]

---

[10] Michel Lambert (1610-1696) was the most prolific composer of songs in the second half of the seventeenth century; he was Louis XIV's master of music from 1661 until his death.

which he had just learned, and sarabands to break the heart. Buried in her sad reflections as she was, however, he chirped in vain. He caused a few flowers to fall on to her bosom and into her hair, but she paid no attention. Finally, not knowing how to extract her from that reverie, which is almost as dangerous on Mercury as lethargy is on our world, he flew so close to her and made so much noise that she perceived him.

I have mentioned that the animals and all the birds on that Planet have almost as much intelligence as our finest humans, so no one is astonished to see them behaving familiarly and interesting themselves in the troubles and pleasures of people. Thus, Zenis spoke to him as to a rational individual.

"Lovely Canary," she said to him, "I can see that you want to distract me from my dolor, but your efforts are futile."

Then, realizing that she was mistakenly speaking the human language to a bird that could not understand it, she continued the conversation in the language of birds.

"No, charming creature," she said, "in spite of the kind interest you are taking in my fortune, you cannot change my fate; let me die, and go tell the cruel individual who is killing me that you have seen me die of the dolor of not having been able to please him."

She knew that the order was impossible, that the song of a bird and all its petty fashions was not capable of making an adventure composed like hers understood, but she nevertheless found a kind of relief in speaking her thought aloud, and had she had the pleasure of speaking to her Beloved, or pronouncing his name, she would have been less unhappy.

The Canary testified his astonishment at her dolor by a thousand different gestures; he tried to console her after his fashion, but without allowing her to glimpse what he was. But when he saw that all his efforts were futile, and that Zenis was falling into a mortal torpor, he no longer took precautions.

"Beautiful Zenis," he said, approaching her ear, "the Emperor adores you; he instructed me to tell you so."

The voice of the Canary was very feeble, as one can well imagine, and he was also speaking in a very low tone, for fear that a secret of that importance might be heard by some metamorphosian like him. However, that tiny sound, which scarcely articulated the name of the one she loved, recalled Zenis to life, passed into the utmost depths of her soul, and returned her in an instant to health, joy and beauty.

It was only a question now of confirming what the Canary had said, for she feared that it might have been a dream. He acquitted that duty like a bird who knew the world and had not always been in a cage. Zenis wanted to take him on her finger, but he refused such a great favor out of politeness. He was content to fly from branch to branch along the route and lead her to the road to the Palace, where he went on ahead of her in order to give the Emperor and account of his mission. He told him about the love, the dolor and the peril of Zenis.

The Emperor was so touched that he took on the form of the little Canary instantly, returning his favorite to his original form, and flew rapidly to Zenis. He conversed with her in the guise of the one that had guided her thus far, read in her eyes the truth of the report that had been given to him and enjoyed the pleasant impatience that she had to see him again.

When she went into the Palace she found in his ordinary form the person who had conversed with her in that of the Canary, and when she still saw that bird nearby she feared having been deceived and thought she might die of dolor. The Courtier perceived her disturbance, and pointed it out to the Emperor, whom she did not recognize under the plumage of the small animal, although he revealed himself sufficiently by his speech, which a bird would never have been able to maintain. She did not hear or see anything anymore, though; the flattering idea that had occupied her on the way had overwhelmed her to such an extent that she was paying no attention to anything else.

As soon as the Empress is chosen she is placed on a very high throne; the Emperor has her conducted there by a Delegate of the Sun who has come to conduct the wedding. That

Envoy ordinarily reads the contract and his presence gives an entire celebrity to the ceremony.

"Do you not promise, August Sovereign of Mercury," he says, "to renounce in favor of Princess *N.* the prerogatives that you have naturally to penetrate the secret of hearts, to read the future and to master wills?"

The Emperor responds: "Yes."

"Are you not content," he adds, "only to employ graces, pleasures and tenderness to win the heart of your divine spouse?"

The Emperor responds: "Yes."

"Will you not grant her the power of Metamorphosis?"

"Yes," replied the Emperor.

Then the Ambassador of the Sun turns to the Empress. "Swear, divine Princess," he says, "never to use the power of Metamorphosis that has been accorded to you to trouble the pleasures of the Emperor, to divine his secrets or to spy on his actions."

"I make that oath," says the Empress.

When that formula is concluded, the marriage is indissoluble, like that of the least of Mercury's inhabitants, so long as the contract lasts—which is to say, two years at the most.

CHAPTER XVII
On Metamorphosis

The Empress can then begin to make use of her gift of Metamorphosis, but usually, she does not make use of it in the first months. It is not until then that the concerns of the Empire oblige the Emperor to go away. Then it is permissible for her to take on all kinds of forms and to go anywhere she pleases without it being possible to be perceived.

One purely political reason dictates that the right of Metamorphosis should be given to all Empresses. It seems that Majesty would be injured if the Empress' actions exposed her by chance—as anything is possible—to the indiscretion of malicious gossip or perhaps the insolence of a satire. That is why it has been judged appropriate to envelop everything in an impenetrable darkness—to which the masquerade of Metamorphosis is more appropriate than any other means.

In addition to the advantage of being able to disappear as often as one wishes, there is another, without which the former would often by useless, which is that the Empress can communicate the same power that she enjoys every time that it can bring her some amusement or utility. It is with the restriction, however, that the Metamorphosis she lends, so to speak, cannot last any longer than her own—which is to say that as soon as she resumes her ordinary form, the one that she has disguised immediately becomes what he was before. Another restriction is that the person whose form she changes can only take one similar to her own; thus, if she becomes a warbler or a nightingale, the transformed individual cannot take the form of a different animal.

Furthermore, the Metamorphosis can only be operated on someone who is willing—but Ladies have an eye so sure that there are things about which they can never be mistaken, and it is always the case that the person to which that kind of handkerchief is sent receives it with pleasure. The Princess who reigns presently has often admitted to her best friend that she must never have chosen badly, since she has always been given very effective marks of gratitude.

The moment the Metamorphosis is over, the matter remains as if it had not happened; it is an item of mischief forgotten by both parties, and it very rarely happens that the same individual receives the honor of that disguise twice in a lifetime. The Empress is curious, like all persons of her sex, and as soon as she has clarified someone's sentiments and manners personally, her inclinations turn elsewhere.

However insensate this practice might be, how many women of our world would give it their approval!

"How many causes for complaint we have," they say. "For a few slight curiosities that we might have in the short space of time that our beauty lasts, is it necessary that we should be exposed to the backbiting of the Precious, our old Grandmothers, our ugly and peevish Aunts and stupid people cut from the same cloth, as if we had committed the greatest sin in the world by amusing ourselves making experiments in order to form the mind and know characters? If people throw stones at us for those bagatelles, it is necessary, then, that we remain true prudes buried in the make-up of our estate, and, like veritable goats, only graze where we are tethered. How unjust our world is! And how grateful I am to the Empress of Mercury for having established such sage Laws by her example."

> She samples all manner of estates that way.
> And it is not acting at a woman that is stupid
> In whatever rank that one considers her.
> Alas, how miserable she would be,
> If, never quitting her respectable pose
> One saw her always on the formal Throne.
> Not to my taste is the most stupid method
> Of being imprisoned in her own grandeur,
> Ana above all to, transports of amorous ardor
> High quality becomes most uncomfortable.

The Empress in pleasures knows herself:
She descends from the heights of supreme glory,
And to enter into anything she pleases,
She often emerges from herself;
The Empress then is not what she appears.
                    (Prologue to *Amphitrion*.)[11]

---

[11] Molière's *Amphitryon* (some early editions retain the spelling used above), first performed in 1668, caused a certain scandal, because it was thought that the author might be satirizing Louis XIV's amorous dalliances in the character of Jupiter: a thesis almost as absurd as the notion that the Chevalier de Béthune might be satirizing the Sun King in the character of his Emperor. *Amphitryon* is a comedy of metamorphoses and confusions, in which the character Sosie, originally played by Molière, is a double of the god Mercury.

CHAPTER XVIII
On Edifices

The materials of which they are constructed are a metallic clay, or, rather, a pliable metal, rendered so by the air of the Planet, which is nothing but the Philosophers' mixture, the universal solvent of all metals. Thus, all of them on Mercury are similar to a clay of which one can easily make bricks, tiles, beams and, in general, everything that can serve in the building of superb edifices. All the pieces of a building are made, if one wishes, by molding, and hardened by the heat of the Sun, but to a metallic hardness; and the same clay of which the bricks, beams and doors are made also serves, when soft, to bind those same materials together.

White bricks are formed from a silver clay; they are also made from gold, mercury and copper. Only iron is used, as on our world, to join together the different parts, to which the other metals cannot provide a strong enough linkage.

It is impossible to describe the many ingenious forms in which bricks are formed, and what charming designs they compose to embellish walls. Our most expert painters do not attain the resultant brilliance or the vivacity, especially when stones of all colors are combined with the metals.

The stones that we call precious here are as soft as clay and likewise only harden over time, with the consequence that it is easy to form all the shapes one desires. One can imagine what effect the assemblage of so many magnificent things, so easy to model, must have.

The ground produces everything needed to build houses; it is only necessary to remove a superficial layer destined for the production of trees, plants, flowers and grass; all the rest is purely metallic, layer upon layer, sometimes mingled with veins, like our marbles. One sees precious stones there of every species, mixed together with an art and design that Nature, more ingenious than elsewhere, renders inimitable and always charming.

The large birds that I have mentioned aid the workers in their labor. They are the ones who carry the materials; it is only necessary to organize them into a base and then dispose them in the order that each imagines. Every street takes its name from the form of the houses it contains. For example, one says the Street of Flowers because all the facades of the houses are ornamented with garlands, vases or baskets full of flowers and interlaced branches. Another is called the Street of Grotesques, another that of Statues, another that of Banquets, another that of Ladies, because all those things are represented there with the natural colors of pebbles, agates and precious stones, combined with a mixture of clays that can vary infinitely.

The great facility of building these houses, whose materials are available to everyone, enables the inhabitants of Mercury to make new ones frequently, in order to have the pleasure of variety. They ask a Salamander of their acquaintance to be kind enough to destroy their house; he does so without difficulty, a torch lit from the fire that burns incessantly in the great lake consumes everything that it touches in a moment.

Needless, to say, the houses—those in the same street, at least—are built on a general architectural design from which it is not permitted to deviate; and in a Realm where land costs nothing, because it does not yield anything, one gives to private houses and public edifices all the extent necessary to the dignity of some and the comfort of others.

People who want to employ in their buildings the different kinds of wood that the soil produces become masters thereof. One finds all colors, and the animals we have mentioned take care of cutting and transporting it. As wood is more difficult to work than the aforementioned metallic clay and soft stones, however, its usage is not very common. The trees are so beautiful in their natural destination that people have some scruples about depriving the land of the brilliant adornment they give it. Those refuges of coolness and gently

71

obscurity seem respectable by the virtue of the need the fiery planet has of them, and it is not without reluctance that one deprives the land of the perfumes they spread there and the gentle harmony they perpetuate by the songs of the birds of all species which regard them as their palaces.

CHAPTER XIX
On the Great Mountain

The one that is so called is prodigious in height by comparison with others, of such a vast extent and more embellished by the gifts of nature than it is possible to describe. The foot of the mountain is surrounded by precipices, and one can only reach it by a narrow path, extremely fortified and guarded by the best troops on the Planet. It is on that mountain that the Sages of Mercury live, who are distributed throughout the universe; the much vaunted Rosicrucians, the Fays, the Mages, the Genii, the Sylphs, the Salamanders, the Gnomes, the Undines—in sum, all the beings that we regard as fabulous—hold their meetings on that Mountain. They regulate the affairs of Society there, communicate their knowledge to one another there, cultivate that which they have acquired, and sometimes live there for centuries without, any thought of leaving, so pleasant is that abode.

The people of Mercury, who love those species of demigods, from whom they receive a thousand benefits, sometimes come to visit them, with the Emperor's permission, and those visits, although rare, further augment the admiration of the people for the inhabitants of the Great Mountain; so they have no difficulty in risking their lives and enduring all kinds of fatigues when it is attacked, which often happens in the following manner.

What we call Sunspots are calcined rocks of an immense size, which the prodigious movement of the star launches to an incredible distance. As those burned rocks are light, they are sustained for many centuries before falling, and during that long interval of time, the ever productive and vivifying ardor of the great star forms animals and humans on those crusts. Beneficent as the nature of the Sun's light might be, however, the inhabitants of those arid burned lands always resent the place where they have been born. The animals there are large and cruel, the humans savage and ferocious, enemies of all equity, devoid of art, morals and discipline, and closely resemble in character the way that we depict Giants and Cyclopes.

These flying lands, if it is permissible to name them thus, do not follow a perfectly regular course around the Sun, but sometimes find themselves closer to Mercury and sometimes further away. It even happens that they sometimes almost touch the Great Mountain. Now, the peoples that inhabit those rocks see from their hideous dwellings the beauties of Mercury and the felicity of that Planet's inhabitants, which gives them an ardent desire to live there. There is nothing that they do not attempt in that design, and as they have wings, they fly from time to time in such great quantities on to the mountain that it is always to be feared that they might make themselves masters of it.

Those perverse humans bear a considerable resemblance to the Demons of which such ugly portraits have been made. It is probable that a few of the Sages who inhabit the Great Mountain and have traveled throughout the world have given us a description of them, and that is why Painters represent to us frightful human creatures with hideous features, bestial visages, horns, tails and trenchant claws, and the entire apparatus of deformity that are attributed to Infernal Angels. That accursed race is born fully armed, like lions, tigers and elephants.

In addition, they are prodigiously strong—but they lack industry, and although they have much more of it than our cleverest animals, it is constant that the people of Mercury, although much smaller and weaker, are their superiors. In any case, the latter are led by Sages, whom nature almost always obeys. It must be admitted, however that it is only with difficulty that they defend themselves against the irruptions of their enemies. I was a witness to the last war, and as I served in it with sufficient good fortune and distinction, I am better placed than anyone else to offer an accurate account of it.

The Sages of all the parts of the world had gone to Mercury for a general assembly; for a few days, already, they had been regulating the interests of Society in public conferences, and distributing the offices that are allocated every year, when, after an obscurity of several hours that descended upon the Mountain, enemy troops were distinctly perceived, which, having abandoned their lands, were flying at top speed to fall upon the Planet.

The assembly of the Sages immediately broke up, and each one went to occupy his post, for everything is regulated in case of an alarm.

As soon as the Sages saw the enemies approaching, they built by the force of their art—which we call magic—a prodigiously high wall of diamond around the Great Mountain, in order to separate it from the rest of the Planet. Troops were immediately assembled and divided into the corps, distinguished by the arms of which they made use.

Generally speaking, all the Warriors on Mercury are armed as we paint Amours; the Sages have also furnished us with that idea. Some carry bows and quivers full of arrows, but those arrows are shafts of light and flame rendered solid, which conserve their natural activity and there is nothing that they cannot penetrate; they traverse the hardened skin and large bones of enemies with as much facility as they pass through the air. Nothing resists them, and the troop that makes use of those weapons is the most considerable.

The members of the second corps carry lighted torches, the flames of which can never be extinguished and whose power of ignition is so dangerous and so sudden that nothing in the world can ward of its effect. They shake these torches when they fight, and any spark, no matter how slight, that strikes penetrates into the depths of hearts and devours them, from which inevitable and prompt death ensues.

The third troop carries simple strips of cloth known as streamers, instruments that do not seem very redoubtable but are, in fact, more dangerous than the other weapons. The slightest touch of that magic fabric initially dazzles and blinds almost instantaneously, with the consequence that, unable to see, one can neither defend oneself not escape; thus, one remains at the mercy of a pitiless enemy, who often insults your defeat and renders your death as ignominious as it is cruel.

The report that the Ages have given us of the weapons of the inhabitants of Mercury have doubtless given rise to the Allegory that causes us to depict winged Amours armed with inevitable arrows, cruel fires, and wearing a blindfold—which we mistakenly put over their eyes, although it really serves to blind those that they wish to enslave.

Those troops, arranged in battalions over three lines, each have seven Sages at their head mounted on chariots. The first seven are pulled by twelve butterflies very neatly harnessed, the next seven by twelve honey-bees released from their labor and the last seven by twelve cockchafers selected from the Stables of Demogorgon, the permanent and irrevocable Doyen of the Rosicrucians.[12]

The Sages could have harnessed their chariots to eagles, vultures or others birds of that sort, but they wanted to show that veritable Wisdom has no need of aid, and that heroic valor is sufficient in itself.

That disposition having been made, and the enemy still approaching, the three troops, with their Leaders, rise up into the air with incredible rapidity; sunbeams are not as light and lightning not as prompt. The enemies are alerted by the sight of these Phalanges sustaining themselves in the air with their wings and hovering there, waiting for them, but they are broken and knocked over in an instant; the abrupt attack of our troops does not give them the leisure to prepare for battle. The Mercurians, who agility renders them almost impossible to

---

[12] Demogorgon crops up in numerous 17th century literary works, usually in a demonic role, but this particular reference probably derives from Jean-Baptiste Lully's opera *Roland*, performed at Versailles in 1685, in which Demogorgon is the king of the fays and functions in the plot of the opera as a master of ceremonies.

attack, have penetrated their ranks and shattered their order before they could close ranks. The combat cannot be sustained for very long, in spite of the surprise.

The ferocity and the rage on one side balanced the agility, skill and veritable valor on the other, but one of the Sages—it was Trevisan[13]—having taken flight more rapidly, rose above the enemy with his troop, while the other two troops, more powerfully armed, took the underside.

The troop following Trevisan was armed with fires, and shook its brands over the cohorts; the penetrating sparks fell like a fiery rain, and while the two corps that had remained below pierced the enemy with their arrows or blinded them, the flying quadroon occupying the median region of the air inflicted inexpressible ravages.

The enemy, pressed from all sides and, so to speak, surrounded by a thousand unavoidable deaths, precipitated their flight toward the summit of the Mountain, and abandoned the air.

They were followed closely, but as a fleeing enemy requires a golden bridge, the Sages sounded the retreat, content to have carried off the honors of the day and to see the ground covered with their mortal enemies, biting the dust.

After that glorious success, the Sages, without losing a moment, garnished the battlements of the diamond wall with a large number of inhabitants of Mercury. As our soldiers were much lighter than the enemies, and had a much more elevated position, and the barbaric people had, in any case, refrained from quitting their retrenchments and the entrances to the Mountain of which they had taken possession, preparations were made to attack them the following day in a regulation fashion.

---

[13] A number of 16th century alchemical works were attributed to Bernard Trevisan, who was supposed to have been active in the 15th century. One of the works in question was "edited"— and presumably faked—by the Belgian alchemist Gerhard Dorn (1530-1584).

In addition to the weapons I have mentioned, the inhabitants of Mercury, when at war, carry long chains whose slenderness renders them imperceptible, and which it is impossible to break. During the night they covered the environs of the fort and the enemy's retreats with them. The next day, at dawn, they put on an appearance of wanting to attack on foot; the enemies, promising themselves an easy victory and emerging full of confidence and fury to meet our troops, almost delivered themselves into the trap. Only the last saved themselves, but it did them no good to have avoided it; thousands of arrows reached them as they fled, with the result that in those two days, the planet was liberated from the inundation of the barbarians, having suffered only minimal losses.

With regard to those who remained in the Mercurians' invisible traps, their lives were spared. The Sages had them take certain powders that softened their natural ferocity for a time; in consequence, they were allowed to spend a few days on the Great Mountain, and even to travel on the Planet.

As they never bring any women with them when they go to war, there is no danger that their numbers might increase on Mercury, since, by the foresight of Nature, they cannot have children with our women. Without that sage precaution, which renders those monstrous men sterile on our world, one might sometimes see pretty women with children six times as large as them.

CHAPTER XX
Portrait of a Sage on Mercury

It seems that the sublunar author[14] that I have mentioned previously was instructed by some Salamander when he expressed himself thus on the subject of virtue:

"Virtue has not yet shown herself to anyone. Only a portrait that resembles her has been painted. There is nothing strange in the fact that she is in no hurry to climb on to her rock; she has been made into a disagreeable individual who only likes solitude, associated with dolor and toil, and, in sum, she has been made into an enemy of the amusements and games that are the flower of joy and the seasoning of life."

He admits, however, that there are devotees who are pale and melancholy of complexion, who like silence and retreat, and who only have phlegm in their veins and clay on their faces.

He goes on: "They have no eyes for the beauties of art and nature; they would believe themselves to be charged with an uncomfortable burden if they had taken on some pleasurable matter. On Feast days they retire among the dead; they prefer a tree-trunk or a grotto to a Palace or a Throne. As for

---

[14] Author's note: "L. P. le Moine, *Dévotion aisée*." The reference is to *La Dévotion aisée* [Natural Devotion] (1652) by Pierre Le Moyne (1602-1671); the L. P. in Béthune's reference stands for "le Père," the author being a Jesuit. He was a prolific writer, whose other works include the oft-reprinted *La Galerie des Femmes fortes* [The Gallery of Strong Women] (1647), which finds some echo in the subsequent chapter on "The Strong Woman." It is not obvious why the author thinks that he has mentioned him previously, although the remark might support the highly plausible thesis that the work was cobbled together from disparate fragments rather than composed in a linear fashion.

offenses and insults, they are as insensible to them as if they had the eyes and ears of a Statue; honor and glory are idols that they do not know and to whom they have no incense to offer. A beautiful person is a specter to them, and those imperious and sovereign visages, those agreeable tyrants who make voluntary slaves devoid of chains everywhere, have the same power for their eyes as the Sun has for those of an owl."

But the Sage admits that those are the features of a feeble and primitive mind, which does not have the honest and natural affections it ought to have.

"True Sages," he says, "have a happier complexion; they have an abundance of that mild and warm humor, the benign and rectified blood that makes joy."

The inhabitants of Mercury, and particularly the Sages, are of that fortunate temper; they have an abundance of mild and warm humor; they have the rectified and benign blood that transports to pleasure. Philosophy is not severe on that Planet; its shows itself everywhere decked in flowers, delights accompany it at all times, following or preceding it. So, far from thinking of destroying the passions, it regards them as a precious gift of the Creator.

"The more we have of them," said the Sages, "the more powerful is the soul that possesses them; they constitute an opulence and a strength. Indeed, without them, what would become of the human race? They are the bond and the soul of Society."

A Sage on Mercury devotes himself primarily to the cultivation of his mind; he sets aside prejudices, the infants of ignorance; he acquires the useful and agreeable sciences; he reinforces his reason by means of the knowledge of the truth, and he labors to furnish it with all the Arts that might extent his intelligence and render it more accurate. But once that difficult task is complete, he only listens any longer to Nature submissive to the Laws of reason.

In following that wise mistress, there is no danger of the passions tyrannizing us; reason can always make them serve our wellbeing, and sets aside the inconveniences that follow in their wake when one allows oneself to be carried away by their impetuosity and caprice.

Let a jealous man, for instance, consult reason, and nothing will seem easier than dissipating his delirium and curing is malady. If the person he imagines to be his rival is not loved, the torment he is inflicting on himself is chimerical; if he is, all his chagrins, quarrels and complaints will surely not prevent it, and will not persuade the one who lives him to flee him and hate him. In truth, one can, having authority over her, prevent her from seeing him, but all the precautions that we can employ to that end will only serve to render us more odious to the one whose love we seek.

If there is one efficacious human means of extinguishing in the heart of the person we adore an inclination contrary to ours, which destroys our hope, it is to do the exact opposite of what jealousy inspires us to do: open all doors, occasion intimacies, dissimulate rendezvous and refrain from letting any indication show that we have the slightest suspicion. Furthermore, let us remain inactive, and certainly, either the Lady will weary of the depressing uniformity of an adventure that nothing opposes, or your rival will fall asleep in a lethargic calm. Then await events, and provided that you cannot be reproached for your suspicions and anxieties, it is a good bet that in the early days, when no resolution has yet been made, she will prefer to take you, being so easily within range, than to go seek further away.

As amour is certainly the principal source of our deviations, one cannot depict its different fanaticisms excessively. The most dangerous that it inspires in the fair sex is when a woman who sees her beauty in decline gets the perilous fancy into her head to attach to her chariot, which has lost its gilt, a more brilliant slave than the tarnished rig warrants.

A few simple reflections on the character of young men would allow her to perceive that a man of that age is the most superb and most despicable of all beings. The sight of that important verity would save her from limitless disgust, and, merely by opening her eyes to the disgraces of her peers, she would understand that all the presents in the two Indies cannot make up in the eyes of her lover for what age has destroyed in her own.

Attention to these moralities of the Sage ought to occupy women as soon as they reach their seventh lustrum; it would protect them from the inconvenience of seeing themselves once again, after the tenth, under the intolerable tyranny of a fruitless and scorned passion. I cannot finish this article better than with these words of the Doctor of our world that I have already cited:

"Youth," says that grave Writer, "can be adorned by natural right. It can be permitted to decorate an age that is the flower and verdure of years; but it is necessary to remain there. It would be strangely untimely to seek roses in the snow; it is only the stars that have the prerogative of always dancing, because they have the gift of perpetual young. The best thing, therefore, would be to take the advice of reason and a good mirror, to yield to decorum and necessity and to retire when night approaches."

Golden words, worthy of being pronounced by a Salamander, which are equally appropriate to both sexes. A man who attains his tenth lustrum ought to leave women to young men, as one abandons dolls to children.

Let us envisage now amour in the most cheerful of its tableaux. Is a young woman entering into Society? (I am still speaking of the Sublunar.) We shall see that all the harm that amour can do to her comes from her ignorance and her errors. The person of whom we speak, brilliant, perfect and adorable, emerges from solitude at the age of eighteen, completely uninstructed with regard to amour. That licentious term has scarcely brushed her chaste lips; she has not even seen any man other than the one who catechizes her, and he has repeated to her a thousand times that it is necessary to flee and detest the entire masculine species.

That speech has something superb and disdainful about it, which makes an impression on the young person, and her beauty persuades her, moreover, that she will effortlessly scorn the entire human species, which she does not know. But as soon as she takes her first steps in society, beautiful youth, adorned, brilliant, intelligent and complainant, enables her to perceive that her pride is not as sufficient a protection against amour as she thought; she perceives the injustice of the project that had made her hate what she did not know, and temperament soon gives her victorious advice, which renders her victim to the first person that hazard presents; a hundred others would be more worthy of that glory, but all are equal to one who knows no better.

If Abbesses, Mothers and Governesses indoctrinated their pupils with the good faith they deserve, they would learn about the traps that are bound to be set for them, the reasons that they have for avoiding them, for the sake of their own happiness, and the manner of saving themselves. The three species of delirium with which amour afflicts us prove that the faults it makes us commit are solely due to the ignorance in which we are abandoned of the means there are of turning the passion to our own benefit.

On emerging from the hands of a Mentor without capacity, Alexander mounts the Throne; his soul, which is only open to sensations, and which has not been educated as to its own interests, receives the first impressions that are given to it, and any idea seems good to it, because it is unable to distinguish those that it ought to prefer to others. In that pernicious state of indifference, it happens that the character of a conquering King is presented to him as a model; he adopts it, and all of his views tend only to war. He arms himself, he advances, and brings terror wherever he sets foot; he desolates fields, destroys cities, subjugates provinces and States, overthrows thrones and eventually immortalizes his vanity and folly by ravaging all of Asia.

If that Prince had known his duties, if he had only learned the rudiments of his métier, he would have known that a King ought only to seek the repose and advantage of his subjects, that the veritable glory consists in their love, and that the most dazzling triumph is in the sincere praise that they give him.

A King who aims at perfect heroism ought not to lose sight of the tacit pact that the people have made with him.

"We shall lavish upon you," they say, "respect, abundance, titles, luxury and voluptuousness, and will yield to you an ample share of our necessities; but it is on condition that you employ everything you have of intelligence and enlightenment to defend us, to render justice to us and procure our happiness. Our devotion and our acclamations, the most precious of all tributes, are at that price alone."

That discourse speaks to the heart and bears conviction to the soul; it is merely a matter of offering that idea to a Sovereign, in order to engage him to follow it—nothing is simpler or easier. But bad Advisers have given birth to the turbulent passion of war, and the lack of experience and reflection have prevented the sight of its inconveniences. It is no longer the appetite for war that it is necessary to weaken in the soul, but the unconsidered impetuosity of courage that it is necessary to repress.

Avarice, which is good for nothing, changes into praiseworthy thrift as soon as it is directed by reason.

Guide prodigality with prudence and it becomes a noble and well-intended liberality.

The timidity that comes from the nobility of the soul and the fear of failure is a fault when it is excessive, but it has little distance to travel in order to become that gentle modesty that someone has called the Lady Surrounded by Virtue.

Without going into further detail, it is clearly evident that the fire of passions is not the cause of their disorders, any more than the strength and sped of a horse are the cause of it running away with a poor rider, whom it throws and unsaddles. The same animal, in the hands of a good master, will obey the bit and feel the spur, and the resources it has, managed with art, will serve for the most hazardous enterprises and furnish the most beautiful excursions.

The passions are like the force and energy of our soul; their vivacity, according to the Sages of Mercury, produces our resources, and their weakness indicates our indigence. What good is the ponderous, taciturn, credulous, placid, insipid Citizen who feels nothing and desires nothing? He will, no doubt, be easily led by the Magistrate, but he will be good, at the most, for making shoes and distributing holy bread equitably.

If one compares to that honest Artisan an impetuous, elevated, luminous genius, impatient with repose, avid for knowledge, amorous of the truth, freed from false prejudices, one will see at a glance that it is necessary to leave the former to his trivial sphere, and that one can destine the other indifferently to command armies, regulating the police, making necessary financial arrangements, maintaining justice or fulfilling any of the vast functions of Ministry. Equally apt for everything, he will be able to turn his mind in accordance with the demands of the employment he fulfills, and that Citizen full of keen sentiments, which he is able to regulate, and passions of which he renders himself the master, will be a thousand times more useful to the fatherland than the most well-meaning and insipid of Compatriots.

Let us know the truth, let us listen to reason, let passion subsist and inconveniences will disappear.

CHAPTER XXI
On Religion

Religion is only founded on Mercury on the enlighten-ments of reason. It is believed that there are two kinds of sub-stances in the Universe, one spiritual and the other material; because one is convinced of that verity by continuous experi-ence, it being as easy to perceive that there is something with-in us that lives, and to know that there are material bodies like the stars and the elements.

They admit two orders of Intelligence, one superior, which is God, and the other inferior, which comprises the in-dividual souls of everything that is animate in the world; they believes them all to be equal, claiming that those of a mite, a man and an elephant are made of the same substance and are all immaterial.[15]

They regard the entire Universe as a Temple where one can adore God. He is, they say, equally present in all places and ever ready to listen to us, but as we are not always in a condition to talk to Him, they believe that it is necessary to assist piety with sensible things. For that reason there are a few magnificent Temples on Mercury, in which everything announces the grandeur and bounty of God.

The only worship they render Him is to have of that sov-ereign Being the most sublime idea they can conceive, to at-tribute to Him all perfections and to be penetrated with the keenest gratitude for the benefits with which He heaps hu-mans, and to love Him as much as the soul is capable of lov-ing.

I believe that I have already insinuated that the inhabit-ants of Mercury think that all the Stars and all the Planets are inhabited, and with a limitless variety, because Nature likes

---

[15] Author's note: "These people admit Metempsychosis, as we shall see."

nothing as much as diversity having thrown it with full hands into those different worlds.

None, according to them, is similar to any other; there is always a Sun and Planets, but that repetition excepted, the rest of the symmetry is infinitely diversified; nothing that can be seen and can be known in one Sun is found in another, There are different Animals, different Planets, other human forms, other senses, other knowledge, new ideas, other sentiments, and all of that drawing nearer to the best and most perfect without ever attaining it.

They say that all those Suns, so beautiful, so vast and so diverse are as many magnificent habitations that the sovereign Master has prepared for us, and in every one of which we shall have nothing to desire of everything that might make us happy, so long as we want to live in that delightful Fatherland. They are also sure that the Supreme Intelligence, which tales pleasure in augmenting our happiness, destines us for a greater one as soon as we have enjoyed the one that we have possessed; that, in truth, they do not know what species of happiness await us, but they are sure that it will be better than the one we enjoy, that that we can only ever emerge from a Sun where we have delighted in living in order to go to lead an even more delightful life in another.

As curiosity, they continue, is the most natural penchant of humans, as soon as they have lived for long enough in one Sun to know all of its marvels and to be, in a sense, sated with life there, they have only to desire to leave; the Sovereign Intelligence never refuses that permission. It is true that He only grants it on certain conditions, which seem difficult to humans; I shall explain the reasons for that, after having said what the conditions are on which it is permissible to pass from one Sun to another.

Firstly it is necessary to consent to lose absolutely the memory of everything one had ever known, and then to submit to passing from one of the Planets of the Vortex that one wants to leave into the one that it pleases the One that governs everything to assign to you.

There we commence by animating the body of an animal, the least on the Planet, and on its death we pass into the body of another more noble. For example, an oyster becomes a sole, a moth passes into the body of a wren and a hare delivered from its terrors becomes a greyhound. In the Sun, that transmigration of one soul into a number of bodies is called the Great Pilgrimage.

It is understood that the soul that makes it only ever lives one in each order of Animals. As there are a large number of different species on every planet, the tour is a long one, but in sum, it is usually completed in a thousand years, and that is when the pilgrim soul reaches the animation of a human body. Then, as soon as it dies, the course is concluded and the soul that finds itself liberated becomes an inhabitant of the Sun that is destined for it, where it is, as has been said, infinitely happier than the one it has quit.

It only arrives there in infancy, as it comes to our earth, but it suddenly finds itself as perfect, or even more so, as it was before its voyage. For in the moment that it is completed, the memory that it had lost returns to it, augmented by the wealth of knowledge that it has accumulated in its journey, and that memory is no longer subject either to loss or to diminution, exact on the occasion of a further voyage, which is a long term operation. For one rarely sees the inhabitants of any sun whatsoever who do not live there for at least a million centuries before thinking of quitting it.

To understand the reasons for the burdensome course that is imposed on every inhabitant wishing to pass from one Sun to another, it is necessary to know that all the subaltern Planets extract, so to speak, the life of everything that respires there from the Sun, on which they are dependent, and that all the Animals that die there pass from one body to another, always to a better one, until they reach that of a human, which is the end of the pilgrimage.

While the souls of Animals are passing through all the steps established in the Worlds from the least to the most noble, however, the bottom rungs would remain empty and the

Animals would gradually disappear from the surface of the earth. It is, therefore, to give life to all the organic bodies on a Planet that the souls that want to quit one Sun to go to another are obliged to go to a Planet in order to take the ultimate order of Animals and animate one of every species. By that simple means, the animal race is perpetuated and the decoration of all the globes is conserved as it pleases the Sovereign Artist to ordain.

A Sublunar Philosopher named Pythagoras once imagined the equality of souls and their transmigration from one body to another, but that circulation had no conclusion; the soul of an Animal animated the body of a Human, and reciprocally, the soul of a Human that of an Animal, without ever leaving the same globe. The inhabitants of Mercury believe in a Metempsychosis superior to that one, as they are themselves superior to Pythagoras.

Never, according to them, does a soul inhabit a member of the same species twice, which might be tedious, and never does it descend from a nobler one to one that is lesser so. On the contrary, when it has once reaches the stage of animating a Human, it passes on quitting it into a Sun, a place of delights where it acquires, on arrival, as has been said, all the memory of what it has been, what it has seen and what it has known in the other Suns through which it has traveled, and the other pilgrimages that it has made, for nothing of what it has learned since the instant of creation is lost to it; it forgets nothing, and it is only during the time of a pilgrimage—which is to say, when our soul inhabits a subaltern Planet—that its memory is labile and it can forget; but all its ideas return as soon as it arrives in a Sun, and in the same instant that it inhabits, everything that it has ever known is recovered and can no longer be forgotten.

Thus, to all that knowledge that it has already acquired, that acquired in its new habitation is added, in which it has encountered millions of novelties, perfecting itself incessantly. By means of knowledge that always becomes more exquisite and more sublime, it always approaches more closely the Sovereign Being, knows Him more perfectly, and loves Him with a love more enlightened and more worthy of His infinite grandeur.

It is for that reason that when one becomes weary of the magnificent dwelling that the All-Powerful has enriched with His gifts, millions of others, all preferable to that one await us; so that one can go forever from marvel to marvel, until, in the end, the soul goes, so to speak to lose itself in the bosom of God, from which it obtained its origin.

There, they say, are hopes worthy of human being, and promises that one can expect of the Omnipotence of God and His limitless bounty.

But I have not yet spoken about the souls of the animals of the Sun, nor those of Salamanders, which are the children of the Solar People.

The souls making the Great Pilgrimage on a Planet are so determined to certain functions so long as they animate the bodies of Beats that they have no liberty to abstract themselves from them. Thus, Animals can never go against their destination, nor displease the Sovereign Being; it is only to humans that He has allowed the liberty of employing the natural enlightenment that they are accorded in abundance well or badly, in order that they are in a condition to refrain from its abuse. When that occurs, therefore, as it is always by their fault, they are punished.

Those rebels against the general Law engraved in the ideas of all beings, are condemned after death to make in the Sun the same pilgrimage that they have just concluded on a Planet—which is to say, to animate a body of each order of animals, commencing with the least and concluding, as they have already done, with that of a human. But then they become Salamanders—which is to say, children of the inhabitants of the Sun. In that quality, they can no longer fail, but there remains a function for them to fulfill, which is to travel to the other Planets to fortify their reason with experience, and work for the benefit, as much as they can, of all the animals and humans there. They must, above all, spend a hundred years on the Planet where they committed their first fault, in order to repair it, and to employ all their industry in procuring the advantage of all the creatures that inhabit it.

Given that, one can judge the imbecility of the humans of the Earth who fear those benevolent spirits so much, which they mistake for malevolent spirits and flee with so much precaution—which often renders the good intentions of those Intelligences futile, for they are deterred by the stupidity of those to whom they address themselves, and although they are not irritated against then, they nevertheless resent them, and abandon them to the baseness of their prejudices.

When the hundred years that a Salamander must spend repairing his ancient fault have expired, he returns to the Sun from which he departed. That is where he completes his self-purification, by cultivating his mind for a few thousand years; then he is free to pass fully into the Sun that is destined for him, if during his human life he had always followed the light of reason.

The long interval of time that a soul employs repairing its fault, the Sovereign Being extends or reduces in accordance with the nature of the fault, but it never surpasses that of a complete pilgrimage. It often happens, when the fault is slight, that a human, on dying on a Planet, becomes a Salamander immediately, which abridges the penalty enormously. It is still a penalty to become a Salamander instead of immediately becoming an inhabitant of the Sun, but it is only just that faults should be published, however slight they are.

With regard to noble and generous souls who have chosen luminous reason and mild humanity as guides for their conduct, their beneficent death only delivers them from a difficult care and open the route for them to the Sun to which they are destined.

After being instructed in that economy of the Universe and the great wealth in which all souls are to participate, you might perhaps be surprised by the extreme repugnance that all animals testify for death. This is the reason for it.

Firstly, we believe, wrongly, that animals flee all kinds of death indifferently; they only dread accidental death—which is to say, one that might overtake them before the term fixed by Nature. Now, that dread is only inspired in them to engage them to conserve their lives for a certain number of years appropriate to their estate. With regard to natural death, they do not fear it, nor are they aware of it; they do not even suspect what might happen in their maladies; the dissolution of the machine takes place before they have foreseen it and without their sensing it.

For humans, it is a matter of necessity that they be forced to dread death in order to oblige them to live; for without the terrors that it causes them, a thousand reasons would oblige them every day to seek it, and they would find it rather than awaiting it placidly., if they could regard it solely as a resource against the evils that happen to them....

I was at that point in the manuscript when I perceived my Salamander in the same place where I had seen him the first time. I ran toward him with my piece of paper in my hand.

"Has something stopped you?" he said to me. "Speak—I am ready to reply to all your doubts."

"I have understood," I replied to him, "that souls pass from a Planet into a Sun, and even from one Vortex to another, but there remains one great difficulty for me in that. The Geometers of our world have demonstrated that if a Millstone fell from the Sun on to our world it would only arrive there after many years. I can see that a spirit travels more rapidly than a mass of stone, but still it can only cover immense distances in a certain span of time. Settle my mind in that score, by some approximation that might serve as a measure. How many months, or days, for instance, does an Intelligence employ in traveling from Saturn to the Sun, where it has to cover two or three hundred million leagues?"

"An indivisible instant," he replied. "You have been to China, you have seen the Emperor sit down at table a hundred times. Imagine that you see him there, that the instant when the idea forms in your soul, is the moment that your soul arrives in China. It could equally well go from one end of the Universe to the other in the same space of time. The invisible chain that links it to your body seems to attach it locally at a certain place, but as soon as that bond is broken, by wishing to be to another point in the Universe, it really is there; space is nothing in relations to a soul."

He went on: "You have difficulty understanding that, but it is one of the verities that is beyond human reach. It is as impossible for me to make you sense it, because of the scant enlightenment that you have, as it would be for you to explain to someone born blind what red or blue is. You find here a true opportunity to humiliate your mind in recognizing its insufficiency, but it is also necessary that an idea so reasonable, which leads us naturally to admire divine power, leads us to love its bounty, which had deigned to assure us of boundless happiness, and to establish the admirable Metempsychosis that has just been explained to you.

"I can see by your expression," the Salamander continued, "that you still in doubt."

An unfortunate smile that escaped me at that moment confirmed that idea.

"O petty sublunar humans!" he exclaimed. "Narrow minds, which you always strive to shrink even further means of ignorance and stupidity, will you never form a noble idea of the Sovereign Being that is worthy of Him? Elevate your mind, my future Compatriot, and believe that the resources of Divine Power are infinite to heap you with happiness. Since you have a continuous experience of His good will in that regard, so do not enter into these base suspicions of His power and bounty, for they simultaneously dishonor your judgment and the most noble of beings."

It only remains for me to make the observation that the Sun can furnish the Planets of its Vortex with a sufficient number of Intelligences to animate all the animals and humans it contains without any difficulty.

You will be easily convinced of that possibility if you make the reflection that the Sun is about three million times larger than Mercury and that each Planet only has a fixed number of inhabitants, equal for all the Planets. The difference there is between them consists of the fact that they are larger on the large planets and smaller on the smaller ones, in accordance with the proportions of their surface area.

The number of inhabitants of the Sun is, however, so prodigious that there is often no empty place in the Planets of its Vortex, in order that someone undertaking a Great Pilgrimage could commence it.

I am omitting, in order not to burden your memory, a great number of details consequent upon the general arrangement, but any intelligent person can easily imagine them, provided that he takes correct reasoning and the good intentions of the Legitimate Sovereign as rules for his ideas; for He has never had any other principle for His works, and that unique method of following reason and doing good to all the Intelligence of the second order is the cause of the formation of the Universe, its immense extent and the prodigious variety that embellishes it.

CHAPTER XXII
On Feasts

I am not talking here about celebrations established on Mercury as acts of religion but those that are devoted to the relaxation and pleasure of the people.

Feasts are one of the principal social bonds between human beings and a very abundant source of pleasures. But on Mercury, as the best fare in the world is communal and costs nothing, it is necessary, on feast-days, to add a new feature to it that renders it more desirable and engages the inhabitants of the Planet to assemble on those days.

There are, as we have said, Birds that serve as purveyors, going every day to the little hills to obtain what the masters to whom they are attached request of them. But there is only one day, which is the first of the week, when they can fly to the summit of a hill that is higher than all the others. There they find the delicious foodstuffs that are reserved for Feast Days; but they never go there if the meal that they have to bring back is destined for fewer than four people; they stop on the other hills and only fill their baskets with ordinary foodstuffs.

It is impossible to say what that kind of food is, because those who have eaten it ten thousand times cannot compare it to anything else, and it does not resemble anything that we can imagine. The dishes at one feast are so different from those at another that it is held to be true on the Planet that the old people who remember the arrival of the first Emperor have never eaten one of them twice.

That prodigious variety extends even further, for no purveyor Bird brings to its master a meal similar to that supplied to another, and as each one takes that domestic of sorts with him to the place where people are assembling to eat, the dishes are all different from one another. It is that reason more than any other that engages the people to gather together, for the more people there are at a table, the more diversity is found there.

Everyone can share with all the guests that which he finds most exquisite, and there is no danger that the sharing diminishes the distributors portion It is merely a matter of sending for more of the same things whenever one wants, which is done by placing a little morsel of what one desires in the Bird's basket. The purveyors take no account of the trouble as long as the day lasts, so one has no need to be sparing, as on other days, on which they only go to fetch the necessary aliments.

The wines are no less good and no less varied than anything else, but what is very singular is that they cannot intoxicate throughout that day or the following night. The following day they become mortal, for the reason that those infinitely delicate liquors corrupt very easily, so it never happens that the pleasures of the table last that long.

In truth, some people prolong it for the greater part of the day, but that only happens among the populace, who prefer the pleasure of the senses to any other. They are, moreover adequately penalized for it, for, in addition to an infinity of distractions that they miss, such as an ordinary day provides—races between the young people, flights that they make, of surprising agility, baths, and the innocent combats of animals in the water and on land—they cannot take part in the general lottery, which is always drawn at sunset. We shall give an explanation of that amusement.

The Salamanders that are completing their terms on one Planet, and are ready to leave it in order to voyage through all those of the Vortex, receive from the Sun, their fatherland, an infinity of precious bagatelles, of which there is not the slightest knowledge on the subaltern Planets, and they abandon them on the ones they are about to leave, on condition that the Emperor will have them distributed in lotteries, to which admission is *gratis*.

The total number of tickets is always equal to that of the inhabitants of the locale: men, women and children. All those wishing to take part in the draw have only to present themselves at the place of assembly before the Sun sets, for at the moment that it disappears the barriers are closed and no one else can enter.

As the number of lots is always fixed at ten tickets, if it happens that a few inhabitants of the place, occupied elsewhere, do not present themselves, as many blank tickets are withdraw, which the missing inhabitants could have drawn—which evidently gives an advantage to those present. That abstraction having been made, everyone draws a ticket, and if it is not blank, his prize is announced, which is delivered to him immediately.

One discovers on those tickets surprising machines, marvelous automata, fabrics superior to those normally manufactured by the Salamanders, instruments appropriate to augment the action of all the senses—such as, for example, spy-glasses that see into the interior of the hardest metals and stones; little lenses that allow the souls of humans to be read; funnels that allow speech addressed to addressed to us ten leagues away to be heard; and trumpets able to fortify the sound of one's voice, but made with such artistry that only the person to whom the words are addressed can hear them.

Sometimes one wins a sense that other humans do not have, or a rare talent, perhaps even a unique one. I knew one man who acquired in a lottery the art of curing bad Authors of the stupid determination to write; he executed it by tearing out a certain hair, which he was able to distinguish from all the others; the remedy was sufficient provided that it was not a matter of Poetry, for in that case it was necessary to combine the removal of the hair with a violent slap.

Another could read in his hand the universal Gazette of everything that was happening on Saturn, including its ring and its five satellites.

It would be necessary to make an entire book of the different prizes and the marvelous jewels that could be won in that lottery. Perhaps I will give at the end of this history a more detailed account of a part of what I saw during my rather long sojourn on Mercury; I shall send it to my reader.

The only inconvenience that is found in the acquisition of these gifts of chance is that they only last for twenty years, at the end of which they lose their properties completely, in the same way that among us, the gift of a good horse only lasts for a certain number of years.

In addition to that amusement, which ordinarily ends with the daylight, one has for the night that of public spectacles whose charm is indescribable—but one can imagine it, after a fashion, when one knows that all the troupes of Actors are equally perfect on Mercury, and that there is none who has not played his role in his turn before the Emperor, who wants to judge the talent of the Actors personally, because it is to their care that the instruction of the people is committed. They are, so to speak, the Preachers on Mercury, where it is held as a maxim that:

> Of fictions, the vibrant liberty
> Often depicts better the verity
> Of which monastic sternness would fashion
> A lugubrious and ponderous lesson.[16]

The Actors on Mercury thus present the moral floridly, and ornamented, accompanied by fine and delicate allegories and sensible and persuasive examples that the themes imprint in souls with the aid of an eloquence appropriate to a declamation perfectly adapted to the subject, and everything that decoration, costume and spectacle are capable of insinuating into

---

[16] Author's note: "Rousseau." The reference is to the poet and dramatist Jean-Baptiste Rousseau (1671-1741), who was famous for his epigrams. The verse cited here, from one of his Allegories, was reproduced in early 18th century updates to Antoine Furetière's *Dictionnaire universel* (originally published 1690), where the present author might well have run across it.

the heart in order to establish amour, virtue and the hatred of vice.

There are a few other Festivals on the Planet, as, for example, at the wedding of the Emperor, after a victory on the Great Mountain, or the arrival of a new Sovereign; but it is always the Emperor who meets the expenses of those public rejoicings, and the people only bring their delight, their good wishes and their acclamations to them.

CHAPTER XXIII
On Gambling

Gambling is not ruinous on Mercury, as on the other Planets, where people almost never gamble except at the expense of others, but it is no less interesting for that, for everything that can be won is always very useful or agreeable, as you will see.

I have said that the Salamanders manufacture all fabrics and ever things that servers as adornment or furniture; but their skill and there activity is not limited to that simple and mechanical labor. They design jewelry of every kind, prodigies of charm and skill, extremely handy bagatelles and an even greater number of other things that are merely superfluous, so to speak, items of luxury and delicacy which only amuse the minds, eyes and taste of the most sophisticated people in the entire Vortex.

The Salamanders compete with one another as to who can produce the most marvelous and original work. In addition, all the superior Genii that inhabit the Sun, and who are what the Salamanders will become in their turn when they have finished their thousand-year novitiate in the Planets, who are all benevolent, send the Emperor innumerable rarities that originate from or are manufactured in the great Empire of Light. They reach him by way of influences that are invisible but reliable couriers.

As the Emperor is accustomed to these prodigies, which are very common in his Fatherland, if he receives them with pleasure it is because he can distribute them to his beloved people, not to keep them or enjoy them. He is capable of making masterpieces of that sort whenever he pleases, but, fully occupied with governing the Planet confided to him, he does not have the leisure to amuse himself with those bagatelles, which are surprising marvels for the inhabitants of Mercury.

It is, therefore, established by order of the Emperor that all the works of the Salamanders and those he receives from the Sun are conserved in public storehouses situated in the cities of the Empire. Those magnificent edifices, and those of the Imperial City, are no better stocked than one another.

All these different curiosities are inscribed in order in Registers that the Salamanders keep, committed to the care of the stores. Each article is a lot destined for the player who wins it, which is determined in the following manner.

It is always the player who makes the largest gain to whom the lot belongs, the others getting nothing. As soon as the game is finished, a domestic Bird of the house where the game has taken place flies of the store, where the Salamander in charge of it gives it the lot inscribed at the head of the List, and that Article is erased. The next lot will go to the winner of the next game played in the dependency of the store.

That Register is only known to the Salamanders, so one never knows what one is playing for, but one is always certain of being content to have won. If the Bird sent to fetch the prize is not strong enough to carry what it is given, Birds from the store assist it, and they convey the lot to the individual who has won it. If the winner desires that it is taken directly to him, he is obeyed, but he deprives those who have played of the pleasure of amusing themselves momentarily by seeing what he has won, and he would have to be in a very bad mood to be so impolite.

It is necessary to know that one can only play one game of that sort per day in each house. If one wants to continue, one plays for money, or jewels, or what one has won from the Imperial store—in sum, anything one thinks appropriate. It is true that people commonly restrict themselves to that first game, because the inhabitants of Mercury have such a great variety of pleasures that they cannot occupy themselves with the same one for very long.

CHAPTER XXIV
Public Schools

If you remember the manner in which things are built on Mercury, the richness of the materials and the intelligence of the Salamanders, you will not doubt the magnificence of public edifices. When one is to be built, the Salamanders assemble by order of the Emperor, are given the design and are charged with carrying it out, without sparing anything. Thus, there is nothing the imagination can invent that is pleasant and comfortable that is not found therein. As the majority of ideas are precise on Mercury, it is felt there that the mind is never more capable of attention than when the body is at ease.

With that is mind, they are not content with magnificence and charm in the furnishing of these Palaces; it is combined with all that delicacy can contrive of the most extensive luxury. There is at least one of these places of Assembly in every city, and they are multiplied in accordance with need and in proportion to the number of their inhabitants. It is there that almost all the people of the Planet come together on certain days at fixed times, although no one is constrained.

The scene opens with the performance of a little comic play accompanied by various pieces of music and dance appropriate to the subject. In that prelude there is no objective but the design to entertain, in order to dispose the mind by pleasure to the instruction that is to follow, and to conciliate by an amusing spectacle the favor of the audience.

When the play is finished, some inhabitant of the Great Mountain—a Sage, Genius or Fay of the first order—explains some of the operations of nature. He unveils the finesses of mechanics, the simplicity of its principles and the relationships full of wisdom and industry that are found between the nature of the subject and the usage to which the Sovereign Architect has destined it.

After having given that palpable explanation, the one who has made it hardly ever fails to find an opportunity therein to praise in an eloquent and sublime fashion that attribute of the Divinity that has the closest relationship with that work of Nature. Sometimes it is the omnipotence of the primal Being that is remarked upon, sometimes the sublimity of His intelligence and the accuracy of His views, and at other times His skill, the fecundity of His ideas or His bounty in the generation of a Work so necessary to the pleasure of humans and so appropriate to their needs.

The whole of that discourse in physics is not much longer than the comic scene that preceded it, not that which follows it, for on Mercury, one always avoids useless speeches, ponderous narrations and the prolixity that is the mother of boredom.

A dramatic performance follows the explanation; there is always a default which is played in contrast to the opposed truth, in order to make the latter loved and the former detested. Lycurgus might have obtained from a Mercurian Sage the idea of sometimes showing the Republicans a drunken lout in order to disgust them with drunkenness and inspire them to temperance in their repasts.

CHAPTER XXV
On the Art of Writing

The Art of writing has no part of human industry on Mercury; it is a pure present of nature. It is sufficient to think and to desire the thought to be written and it will place itself on the paper of its own accord. There is, therefore, no other ceremony to perform to write Letters, speeches or a Book than to set paper before one and place writing equipment on the paper; then, everything that you imagine will be written, as if you had taken the trouble to trace all the letters.

A letter, once written, will carry itself to the person to whom it is addressed, and it informs them by means of an interior sentiment from whom it comes. Then, if they wants to know what it contains, the same interior sentiment informs them; but if one does not have the leisure to read it at the moment, one put it in one's pocket, and when one has nothing to do one has only to turn one's thoughts in that direction, and what is written in the letter will reveal itself.

If, by chance, one does not remember to read it, every time one puts one's hand into one's pocket, one will not fail to find it between one's fingers, in order to provide a reminder that it would like to be read, and will not rest until it is either read or torn up—for then it no longer has any virtue, and all the writing disappears. The same thing happens if some curious individual to whom it is not addressed decides to open it, for all the artifice resides in the seal, with the result that as long as it remains entire the letter can be read, but as soon as it is broken, the whole discourse evaporates and the paper remains blank.

When it happens, therefore, that someone wants to show a letter to a friend, it is necessary for him to refrain from opening it and giving it to him sealed; it is necessary, too, that he consents to it being read, and then the confidant is informed of what it contains.

The same thing happens with a Book. If the person to whom it belongs does not want anyone else to read it, he has only to desire that the pages remain blank for anyone other than him, and the Book will no longer appear to be anything but bound paper. That is so commonplace that if someone lends a Book to a friend without having given him at least tacit permission to read it, nothing will be seen to be written therein—but that does not happen often. Everything that is printed and sold in Bookshops is legible to everyone, unless the purchaser issues a contrary order.

Another great convenience that Mercurian books have is that they open directly at the place where one wants to commence reading, and the page turns of its own accord when it has been read. In the same way, without one being obliged to mark the place where one stops, it will reopen there went one picks it up to continue reading.

The mothers-in-law and husbands who use so much trickery in our world in order to read letters surreptitiously have their noses put out of joint there, for nothing annoys that kind of person more than the despair of being able to discover what they want to prevent.

On the other hand, jealous lovers develop squashed noses because they are forever running into the doors and windows through which they want to pass in order to spy on those they love. To explain this fact, one needs to know that all the approaches of a rendezvous, although seemingly open, are naturally closed. A perfectly transparent but very wall forbids entry, provided that those who have an interest in not being surprised have taking the precaution of wanting that impenetrable wall to be formed; that is what is known on Mercury as a "*pot au noir*."[17]

---

[17] The term *pot-au-noir* [roughly, black spot] originated as mariners' slang for the geographical region known in English as the doldrums, and was transferred to metaphorical common parlance in much the same way; I have left it untranslated be-

It does no good to put out one's hands in order to feel whether that wall is there, for the hands and the rest of three body pass through with the same facility as in free air; it is only the nose that bumps into the invisible wall. Now, as it is not usual for a man to go where his nose cannot, Nature, which does nothing futile, is content to impose that small difficulty on the perverse intentions of the jealous.

It is apparently from that custom that the Sages of our world who frequent Mercurians have derived cautionary warnings against "poking one's nose where it doesn't belong," which are delivered in an ironic tone, to signify the futility of such desires.

But, you might say, if one is certain of finding an invisible obstacle to investigations one carries out contrary to the liberty of others, would people on Mercury not be deterred from making such attempts? That is fair comment, but it sometimes happens that two people in love are so occupied with one another that they forget any other concern, including that of their own security. Do we not see the same thing in our world, where more than one pretty woman has been taken by surprise after having forgotten to bolt her door? It is sufficient for that negligence to be possible, and that it happens once in ten thousand cases, for a jealous individual who has time to waste to attempt to satisfy his mania at the expense of his nose.

A similar imprudence of a different species is very common on our world. All gamblers are aware of the composure that one requires to win at Pharaoh;[18] it happens, however, that an unfortunate banker has a big win by the greatest fluke. The

---

cause the phrase crops up later in a different context, and the English word would not be appropriate in either instance.

[18] Pharaoh, or Faro, was a gambling game popular at the court of Versailles during the reign of Louis XIV; it bears some resemblance to the modern games of pontoon and baccarat, in that a banker plays against a number of other players simultaneously, thus risking a great deal on each hand.

false favorite of fortune then ruins himself like a hundred thousand others. Why, he says to himself, should I not win today? I did well with the bank yesterday. In that instance, reason is against you, and the hazard that enabled you to succeed once is more submissive than you think to certain rules and a definite number of combinations.

If you want to justify what is advanced here you only have to take two perfectly square dice; you will see that in forty throws you will not fail to bring about the doublets of which you have thought. That which we regard as blind chance is nothing but a necessary consequence of general Laws, which determine that a particular combination will inevitably arrive in a certain number of throws.[19]

Thus it happens that having lost for a long time at Pharaoh, one will eventually win, but as the combinations of that game are very numerous, and one does not count up the daily losses in the orders prescribed, it happens that before encountering the day when one wins a thousand pistoles one has lost two thousand, because that day is perhaps only one in a hundred, and instead of risking ten pistoles every day, which would be the correct proportion, one loses twenty, thirty or more. Furthermore, the indulgence that concedes the House at least twelve per cent gratis increases the difficulty of winning at the same—or, rather, demonstrates its impossibility mathematically.

It is by virtue of reasoning founded on the same principle that jealous individuals are subject to squashed noses on Mercury—but I shall return to the Art of writing, from which subject I have gradually deviated.

If one wants to erase something that one has written, the words that one takes back evaporate and those one substitutes for them take their place. In that case the lines draw apart and close up of their own accord, as required—which is very useful, for by reading over a Letter written in haste once or twice,

---

[19] This is not true, but it does not affect the validity of the general argument.

one can take out all the repetitions, badly-turned phrases and unexpressive words, and reestablish in according with reason the order of a badly-formed argument, in which one finds at the end what ought to have been at the beginning, and items preceding that ought to follow. As a result of that facility, people on Mercury write very well: a fortunate talent that is almost entirely due to the habit they have of being able of erase, which Nature facilities in the people in question with so much advantage.

Many people who never reflected on the power of Nature might have difficulty believing all that has just been said about the manner of writing, but they will soon be convinced of the possibility of that usage when they know that, by virtue of an institution of the Great Architect, Books and the entire art of writing are as submissive to the will of the inhabitants of Mercury as the parts of their body are to the intelligence that animates them.

One does not know by what artifice one moves an arm or a leg; all that one can say is that those actions are executed with an admirable facility as soon as we desire them. It is the same on Mercury, with the talent of reading and writing; it is, so to speak, a sixth sense, or an extra organ of which we are ignorant because we are deprived of it; but should one dare to say that Nature can only give five of them to humans because we have no more than that? We feel, on the contrary, that we lack an infinite number.

For example, one might sense what the people who are looking at us are thinking about us; one might sense what impression a certain step we want to take would make on another person; we could do with another sense to tell us whether some salt, alkali or sulfate is useful or harmful to us, and whether some liquid will aid or interrupt the circulation of our blood.

If we had an interior sense to assemble easily all the relationships of numbers and geometrical figures, in the same way that we have one that persuades us invincibly that two and two make four and that a line falling obliquely toward another will intersect it at a certain point, the study of Mathematics would be mere child's play to us, and it would be sufficient to see the most difficult propositions to understand them as easily as we perceive red and green by opening our eyes in daylight.

But it would take too long to examine the innumerable list of senses and organs that Nature could have given us, and might perhaps have distributed in all the globes that compose the Universe, to a greater or lesser degree—for it is not impossible that there are creatures that possess a thousand different senses, while we only have five, a thousand portals by which the soul could perceive objects, or, reciprocally, by which objects could vibrate the little highly mobile threads of the nerves in order that their agitation might reach the soul and give it a certain conception or sentiment. Because the thinking being is always highly disposed to think and to feel; it only lacks instruments by which to perceive objects, and the objects channels full of spirits sufficiently mobile to be agitated by the slightest movement.

Let no one be astonished, then, by the power that the soul has in the bodies of the inhabitants of Mercury to imprint thought on paper, since we feel that among us it imprints them on the memory, which is, in effect, nothing but a tablet artfully worked. In any case, whether one doubts that truth or accepts it, it nevertheless remains true that humans do not write in any other way on Mercury. Only the fish there write like us; the sluggish and slothful people in question adapt well to that slow manner of writing; it gives them the leisure necessary to reflect and the art of expressing their thought more rapidly would be no use to them, for the coldness of their phlegmatic imagination cannot animate it sufficiently to need such an expeditious Secretary.

CHAPTER XXVI
On Laughter

Laughter, the most precious of the gifts of Nature, is no less familiar on Mercury than among us, and everyone carries at birth a certain dose of gaiety and good humor. But the inhabitants of that Planet have one great advantage in that regard over all the other peoples in the Universe, for they can buy laughter, joy, expansion and cheerfulness. There are Merchants in every City who sell that inestimable commodity by the grain.

When one wants to take some, one allows it to dissolve in a spoonful of a clear liquid which is known as complaisance water, and which falls every evening like the dew on that fortunate planet. It is ordinarily on awakening that one takes the first dose of that elixir, instead of tea; one takes another when one sits down at table, if one is not eating alone; one never fails to equip oneself with a supply before going out into Company.

Unfortunately, it is not very easy to have such powders well prepared, for the Artists who sell them are not equally well-equipped; people often get poorly prepared drugs, in consequence of which, for instance, when one wants to buy veritable laughter one only gets forced laughter, pointless laughter—the most insipid kind—habitual laughter or, worst of all, long bursts of laughter.

If one addresses oneself to a first-class Druggist, however, one finds nothing in the shop but quality goods; it is furnished with thin smiles, delicate smiles and malicious smiles, and even goes as far as bitter smiles, although they are scarcely used on the Planet. Such people also boast of having silly laughter; it is true that no one ever buys it on its own, but when it is mixed with other drugs in very small quantities it sometimes gives them an edge, and it is not impossible that it might improve them, provided that it is well prepared.

I know a distiller called N*** who had all these powders; he was the greatest Artist on the Planet, but he had one fault very harmful to the sales of his elixirs, which is that he had only to show himself and it seemed that everyone had been furnished by his shop, so much joy would suddenly spread through the assembly. He had, however, not sold anything or given it away; it was sufficient to see and hear him; his attitude and mannerisms had the same effect as his stock-in-trade.

The majority of people prefer that purchased laughter to the natural, which is not always of good quality. There is, however, one kind that Nature furnishes to everyone and which has a very good effect when it is diluted with the elixir of youth; that is the perpetual laughter of childhood—but it only lasts for a time. For someone born to ample fortune and long prosperity there is something scornful and conceited about it which renders it hateful.

Sardonic laughter, the child of self-love and envy, and the ironic laughter that is child of hatred and malignity, although one obtains them from Nature, are repellent on Mercury; people avoid those who make use of them, and encountering them is considered to be a bad omen.

There are Quacks who have tried to sell wit in the same way that laughter and gaiety are sold, but they have been ruined by that commerce, for want of customers. The Emperor has forbidden it as contraband merchandise, because wit ought not to be studied and cannot be stored without considerable depreciation, so when it arrives in the shop it can only be retailed as poor quality merchandise, which spreads distaste and boredom—epidemic diseases of a sort—among the Public. The Edict added that, that talent of wit having descended from the Heavens, it is not permitted to humans to counterfeit it.

CHAPTER XVII
On Fashion

I have already said that there is no general Fashion on Mercury, but that everyone dresses in accordance with their own whim and invention, as in our Masquerades. The Tailors of the Planet are principally occupied in devising clothes agreeable and suitable to individuals, in order to make the most of the charms and hide the petty faults of each one.

Although it is true that beauty is more widespread there than anywhere else, that does not mean that there are no deformed individuals there, or those who at least leave something to be desired. That is always a fault, which it is good to disguise by and innocent Art, since Art is only given to human to second Nature, or to aid her when she is lacking.

By the same token, every individual has some advantage that others do not have, and as clothing is to people what frames are to paintings, one always chooses that which ornaments most effectively and brings out more fully the graces of Nature. But as diversity is in all things the most general source of all kinds of enhancements, that which is established in the adornment of women and the clothing of men is almost infinite, for the coiffure as well as the rest of the apparel.

For that reason, promenades and assemblies are always a very cheerful and very agreeable spectacle, as much because of the great variety of colors and the admirable fabrication of fabrics, which are always in exquisite taste, and the Art of putting them to work, in which the couturiers of Mercury excel to a far greater extent than what is contrived in that genre in all the other Planets, and even at the Opéra.

Although all sorts of adornment are indifferently acceptable, there is no risk that women ever dress like men, or men like them. Propriety and decorum are too precisely observed on the Planet for anyone to commit such an offense against visual sensitivity, which is the true judge in that matter. In fact, what suits one sex does not suit the other, in relation to the different conformity of the figure; so, although there is no question in that of any decency in relation to mores on Mercury, there is one founded in good taste, and for that reason, no one ever departs from it—with the result that there is always a widespread difference in the garments and coiffure that distinguish the sexes.

The different professions are also recognizable, but that is by virtue of certain particular marks, such a ribbon, a brooch, a bouquet or a feather in the hat, adapted to the garments that everyone wears to their owe taste; a judge does not dress any differently than another man, and no color is forbidden to him or ordained, as among us.

Philosophers and Sages adapt themselves to that custom without difficulty. As the knowledge of the Mysteries of the Cabala has rejuvenated them, or they achieve that result by possession of the philosophers' stone, they put on as good a show as any agreeable person in the land. Cardan,[20] for example, who was, it seems to me, clad in black buckram on our World, is often dressed in a celestial blue that suits him very well. Descartes, the last time I saw him, had a gray linen suit garnished with silver filigree. The devout Comte de Gabalis combs his beard every day and distinguishes himself from the Devotees of our world by the delicacy and whiteness of his underwear, which he imports from the Milky Way, where the most skillful laundresses in the Universe are found.

The worthy Flamel has renounced the dead-leaf-brown soutane that he wore beneath the Charnel-Houses of the Holy Innocents,[21] and ordinarily dresses in agate taffeta, which suits

---

[20] Gerolamo Cardano (1501-1576) the mathematician who founded probability theory, in the slightly-mistaken fashion set out by the present author in his chapter on gambling. He also wrote books on medicine and alchemy.

[21] Nicolas Flamel (c1330-1418), who had a house overlooking the cemetery of the Holy Innocents—famous for the elevated ossuaries surrounding the graveyard, which provided a kind of

him quite well because he suffers somewhat from acne, not without a suspicion of a red nose. For his eternal other half, his little Perenelle, it is more than seventy years since she resumed the color of Rose, with a form determination never to quit it. Her clothes are made of gauze or butterfly-wings, which are worked infinitely well in that land, and she achieves prodigies with her hair, although it is a trifle frizzy and very thin over the temples. She has presented several requests to the Emperor to have them better furnished, but he always replies, in order to get out of it with a polite refusal, that he refrains from trespassing on the prerogatives of the philosopher's stone and that the faults of Nature that it cannot repair are beyond his jurisdiction; thus, to all appearances, the little Maid continues to live with deprived temples and a forehead poorly disposed to the point so essential to the coiffure.

Common sense and reason sustained by public authority issue from time to time a few general precepts against the enterprises of Fashion, their enemy, which often comes from our world to make ridiculous irruptions on Mercury.

Our last proclamations declared that, hair being destined by nature to accompany the visage, it was necessary to refrain from distancing it therefrom. They also forbade Ladies to wear garments too tight-fitting, alleging the privilege of noble parties whose excessively narrow confinement might be prejudicial to health, the mother of beauty. They also prescribed a

---

covered promenade for strollers—was a prosperous dealer in paper and manuscripts, who was only credited posthumously with an entirely false reputation as an alchemist, but subsequently became more famous in literary works than any actual alchemist. His fortune was partly derived from his marriage to a rich widow named Perenelle, who died in 1397; her will, leaving her money to Nicolas, was then famously contested by her family; she appears as his collaborator is the fanciful accounts of his supposed alchemical adventures—including the anecdote subsequently included, somewhat anomalously, in the present text.

great moderation in the volume of coiffures, and remarked that, a small head being one of the great gifts that Nature accords to her Favorites, it was an enormous fault against good taste to increase its size and drown its delicate features in a superfluity of coiffure. They prescribed too the austere mediocrity of Rouge, which they did not permit in the great excess that went as far as the color of offended modesty.

There were also a few Tariffs regarding the number of handkerchiefs, and an Alphabetical Table for their placement on different occasions, but I have forgotten them, as well as an Edict relating to the measurement of fans, to which excessive length an appearance of an offensive weapon ill befitting the tenderness of the fair sex.

At the very time when everyone, deferring to the Proclamations, had consulted reason and good taste with regard to adornment, and the people of the Planet had never been as well dressed, Fashion arrived, legs akimbo, astride Extravagance; its coiffure was no less than waist-long, comprising in addition a fifth of the total height; imperious Scarlet shone on her cheeks; her hair was carefully gathered into a prison of fustian holding it far from the visage; her waist could be encircled by two hands, and the rest of her adornment was admirably assorted.

In that state she dared to show herself in public, but to her misfortune, fine Habit was already walking there, between her Favorites, Good Taste and Reason. They had no sooner seen that impertinent composite of falsity and ridicule than they resolved to take her down a peg or two, and without anything being communicated, everyone imagined some prank. That of Reason was to cut the laces of Fashion's corset. Good Taste, who, by chance was sporting a pretty little hat after the fashion of the Empress, planned to detach the big one that Fashion was wearing and give her another. Sensible Habit wanted to remove the hair from under bonnet and wipe off her rouge at the same time—but whoever attempts too much achieves little, and he did none for having wanted to do too many. No sooner had Fashion felt her laces cut and her hat removed than she fled at top speed, regained her mouth and returned to our world with her natural waist, free of the shackles of laces, and wearing her little hat.

Scarcely had she appeared in that new accoutrement that our pretty women, who only ever consult one another with their eyes, thought it as an agreeable novelty that she was bringing from Mercury, and departed immediately to loosen their laces and prune their hats. Since then bodices have passed for an obsolete and proscribed invention; since the reformation of hats, hair has gradually reclaimed its ancient right to approach the face, which cannot be praised too highly.

My Sage claims that if Fashion takes it into her head to take Petticoats to Mercury, in accordance with the latest creation, she cannot fail to be universally cheered.

PART TWO

CHAPTER I
On Epic Poetry and Romances

The composition of Works of the Imagination appeared to the Emperor to be such an important matter for Policing that he has not disdained to prescribe the principal Regulations by means of a Decree which the great Descartes was charged with drafting; he did so in the following terms:

Whether an Author intends a Work to form the Mind and Mores, or whether he has no other objective in composing than to amuse himself and others—these two objects being equally important to the wellbeing of society, which is the dearest of our cares—we are persuaded that Imperial authority cannot be better employed than to prevent by an irrevocable Law the faults that might be committed in that genre.

To these effects, we enjoin every Composer of Poems or Poetic Romances:

1. To make a hero not a demigod but a human being. We forbid him to execute any enterprise above human force. We enjoin him only to perceive natural objects in the places that he traverses in the rapid course of his conquests, and not vain chimeras beyond all belief.[22]

---

[22] Not being a Mercurian, the author of the present work was under no obligation to follow rules made there. It is, however, perfectly evident that these rules are being addressed to Earthly authors, not Mercurian ones, so it is not obvious why the author is unprepared to offer them the same latitude as he gives himself, with the support of the same excuses.

2. We forbid him all commerce with the Gods, Genii, Fays and other elementary peoples, whose existence is not established in the other Planets. If he is brave, he must be so without the aid of Mars or Minerva; let him not traverse the sea under the protection of Neptune, but with the aid of the wind; dreams should not instruct him as to the future or give him any precepts for the present.

Let his arms not come from Heaven, and let him only carry a shield of shiny steel without any figures sculpted or engraved, as being in that regard an excessive waste of time for workmen to employ in embellishing an instrument overly exposed to the trenchant edges of swords, on which figures would soon be maimed—an accident that can only happen to the great scorn of the fine Arts, whose productions deserve to be preserved more carefully.

Descents into Hell and flights to the Empire of the Moon are similarly forbidden to him; he will, in consequence, have no dealings with Magicians and Demons.

The hero will be formed, in possible, sufficiently sensate to have no need of the advice of Angels or to be instructed by them as to the map of the country into which he takes his army. He will know without them the forests where one can find wood to make war machines, and also the places filled with forage and appropriate to the subsistence of his troops.

Hell will not enter into negotiations in his regard and will allow him to lead his soldiers peacefully if the roads are clear.

If the Hero of the story has not yet attained his eighth lustrum, the Poet can suppose him to be amiable, and even amorous, but in that case he will abstain, no matter what happens, from forming himself on the model of the insipid Bergers of Lignon,[23] deviating in that regard from the right established by long custom, from which we have departed and are departing by these presents. The Poet will also pay atten-

---

[23] The reference is to Honoré d'Urfé's classic pastoral romance *L'Astrée* (1607-1627), whose hero Céladon is a "Berger" [shepherd] on the banks of the river Lignon.

tion to leaving us unaware of the education of his Hero, even if he executed feats of arms at the age of thirteen better than our best fencing-masters and was more eloquent than our most skillful orators. If it is possible to conceal the sickly insipidities that the heroic characters have written, so much the better.

It would be even more useful, in order not to make the Reader yawn, to refrain from comparisons drawn from Flame, the Lion, Tempests, Torrents, the brightness of Day, the horror of Darkness, etc., with regard to the scant conformity that is always encountered between these images and the events they represent.

Verses will be precisely rhymed; furthermore, the Author ought to answer for his hero, body for body; if it happens that he brutally slays and estimable Enemy who asks him for mercy or performs some equally cowardly action, the Poet shall be held responsible and condemned to pay the cost of the funeral of the man killed contrary to the rules of war.

Any Christian Poet[24] who names Pluto as the Prince of the Inferno shall be condemned to an arbitrary fine.

If he introduces into his Work adventurous Princesses so profligate as to run around the fields in close company with some bravo and get mixed up with drawn swords, even if it is a question of Tomiris or Zenobia,[25] he will be liable to carry a

---

[24] This admonition, like many of the others, can only apply to Earthy authors, and might seem odd even in that context; however, Pluto was frequently named as a Prince of Hell in 17th century French literature, the popularity of the notion going back at least as far as a famous manuscript dating from 1544, *Ceiberus Portier d'enfer & Pluto Prince des Diables* [Cerberus, Hell's Doorkeeper, and Pluto, Prince of Demons].

[25] Tomyris, a Scythian queen who successfully defended her homeland against invasion by Cyrus the Great in the 6th Century B.C., is mentioned by Herodotus and other Greek historians, and was credited by the French Medieval poet Eustache Deschamps (1340-1406) as one of the "nine worthy women" established as counterparts to the *Neuf Preux* [Nine Worthy

spindle for four days, in order to make reparation to the sex he has attempted to denature.

No Episodic History shall be interrupted; the poet should make it short enough not to weaken the principal action.

Given of the great resemblance between serious Drama and Epic Poetry, Tragedies will follow the same rule, and the first twenty lines will acquaint the Spectator with the names of the principal characters, as well as the location of the Scene.

The gigantic exaggeration that commences *La Mort de Pompée*[26] will be written in large letters on the chimney-breast of all Dramatic Poets, in order to be avoided in perpetuity. The decency of the first two lines of *Mithridates*[27] will serve as the contrary model.

Frantic amour will not serve as an excuse for the crime of any Heroic character, and Cinna will be hanged if he offers that pretext for assassinating Augustus[28] one more time.

The dress of any Episodic Princess who sticks her nose in where it does not belong will be slashed.

A Poet convicted of having written a single Verse of the Play before having written it in prose will we shaved dry and soaped on alternate days for six months.

The heroic Rustics of Idylls will abandon their flocks to the care of peasants, as Tragic Heroes will abandon pointed hats to Polichinelle.

Amour being only a passion, like ambition and avarice, it will be indifferent in future to conclude a Comedy with a marriage, the punishment of a miser or the fall of an ambitions man.

Knights] appointed as the models of chivalry. Zenobia was a Syrian queen who led an ultimately-unsuccessful revolt against the Roman Empire in the third century B.C.

[26] The tragedy by Pierre Corneille (1642).

[27] The tragedy by Jean Racine (1673).

[28] As he does in Corneille's *Cinna ou la Clémence d'Auguste* (1639)

The Decree that the Emperor signed had several more clauses, but I shall content myself with reproducing the principal ones. A few more will be found in the next chapter.

CHAPTER II
Plays

There are Theaters on Mercury, as on our world, where plays are performed featuring all the different characters, but the stage is not yielded, as among us, to just anyone. The Art of diversion and pleasure being regarded on that Planet as a very important Art, these are the regulations that are established for Plays. I shall give them such as I find them in the Registers of the Empire.

1. The *Poetics* of Aristotle shall serve as the invariable rule for Dramatic Plays.

2. Two Genii of the first order will swear an oath in our presence never to admit to the Theater any Poet who has not exhibited the talents appropriate for an Employment of that consequence.

3. As Poets on Mercury do not put on the impertinent airs and ridiculous figures that they have in the majority of the other Planets, they will undertake to appear in their Plays themselves, but, given that one Actor cannot perform an entire play, the established order that we are about to describe will be followed.

4. The Sages who travel to all the Planets and who know better than anyone else the adventures that happen throughout the extent of the Vortex will be requested to give subjects to Poets.

5. The Genii destined to preside over a certain number of Dramatic Poems will be charged to go in search of Subjects to the Great Mountain, and give them to the troupe that they govern; each Poet will work on the Scenes that he will perform.

6. When the Play is complete, the Genii will examine it, and if they approve of it, they will permit it to be performed.

7. One or several Troupes of Actor Poets will be established in every City, in accordance with necessity.

8. Each troupe will be directed by one or two Genii, as aforementioned.

9. No troupe will exceed the number of twenty, it being unnatural that there can be more than twenty principal Actors in a good play; if it is necessary to represent, for example, the horse Pegasus or the Serpent Python, it will be the role of a vagrant paid by the hour.

10. The Protective Genii of the Troupe will be charged with the Decorations of the Theater and erecting for each Play an edifice appropriate to the subject, embellished with the most marvelous inventions of Fable and the Land of Fiction.

11. If the Magical Art, the power of the Genii and the virtue of the Wand are found to be insufficient to execute the present Decree of my full power, certain science and Imperial authority, I augment infinitely the limited power that nature has given to those Beings over the Elements.

Signed by the Emperor,
and sealed with the Imperial Seal.

There can be no doubt that with such wise precautions, the Theater has reached a degree of perfection that others never achieve, so no one has yet needed to yawn there. The sad usage of whistles is unknown on that Planet; that is an effect of the enlightened choice of the Genii and the attention with which the Planet Mercury has been purged of bad Poets; it is, however, open to anyone who wishes, as a consequence of the liberty that minds enjoy, to "waste ink and paper with impunity,"[29] provided that he does so in secret, and that the paper an Author splashes remains in his portfolio. But if poetic effrontery pushes him to distribute in the world a Script that is at all soporific—or has it printed, which is worse—he is then regarded as a disturber of the public peace, and is denounced in

---

[29] The quotation is from one of Nicolas Boileau-Despréaux's satires

that capacity to a Magistrate, who always sends him to the Genii. Those severe Judges, without appeal, condemn him to penalties proportionate to the nature of his Verses and the degree of insipidity found therein. Not so long ago a new Tariff was drawn up, a few Articles of which a Sage of my acquaintance recited to me, as I was absent at the time, occupied in calculations to fix exactly the number of the Atoms of Epicurus.

For a bad Sonnet the Poet will have his nose squashed by the art of magic and in that state will be seen for three consecutive days in the Theater Pillory, with a heavier penalty in case of recidivism.

For a limp Epigram, as many *croquignoles*[30] as lines, and five strokes of the rod, if it is satirical.

For a dedicatory Epistle longer than six lines, a pecuniary fine of forty-eight livres, in the form of compensation to the advantage of its recipient.

For Stanzas on an absence, jealousy, or joy, six grains of Emetic, in accordance with Hippocrates' aphorism, *vomitoria vomitantibus.*

The author of an Elegy will wear a long black robe embroidered in gray for six months, and will enjoin all the Inhabitants to avoid encountering him, for fear of bad air.

Tender verses, good or bad, will be neither punished nor praised if the Author can prove that he was in love when he wrote them, in view of the fact that a man in delirium merits neither punishment nor recompense.

Any rhymed praise, and any insult in verse, will be declared null and devoid of effect, but the Poet will be punished as a forger.

---

[30] A *croquignole* is a kind of pastry, known in English as a cracknel, but French dictionaries derive the term etymologically from two Old French words which, in combination, mean a light slap in the face, and that is obviously what the author means by it here.

Any Impromptu will be whistled publicly, in view of the impertinence of the act.

Any Rhymer of cold sense convicted of love letters, Madrigal, Idyll, Anagram, gallant letters or other stupidities will be relegated to the north of Mercury.

The Author of a bad Comedy will serve twenty years in the Italian Troops.

A failed Tragedian will be devoted to the service of the Théâtre Français to snuff out the candles when the good Plays of Corneille, and Racine are performed.

An Epic Poet who has not enriched his bookshop will serve in the capacity of shop assistant, working for bread alone, for as many years as there are Cantos in his Work.

It was some time ago that Descartes brought to Mercury, on behalf of the Queen of Sweden,[31] the invention of Italian Operas; it was whistled, and noted in the margin of that Princess's renunciation.

The Examiners agreed, however, that an excellent Play put to music, but of mixed taste, composed in French and Italian, might succeed; it was added that the Comic genre might suit Opera better than any other, because it would quadruple the advantage of the ridiculous idea to have it all sung, which was regarded with unanimous consent as a plenary impertinence.

There is another kind of Actors, who play at Fairs, but it is forbidden for them to speak other than in the general language, which is that of animals. It is also for themselves alone that they perform, or for some of the inhabitants detached from the Sun who were taken as prisoners of war on the Great

---

[31] Christina, the monarch of Sweden from 1633-1654, wanted Stockholm to become "the Athens of the North"; she invited Descartes to found an Academy there, and he arrived in December 1649, but died there only a few weeks later, apparently of pneumonia. She also invited an Italian opera troupe, but it did not arrive until 1652.

Mountain: those who have scorned the instructions and advice of the Sages, have conserved all the faults of their birth, and whose ferocity has almost doomed them before they were given the liberty to travel the Planet.

Those poor individuals, whose minds are inferior by several degrees to the minds of Mercurian animals, bear a fairly close resemblance to the populace of our world.

CHAPTER III
On the Education of Children

As soon as they are able to talk, children are taught three different things, which in their regard are almost the same: one is to know the Letters, the second is to attach certain ideas of magnitude and number to them, and the third is to form the letters in order to make use of them in Algebra, with which they are familiarized as soon as they are born, in order to remove them from the difficulties of that simple Art, whose utility is so extended.

As the different notes that serve for these operations are fairly numerous, and that the young must at least be accustomed to attach them to the ideas appropriate to that science, it is difficult to succeed, but that is how the education of youth is outlined.

The work requires some application to begin with, and the majority of young people imagine that it is beyond their scope, but that is a great error and very harmful to the progress of the Sciences. In the foundations of Algebra, of which people are so fearful, there is nothing but the Art of knowing, for instance, how much longer or shorter one line is from another, and how many times the small is comprised within the large.

That is simple, and to mark that it has been discovered, one makes use of notes that are the simplest in the world, knowing our Letters. However, because one does not employ them in Algebra to make up words, and one mingles with those letters a few other marks, Algebra is reputed to be a thorny Science very difficult of acquisition, although it is true that it facilitates the study of Mathematics infinitely, including that of Arithmetic, although the latter is taught to infants as soon as they can read—but on our Earth, almost everything is done without forethought.[32]

I cannot, my Sage continued, refrain from inserting a singular but perfectly true fact here.

A short time after the Art of printing became known in Paris, when someone wanted to print Euclid's *Elements*, with the figures—which are, as everyone knows, circles, squares, triangles and all sorts of lines—a worker at the Printer's, not knowing what the Book was, because the text was in Latin, which he did not understand, imagined that they were magical characters and that the Devil might carry him away during that work. Fear made him ill; his Master, knowing the cause of his illness, explained the fact to him, but he was not understood and the illness grew worse. Finally, they had recourse to the imbecile's Confessor; he worked in vain to cure an imagination struck without resource, with the result that the patient died within a matter of days.

That is where error leads, and it is for that reason, above all, that one strives to avoid it on Mercury.

The principles of Algebra are therefore taught as early as possible, because that Science renders the mind more precise, accustoming it to see things as they are, and giving it an extent that it would never have without that study.

If people are ignorant of a great many things that they ought to learn, it is no great evil, for there is a great deal of knowledge that makes almost no contribution to the happiness of life; but if humans are accustomed from infancy to judge everything at hazard, purely by opinion and without any principle, that is a public misfortune of the greatest consequence. For not only is a person who cannot reason inaccurate, apt to make important errors against fortune and his own wellbeing, but also, his false reasoning rebounds on everyone that surrounds him: friends, relatives, neighbors and servants all feel and suffer from his false ideas; and mental incompetence, if

---

[32] This insistence on the essential role of Algebra in mathematical education is derived from Descartes.

one can put it this way, is a species of contagion that always extends further and further, and which tends gradually to the degradation of the entire human species.

It is to avoid that misfortune, the greatest of all, that the people of Mercury are so firmly determined to equip their children, with everything that can put them in a state to make the most accurate and extensive usage as possible of their intelligence and their reason, with is nothing but the result of true and considered ideas.

On Mercury, little priority is placed on the study of Languages. It is not that one cannot easily find people who apply themselves to it, as it is agreeable and useful to have in the estate of Poets, Painters and Musicians, but those who want their children to grow up as human beings and not Grammarians, do not occupy them much with that study. They like them to know their own language well, and at a certain point they are permitted to learn a certain number of those that are most commonly used, but they do not approve of children charging their memory with words and pretending that speech is knowledge.

The study of History succeeds that of Languages and Geometry, but little effort is made to delve deeply into History. They are content to have in mind a general plan of the sequence of Empires that precede the present government, and it is noteworthy that the History in question has a limited number of important epochs, which everyone retains without difficulty, after which one does not burden oneself with names or chronological calculations, and only attaches to mind and heart to the former by virtue of the reflections one makes on the principal events.

One chooses the most illustrious in each genre and one has several of the same species, in order to get a better sense of the principles and the invariable resultant consequences, such as treason, leading to shame and danger; of sagacity, producing useful discoveries and honor; of blind obedience to the passions, generating a multitude of inconveniences; of the empire of reason over them, leading to all sorts of glory and advantages; of precipitation, causing blunders; and of attention, producing almost assured success.

Furthermore, one does not pride oneself, on Mercury, on knowing positively whether some person, the son of some other, carried out some good or bad action, nor whether the things happened in some particular Olympiad or year of the Hegira.

Those people generally say that to merit the esteem of people it is necessary to perform good actions similar to those one finds in History, and avoid those that attract criticism, but it matters little to know the names of those who performed the actions in question or the year in which they did it, because those details have nothing to do with the fundamental issues, and that with regard to a great man, committing his name and the dates between which he lived to memory is futile.

They add to the antipathy that they have for the pedantry of History, that the ancient is so uncertain and the modern so often false, when it is written by cotemporaries whose passions falsify it, that when one attaches oneself to knowing in depth, one often retains nothing but pure Romance.

They are, however, scornful of a person who confuses all the names, mistaking, like Molière's Comtesse d'Escarbagnas,[33] Martial for a perfumer or an author of the twelfth century; but fundamentally, except for those who make a profession of knowing History, because their narrow and limited genius is only good for furnishing their memory, few people attach themselves to it.

On Mercury, Historians and Genealogists, are viewed like furniture repositories, or, at the most, Dictionaries, to which one has recourse when necessary but which are not of very agreeable usage in society, their eternal citations being boring.

But still, say the Sages, who sometimes remain stubborn in regard to our manner, if you confuse names and times, you will be deemed to be ignorant.

---

[33] In the eponymous 1671 comedy.

"What!" you reply, indignantly. "One will be scorned for having mistaken a date, or having substituted one name for another, even though one has an infinity of other knowledge, order in one's mind, a reliable Logic and sane ideas on all subjects? When one knows how to envisage an incident from all angles, when one has the capacity to anticipate all inconveniences, and has mental resources to turn all hazards to one's vantage? Such an ignoramus is, on the contrary, well made for any kind of employment; it is to him that the prerogative ought to belong to make Laws and govern; it is him who ought to set in motion all the great mechanisms, it is him who ought to preserve peace and decode on the occasions to take up arms; in sum, it is by virtue of his conduct that the Empire would flourish and the People would be happy, of they were not governed by the superior Genius that rules the Plant. Such a man has, so to speak, something of the Divinity, and you will never find his peer in a person who possesses Languages, nor cold Chronology, the Nomenclature of all the centuries."

To justify that fashion of thinking, one can also use this reasoning. Humans have only a certain measure of capacity; they can only give a certain portion of their leisure to the culture of their Mind; that is certain. It is no less true that the mind only improves itself by means of the reflections it makes, in comparing, in an infinity of ways, what is true and what is false, what is good, or better, or bad, and what things are just or unjust. Now, can a man who employs all his time in arranging in his memory names, dates, innumerable events and genealogical sequences conserve sufficient leisure to make some usage of the materials he has amasses?

But with a well-cultivated memory, someone will insist, all that costs almost nothing, and leaves plenty of time for reflection.

Pure illusion, reply our Sages; the life of a man is scarcely sufficient to learn History; furthermore, a mind accustomed to make such futilities its principal object, and which has nourished itself for thirty years on those indigestible aliments, is no longer capable of the noble ideas that inspire healthy Morality, nor of knowing the veritable Truth. For that is not merely a matter of knowing how to talk and to define it; it is necessary to have practiced it for a long time, to be familiar with it, and to make it a habit that becomes, so to speak, the very substance of your soul.

CHAPTER IV
On the Education of Children Continued

After a child is sufficiently instructed regarding History, he passes on to Logic. Simple, clear Rules, few in number and supported by examples to render them sensible, teach young people to guide their intelligence, to understand enlightenment, to differentiate the true from the false, and, in consequence, to speak reasonably and do the same in all the actions of their lives.

Practical Morality being entirely contained in the Lessons of History, they do not bother to occupy themselves with that idle Morality that can be called intellectual, in which one only occupies oneself with frivolous questions, ordinarily more appropriate to sustain the imagination than to form the heart and sentiments.

They treat Metaphysics, which presents us with very imperfect ideas of the Divinity, with a similar scorn. They correct that Science, and it is with the aid of good Physics that they learn to know God and the intelligent part that animates us.

The study of Nature, which succeeds Logic, sustained by the knowledge of Mathematics, enables those People, who are naturally endowed with a great accuracy of mind, to make great Progress in Physics. They learn to know causes by their effects, and sometimes to anticipate effects by means of the causes that they know. By means of the well-managed usage of that Science, they are liberated from an infinity of the errors and prejudices that are so common on our Earth.

When all these preliminary studies are complete, a young man is permitted to read the Poets. He learns to know that much-vaunted Art, and how it often deviates from the objective to which it aims, which is to please and instruct, and to render vice odious and make virtue loved. But that idea, say the Inhabitants of Mercury, is only, s it were, the Romance of

Poetry, or the deceptive mask, which is abused almost every day.

A Sage I once knew called Art the ingenious imposer of reason by the cadence and harmony of words. "It seems," he said, "that the enthusiasm of Poets is gripped, either by a vertigo or I don't know what spirit of seduction, which draws them out of themselves and almost makes them forget reason, to follow the number and the measure of the Fanaticism that draws them, taking them away from their subject and perverting the notion of it, with the result that, with the best intentions in the world for the accuracy and solidity of reason, a Poet finds himself led by a kind of magical violence into falsehood and puerility."[34]

The Poetry that ought to please does not attain its goal, therefore, when it strays from accuracy and amuses itself with trivial bagatelles, for a sane Reader only seeks the truth and solid ideas.

Nor is it instructive when it disguises objects, and instead of depicting them as they are, it only presents an embellished mask that often renders them unrecognizable.

It is true that in those faults it is not the Art that it is necessary to blame, and that the Workman has all the fault; so Poetry is not scorned on Mercury, but the young are advised to read it with precaution, in order to protect oneself from the seduction that it often spreads with full hands.

It is a great pity, say our Sages, that the Pupils of the Muses, with so much imagination, charm and fire, do not apply themselves sufficiently to forming their judgment. If they made some reflections on such an important issue, they would see that the frivolities to which they devote themselves dishonor the Art that they profess, and that the tender nonsense, the rustic puerilities, the insipid praise and the negligible little rhymes in the manufacture of which they grow old, defame both the Art and the Artisan.

---

[34] If this really is a quotation, it does not seem to come from a published work.

The Inhabitants of Mercury do not refuse their approval, and crowns, to the Poets who render themselves worthy of them, but they judge as so many grinders and bauble-mongers those who give them nothing else.

Ignorance and stupidity do not pass on Mercury for charms, as on our world. Girls are brought up there in the same fashion as boys, with respect to everything concerned with the mind and accuracy of reasoning; one does them the honor of believing that they have sufficient temperament and health to acquire a certain amount of necessary knowledge; it is even judged that they will not lose either their complexion or the curves that create beauty in forming reason or in rendering their hands more adroit.

Following that system, instead of teaching them to spin, to embroider or to make tapestry, they are taught to think precisely, to reflect, and they are led as far as possible to know a large number of things and to talk about them reasonably. There are few of them that have not learned one of the languages that the Sages speak, as well as that of the Court, which everyone knows, and no one has yet observed that that study, and that of Philosophy, has rendered their eyes less brilliant and their complexion duller. The contrary seems to be the case: that the light of their intelligence, which expands through all their actions and their speech, makes them more amiable. I know, at least, that the neither the mildness of their humor, their gaiety or their appetite for pleasures is diminished. I have sometimes heard lovely individuals talking, while getting dressed and arranging their beauty spots with the greatest artifice, to the great Descartes about sublime things, and the most abstract intentions of Metaphysics.

These facts ought to be taught to the beauties of our world, in order that they might know many things without becoming ugly; but it is very difficult to be very pretty when one is stupid and utterly ignorant.

The first care that is taken after having formed their mind is that of affirming them as much as possible against the illusions of self-love. All the women on Mercury are subject to that epidemic malady; it ordinarily attacks them at the age of fifteen or sixteen, and returns from time to time in fits. There are even cases in which it is lifelong.

That infirmity is dreaded almost as much as our small-pox; it in not that it spoils the features or destroys the freshness of the complexion, but it expands something unwholesome and repulsive throughout the person that it afflicts, which deters amour and amity for five paces around—which is reckoned a great misfortune on the Planet. Fortunately, the Art of curing the malady is not difficult, for it only consists of giving everyone a firm idea of her own intrinsic value, persuading a beautiful person that she is not a Divinity and a pretty woman that she is only that.

Following that tariff, anyone with a little intelligence maintains her complaisance and good humor, and those who have more talent and genius than others nevertheless have the modesty to believe that they can sometimes be wrong. In that state of mind, stubbornness is not one of their faults, and, without attracting their scorn and aversion, once can dispense with being always of their sentiment, which is very useful for the mildness of life's commerce.

The Stage is charged with what remains of the education of the fair sex; they see their ingenious and true depictions of all the passions. It is there that they learn that they ought always to be grateful for the empire of reason, but that it is necessary above all to guard against those that put our happiness in the hands of others, such as ambition or amour.

Those two Tyrants submit us to so many people, and cause our fortunes to depend on such a large number of imperceptible bagatelles, that it is almost impossible to find a moment's respite from their consequences. The ambitious man is the slave of his Master, the Favorite, the Minister, the Mistress and servants. It is necessary to compete more strenuously against his peers, to get rid of his Superiors and generally to dread all those that justice, hazard or ambition alone might put in competition with him; for, however inferior they might be to us in all things, they might supplant us by means of cun-

ning, presence of mind or, as they saying has it by the under-
sides of the cards; nothing is more commonplace on the road
to Fortune. It is therefore true that in soliciting favors, our
happiness not longer depends on us, since we are delivering
ourselves to so many hazards.

Amour is no less contrary to our repose than ambition; it
always attracts by means of a route strewn with flowers. Beauty, joy and amusements accompany it; a reciprocal seduction
sustains us for a while in a delight to which our pleasure
yields, but those enchanting moments are less durable than the
calm of the Ocean. Habit soon arrives, followed by loss of
savor, which never progresses without distaste as intolerable
ennui.

That dangerous company takes possession of our heart,
and as our sex is more disposed to receive it, it is also in us
that it ordinary commences to establish itself. That gives birth
to inattentions, apparent distraction, thoughtlessness, sometimes impoliteness are certainly indiscretions; ill humor then
follows and that contagious disease produces clarifications,
dry responses, reproaches and an infinity of reciprocal imper-
tinences, of which each one separately would be quite incapable.

One that subject, the story is told of a singular imagination of Artemisia after the death of Mausolus, her husband,
whom she had loved perfectly. As that Princess was still
young and very beautiful, her temperament and the virtue of
celibacy were not at all in accord; however, in order to act in
cognizance of the circumstance, she charged a famous Mathematician to calculate accurately the pleasures and chagrins
that amour can cause, and in order to help him in that calculations she gave him a exact journal of her life since her marriage.

After a very attentive computation, the Geometer report-
ed that the most perfect attachment between the best matched
individuals produced approximately thirteen fifths more pain
than pleasure. The Arithmetical rule, expressed in simpler
terms, signifies that two people who love one another dearly

have in any one year only two months of happiness and perfect calm, and ten of anxiety, contretemps, trifling disputes and despairing torments.

On that exposition, the beautiful Queen of Caria, whose natural tastes inclined her toward a second marriage, concluded in favor of celibacy, but in order to distract herself and occupy her pleasure with some pompous bagatelle, she built the famous mausoleum, with was in its time the most sublime monument to human impertinence.

CHAPTER V
Burials

Death being a voluntary action here, it occasions nothing lugubrious in its wake. On the contrary, the friend of the deceased rejoice in the passage that their Companion has just made, to a kind of life more to his taste than the last, since he has quit it. In accordance with that opinion, which is very reasonable, they include nothing in funerals that is not appropriate to inspire joy; all the symbols are cheerful. A Pyramid is set up in front of the deceased's door, decorated with verdure, crowns and garlands of flowers, mingled with pleasant representations and emblems. Songs are sung in praise of death to sprightly tunes, and his good qualities are recounted, while never failing to make a satire of his faults; that is like the small comedies that follow the main item in our Spectacles. People laugh at it and profit from it.

The most beautiful part of the Spectacle is the arrival of the deceased's ashes, which the friends carry in a kind of precious and magnificently decorated urn; it is placed, uncovered, sat the top of the display. When that ceremony is concluded, pleasures, dances, music and all kinds of games and other such exercises recommence, and last for the rest of the day. Finally, everyone retires, leaving their friend's ashes in the bosom of the air, which takes responsibility for them and scatters them, by unknown routes, into the treasures of Nature, which makes a new individual out of that handful of dust. Thus the human race is perpetuated.

Those cold Relics being soon dissipated, the apparatus of the Funeral is destroyed; it is then that those who were sufficiently touched by the death of the departed individual indulge themselves by weeping are denounced to the Magistrate, who sentences them as ingrates to a pecuniary fine payable to the heirs. It is said, with reason, that anyone who loved the deceased enough to weep after his death doubtless had many obligations to him, which consisted in the pleasure of his conversation, the mildness of his commerce, his amity, his good offices, etc., and the Weeper, it is said, enjoyed all of that, otherwise he would not regret it; he has even enjoyed it for a considerable time, since he is so accustomed to it that he cannot let it go. But is it not just that the defunct, who lived so much for the pleasure of his friend, ultimately had the liberty to die for his own satisfaction? And is it not a great ingratitude to be sorry, in one's personal interest, for the benefit that has been received by our intimate friend? That is why the Police punish those who are afflicted by the death of another.

Our Sages have sometimes asked why tombs are not erected on Mercury as they are on the majority of other Planets—to which the Mercurians reply, briefly but decisively: "If Tombs and Epitaphs were eternal, the Planet would be incapable of containing them all; if they are perishable, it is not worth the trouble of building them."

CHAPTER VI
The Story of Termetis and Nixée

Termetis was more beautiful than an Amour, and just as amusing. He was, in consequence, pursued by all women, and no matter who caught him, he was carried away. The amiable Nixée was the only one who did not participate in that frenzy. As she had more taste and discernment than the others, she avoided the trap of those superficial attractions. Termetis was put out, and made futile efforts to add her to his Catalogue. I do not know how many malevolent tongues had said to her "all that glitters is not gold," but it is certain that the Proverb and a few well-matched speeches had depreciated him in Nixée's eyes, and she could hardly stand him.

Such treatment appeared insupportable to him, for these Tyrants of hearts before whom every virtue trembles suffer contradictions with great impatience. So, Termetis was smitten for the first time in his life, but Nixée laughed at him, droving him to despair. The others were aggravated, and mocked him for his unhappiness, and for a fidelity that was not demanded of him, but nothing made any difference; it was impossible to cure him.

After years of perseverance, which had not brought any success, he became determined either to vanquish the stubborn disdain of his Queen or to die; as the latter alternative seemed surer and much easier, that was the one he attempted first. He went to the Great Mountain during a time when it was being very fiercely attacked.

Termetis placed himself everywhere that the peril was most evident, performed prodigies of valor, and was soon chosen to head the principal Troop, whose Commander had just been killed. The battle was a long one, and only ceased because of the extreme lassitude of both parties. It began again the following morning, and lasted all day, and Termetis, who was only seeking to die gloriously, led his soldiers further than they believed themselves to be capable of going. They got all the way to the Crust that the Enemy had abandoned, occupied their own terrain there, and when their enemies, vanquished and driven back, thought that they could find a refuge in their Homeland, they found nothing there but death and chains.

That new prodigy of courage and good conduct was praised even by the Emperor, which is the acme of glory on Mercury. But the Prince was not content to have given praise to Termetis; he wrote to him and promised to grant him the first three wishes that he expressed, provided that they did not include the gift of Metamorphosis, because the number was full.

Termetis, who only wanted that gift, by means of which he might hope to render himself lovable in Nixée's eyes, considered the Emperor's letter and promises as useless, and thought of nothing but dying, as many overly excitable people do who always see things in the worst light. He was returning home, overwhelmed by sadness, with despair in his heart, cursing cruel destiny, when he saw two small aged individuals, a man and a woman, arguing in the shade of an orange-tree, with as much vehemence as if they had been at it for fifteen years, and as if they wanted to scratch one another's eyes out.

He approached them, with the intention of bringing them into accord, if possible, but they were no animated that they did not see him, even though he had been there, listening to them, for a long time—with the consequence that he had already learned that the dispute consisted of knowing whether the Charnel-Houses of the Holy Innocents still existed in their ancient form in Paris, or whether it was true that a market had been made of them in the heart of the City, as a few Savages newly arrived from the great Moon that is our Earth had alleged. The little man was sustaining the former, the little woman the latter.

Finally, they perceived Termetis, to whom the old woman addressed herself first, asking him whether he had not heard mention of what she was asserting. He said that he had not, but that he could not imagine how two people who seemed so sage could get so excited over such a trifle.

"Trifle!" cried the little old woman. "It is, indeed, a trifle to you, to whom they mean nothing, but to me, who built them, it's not the same. For it is my work, as is the Church that strands there, and also the fine and beautiful houses of the quarter. It is true that my husband Flamel, here present, furnished me with the money, having found the authentic Philosophate Stone...."

"You mean Philosophical," Termetis put in.

"Philosophical, if you want to call it that," said the little woman, "but that's no reason to contradict me."

Termetis realized then that he was dealing with a man who was much more important than he had imagined. He spoke very politely to Flamel, and begged his pardon for coming to interrupt him and interfering, perhaps indiscreetly, in their dispute.

"No, my child," replied the old man, "I don't hold it against you, but do me the pleasure of telling me which of the two of us is right; we take you for our judge—isn't that right, Perenelle," he added, addressing his wife,

"Yes," she replied, wholeheartedly.

Surprised to have to decide a fact of which he did not have the slightest knowledge, Termetis wanted to excuse himself, but they both begged him so insistently to make the pronouncement that he yielded to their pleas.

"If you ask me," he said, after a period of silence, "the best way to know the truth is to go and see."

"Good," said Flamel. "That's a fine decision; truly, we would have gone ourselves if we could, but although we're Sages and Philosophers, we're retained here by indissoluble bonds. Hermes, who, as you know, is the foremost of Sages, and ought to be regarded as the Genius of Nature, is the one who obliges us to live on Mercury, only able to leave after a sojourn of a thousand years. I don't know who told him, when we were on our Earth, that we were making great expenses on magnificent buildings, extraordinary alms and large foundations, but he began by criticizing our imprudence and then, seeing that it was continuing, he talked to me about it.

"I promised him to be wiser in future, but the woman you see here"—he smiled as he inserted, in parentheses: "these animals are made to turn men's heads—persecuted me so much that it wasn't possible for me to keep the promise I'd made to the Master, and when he saw that I was incorrigible in that regard he removed me from my home one night, along with my wife, and brought us here. He told us on the way that he was only doing it for our own good, with the design of preventing some avaricious Prince or other powerful people envious of our secret from seizing us, forcing us to reveal it to them and, in sum, usurping divine knowledge that ought never to be acquired other than by pure revelation, by assiduousness or genius, or by virtue of the amity of some Sage who might divulge part of it in order that one might try to clarify the rest—as happened to me, for I got the primary substance from a Jew, but owe the rest to my long studies and my attention."

"I'm sorry," Termetis replied, "that you've been exiled for such a long time from your homeland, for you seem to me to be at least two or three hundred years old."

"Very nearly," said the little woman, blushing at the antiquity of her baptism.[35]

"Since that's the case," said Termetis, "I promise, if you wish, to obtain a passport and a carriage for you, so that you can go home and return here. You know the Emperor's power; he has promised me, as you can see in this letter with which he has honored me, to grant me three gifts. The first I shall ask of him will be your voyage; doubtless he won't refuse me that."

The wizened couple fell at Termetis' feet. He lifted them up again, and, assuring them that he was very glad to have encountered such a favorable opportunity to oblige such important people.

---

[35] As Perenelle Flamel died in 1397, the "very nearly"—if it is not a wild exaggeration—suggests that this part of the story must have been composed before 1700.

Flamel certified the truth of the matter by means of the Emperor's letter, and, penetrated with gratitude for Termetis' generosity, offered him all his knowledge and what remained of his projection powder. Termetis, who could not see how that secret would render him more lovable to Nixée, thanked him but refused.

Very surprised by that refusal, Flamel asked him why.

"Because for my happiness," Termetis replied, "it's not a matter of transmuting metals but of changing the inflexible heart of a woman that I love passionately, and who can't abide me."

"Death of my life," replied Perenelle, "she must have very poor taste not to find you to her liking. There's something behind this. How long than you loved her?"

"Three years," said Termetis,

"And she doesn't love you?"

"No."

"That is, with respect to the Company, a great...she's surely wrong, or must be bearing a grudge against you. Listen: Flamel, don't you have some of that Household Elixir[36] that you take so often?"

"Yes," said the man, "but it won't make any difference— at least, I didn't take any at his age."

"That's true," said Perenelle, "but you were loved; I'm the proof of that. He isn't. Give him a little; it can't do him any harm. Believe me, handsome boy, take it. You won't recognize yourself. I know what I'm talking about; when Flamel takes four or five drops, he becomes so embellished, so far as I'm concerned, that he's an entirely different man. They say

---

[36] I have translated "*elixir de ménage*" literally as "household elixir," although the English term does not accommodate all the nuances of the French one, which carries the implication of domestic harmony and extends to other kinds of suitability— but it would have to stretch a long way to take aboard the effects that the potion seems to have when tried, so Perenelle is obviously employing it euphemistically.

145

that it amends Nature, that it's a ferret that hunts down faults and gets rid of them. Anyway, what do I know? I don't understand all that, but I know what I've got out of it."

Termetis did not have to be asked twice. He took it. Flamel gave him a large bottle and promised to bring him more when he returned.

With that assurance, they all set out. Flamel's request was granted by the Emperor. The three of them separated, each going their own way.

The next day, Termetis took a dose from his bottle. Scarcely two hours after drinking it, he perceived that his hands, which had been a trifle large, had elongated and become paler; he looked at his reflection in the first spring he came to, and found that his eyebrows were thicker, his hair longer and better furnished. What marvels might he have seen if he had bathed?

He was not unaware of them for long.

He thought that the time had come to go and see Nixée. He exercised great diligence and went to her home. He was told that she had just gone out, and that one of her friends was waiting for her. It was one of those who had desired him, and in spite of his great passion for Nixée he could not resist the present opportunity; the elixir was too pressing and the Lady too weak.

During the time when he was performing prodigies, Nixée came back, and found the two young people so intoxicated that they almost did not perceive her. Termetis, who saw her first, leapt up in order to go and hide.

Nixée, who was a good Princess, was content to offer a few reproaches to her friend for not having warned her about the rendezvous; the latter swore that it was only a chance encounter, but that it was well worth it, and gave details of the adventure. Nixée, in her admiration at that detailed account, exclaimed that it must be very true that travel made men.

The traveler came back in, threw himself at the feet of his Mistress, who forgave him on condition that he mended his ways, or chose his battlefield more politely on another occasion. She was so content with her Lover that she swore subsequently that she would never have thought it, and that she would judge things for herself in future before believing them.

CHAPTER VII
On the Emperor's Prime Minister

That position is much sought after, as you might imagine, given the great honor, abundant credit and large salary that are attached to it. But as there is no fortune that is not subject to some inconvenience, there are a considerable number in that employment, as you shall see.

As soon as the Emperor has appointed a Prime Minister, he is sudden gripped by a contagious malady to which other men are not subject; several of them die of it, others are never cured, and even those who recover do not do so without having been very ill.

The disease is called the Swaggers; it commences with joy and concludes with pain. I shall describe some of its symptoms, but not all, for they are innumerable.

The Swaggers is preceded by violent vapors, which go to the head and confuse it completely. First, a species of delight grips the invalid; one sees a joy in his eyes that he cannot contain, and which stifles him, because the decency that his new tank demands forces him to put on a serious countenance. That retained laughter spreads throughout his person, however, inflating it, stiffening it and elongating it to the point that the new Minister thinks that he had grown a good four inches in twenty-four hours.

Scarcely has he enjoyed the advantage of his height, however, than his eyes begin to wander; something grim charges his Physiognomy and darkens it; the sound of his voice changes, and it takes on an affirmative tone that frightens little children and at which other people find it difficult not to laugh.

When the malady reaches that point, it is seen to augment visibly. Then the invalid loses his memory, forgetting the faces of his best friends; he calls his oldest servants "you there," their names ceasing to be familiar to him. A restless movement agitates him considerably. He no longer hears any-thing that is addressed to him and cannot respond. He stamps his feet, strides back and forth in his room in the midst of new Idolaters of every rank. He still extends his hand, and shakes any that are offered to him, but that is the last comic scene in the play; he goes into the wings and disappears.

It is then that the Swaggers reaches its climax and the force of the disease changes the Minister's constitution com-pletely, giving him a new character.

Affable, polite, cheerful, laughing and verbose to begin with, he becomes affected, rude, somber, haggard and taciturn; he avoids everyone, instructing a bizarrely dressed man he posts at his door to keep everyone out.

That Cerberus catches has Master's disease by contagion and becomes a grim and surly as him. He defends the door like a frontier post, repelling those who lay siege to it with the formula: "No one can go in," which encompasses all rhetoric, and sends away five hundred people.

In the meantime, the mysteriously-enclosed Minister turns on his heel, cuts his fingernails, murmurs a comic song, writes to his Mistress and takes directly from his Secretary's hand the report that he has been charged with preparing for the Council. These important functions being fulfilled in three or four hours at the most, the Clock chimes, my man takes his coat, asks for his snuff-box and checks his countenance. The door opens, and when the Statesman appears, everyone has-tens toward him, the greatest first. A few of them speak to him; he smiles without listening to them, and accepts respon-sibility for concluding some affair that will not be concluded for forty years. A quarter of an hour suffices for that difficult employment; he is awaited; he cannot stop; the Council is about to sit; he vanishes, giving the slip to the crowd that awaits him every day, and will wait for him tomorrow and the same time, with no greater success.

The Swaggers does not stop there. The disease progress-es, and in very little time the patent becomes more intractable. He becomes proud with his Superiors, insolent with his equals, impracticable to his friends and invisible to everyone else. That engenders hatred, jealousy, and then public protests. The Prince listens to them for a time, and becomes weary of them; he dissimulates, and hopes that the complaints might die down, but they increase. It is finally necessary to yield to them; the Master, overwhelmed by the cry of all the Estates, withdraws the hand that sustains the Minister; he falls, and his fall drags down all those that his malady has afflicted. The inflexible Janitor, who handles the greatest men rudely, welcomes a man of the people.

The disgraced Favorite, who scarcely responded with a movement of the head to prostrations, now salutes all comers. He asks for the favor and protection of all those that he did not deign to honor with his own, and his family, with which the greatest names coveted the glory of being dishonored, can scarcely make humble alliances. Thus fortune is often pleased to humiliate more profoundly those she had elevated the most.

CHAPTER VIII
On Amour

Amour is not regarded on Mercury as a matter more serious than other occupations of life; it is reckoned an amusement, like gambling, good food and a taste for spectacles and other dissipations. It is not condemned on the Planet, but people nevertheless laugh at the ridicule that it often acquires, for there is no sentiment more liable to reveal character and to expose its faults. One knows no scruple in its pursuit, but one dreads the consequences; that ensures that the secrecy of gallantry is scarcely less guarded than that of an affair of State.

Lovers, therefore, do not confide publicly their dolors or their pleasures; the brazen catalogues that advertise the conquests of a pretty woman, and the coarse arithmetic of a young blockhead whose calculates his daily amusements publicly, are unknown on Mercury.

In sum, nothing is less free in appearance or more private in fact than amour on Mercury.

A husband does not lock up his wife; a new Lover does not refuse his door to anyone, even his predecessor; mothers do not pester their daughters; it is equally open to either sex to go out and to fly with all the strength of their wings, without fear of being followed on the ground or in the air.

It is true that these facilities are only used by night; one encounters them every day, just as one does here, but while the Sun shines, amour hides away. It is, at the very least, postponed until dusk—but as soon as the Sun sets, there is every likelihood that, within two hours, the inhabitants of Mercury will be in intimate circumstances.

The jealousy of our world is unknown on that Planet. It is true that the delicate fear of losing a beloved person is not banished, and that people are as sensitive as they are here to the slight anxieties that love sustains in them and render them attentive, but two people who love one another, have sufficient mutual esteem not to fear veritable treasons; in any case, it is an established custom that the first whose taste has worn away admits it without prevarication. Thus, jealousy, which only consists of dread and suspicion, has no place, since everything is clarified right away. In case of separation, one despairs if one wishes, but at least one is not jealous, and the Connoisseurs all say that to spare a deserted lover jealousy is to extend mercy to a condemned man who finds himself on the scaffold.

If some pain remains in amour, therefore, it is, at most, that of the commencement of an affair of the heart, where uncertainty does not leave the soul in a very placid situation—but anxieties of that kind have more pleasure in them than bitterness. It is true that, when the Emperor offered one day to teach the Art of consulting the fate of new engagements, in order to know from the very outset whether they would come out well or not, he was humbly requested to leave things as they were—which seemed all the more reasonable because that kind of uncertainty is usually not very long-lasting. It has been known for women to remain on the defensive for the entire months, but such a thing, although true, is reckoned to be so rare as to be incredible. Our men are so adroit, and the Ladies of the Planet so enthusiastic that something trivial is sufficient to make up their minds.

One anxious blonde, who persisted in her irresolution for more than a month, had two Lovers who pleased her equally. The one that she had seen most recently always seemed preferable to her, but when they were encountered together, she could not decide to give up either one, and unfortunately, the custom of having both had not yet passed from our world into theirs.

In that embarrassment, one of the two who found himself alone with her one day went so far as to say: "Amour, beautiful Zénis, increases beauty, and joy maintains it, while seriousness and boredom destroy it. Nothing in the world is a beautiful as you, but some people have said that the uncertainty you are in, as to whether to choose Alcime or me, is giving you a certain somber aspect that you did not have before. I

152

have not perceived that change myself, and it might be those envious of you that are putting the rumor about, but...."

"No, Télexis," she interrupted, "they're not mistaken. I've perceived myself they they're right, and I'm glad to have confirmation of the reproaches that my mirror has been making for several days, but since you've made me perceive that a longer uncertainty might be capable of doing me frightful harm, let's finish it. Receive my heart with all the testimony of my most enthusiastic tenderness."

Alcime arrived shortly thereafter, and Zénis did not hide the preference that she had given to his rival. He was wounded by it, but as the harm was irremediable, he went to seek elsewhere the consolations that our Beauties hardly ever leave the afflicted lacking.

As maladies and weaknesses of temperament are virtually unknown on Mercury, two essential causes of sullenness have been removed from the commerce of gallantry. It is not that the source of pleasures is any more inexhaustible there than here, but it is much less limited.

In any case, ingenious Nature, always attentive to the happiness of that favorite People, permits men to hoard pleasures—which is to say, to reserve those that are not expended in daily usage in order to employ them when they please, just as, in our world, one can economize for an entire year in the Provinces in order to live for three months splendidly in the Capital.

As for Ladies, the common mother has judged them so rich with their own funds that she did not think it necessary to provide them with that sort of economy.

CHAPTER IX
On a Few Singularities of the Planet

The Palace of Nature[37]

At an almost equal distance from the two Poles, there is a great mass of rocks covered with moss and trees of every species, laden at all times with flowers and fruits.

That mountain is pierced on every side, and the intervals that the rock leaves between them form irregular Porticos, of which one can never weary of admiring the noble and magnificent simplicity. Those superb lairs are the Palace of Nature; she works there incessantly on all her productions, and it is from there that she distributes them to all the globes of the Vortex.

That palace is eternally open to all those who seek Nature, but it is necessary to have passed over rude pathways, to have climbed rocks and traversed torrents before being worthy to approach her. She has not wanted her dwelling to be equally accessible to all men, but only to those who seek her ardently. She calls them her children and treats them as a veritable mother, all the doors being open to them. It is permissible for them to watch her work and to interrupt her as often as they please, but as she does not like questions, the best thing is to study her by watching her proceed and interrogate her without speaking, by examining her Works, and trying to figure out what means she had employed to carry them out. To come to her with great familiarity, however, it is necessary to have known her at length and to have seen her many times.

---

[37] The presence of this unsupplemented subtitle and the abrupt swerve in the work's narrative strategy (albeit not the first) might be indicative of the insertion here of what was originally a separate work, and the rest of the text might well have been cobbled together in a somewhat arbitrary fashion.

As she grants Sages the honor of admitting us to her most intimate confidence, and we see her as often as we please, it is easy for me to paint her portrait.

She is an individual of large stature, very beautiful, with perfectly regular features full of charms. Health, innocent joy and tranquility, which never abandon her, are fully occupied in grinding the beautiful colors that one sees on her face, renewing her bosom and conserving the ever-renascent glamour of an eternal youth. Her height is well above the average, and gives her an air of majesty, more noble than piquant; what many people say is that her attractions are a trifle massive, and that her beauty would be more agreeable in lesser volume, such as Candace and Minerva must be, and very nearly M. de N.[38] As for her humor, it is gaiety, sweetness and complaisance personified; justice and equity form her character, and just as amiable youth repairs sufficiently a few strokes of the sculptor's chisel that her person lacks, the foundation she possesses of all the essential virtues amply compensates for the slight polish and adornment that one might think desirable.

That is Nature.

Very near to her Palace is that of Art. Once, it was situated in the opposite hemisphere of the Planet—which is to say, as far away as it could be from that of Nature. That point of the History of Mercury is largely unknown, so it will give pleasure to those who like to know everything.

Nature had a great version for Art because he had had the temerity to retouch a few of her Works and had spoiled them, by leaving the traces of his labor exposed. As soon as he puts his hand on something, he imprinted it with his mark, and by virtue of a vanity insolent in a Student, he rendered himself as recognizable in the works of Nature as Nature herself. One could easily see in everything he had made the strokes of the brush, the marks of the chisel and the impressions of the file, which made many people believe, to the great scandal of the

---

[38] Perhaps "Maria de Navarre," or Maria-Theresa, Louis XIV's first wife.

truth, that Nature only works gropingly and cannot deliver the free thrusts and bold strokes that are the true price of good Works. The well-founded jealousy and ridiculous stubbornness of Art in not submitting to Nature had caused them to quarrel, and she could not abide him.

Humans who had more need of her than of him, being close to their mother, insulted her enemy wherever he dared to show himself, to the point that, by dint of persecuting him, they obliged him to hide one the other side of the world. Scarcely had he retired there than he built a Palace that cannot be described, because the marvels one saw there surpass anything that can be imagined, and the marvelous idea of Castles in Spain does not come close.

As the Master of the house was greatly offended by Nature, because of the general aversion that she had attracted to him, that enchanted Palace held nothing at all of hers. Its gardens were in the air, waters spurted instead of flowing, the trees were shaped in human form and instead of the enamel of meadow-grass, that of precious stones carpeted, so to speak, the promenades. One trod on rubies; a thousand brilliant stones formed the plants and flowers, and when anyone desired to lie down on the cool grass, they found themselves on a mosaic of emeralds. It is true that the portrait resembled Nature so strongly that the eyes were deceived by it, but it was not her, and the other senses always murmured that it did not contain anything that the eyes had promised them.

The rancor of Nature and the sulkiness of Art endured for a long time. Things were at that point when Good Taste, one of the Followers of Nature, and her most zealous Partisan, got it into his head to travel, in order to complete the formation of his mind. After having visited all the Planets and stayed for some time in Paris, he took flight toward Mercury and stopped on the exact spot where Art had built his Palace. They had been friends for some time, having spent their lives together and serving the same Master. The Voyager was struck right away by the prodigious magnificence of the Palace, but instead of admiring it he remained surprised by the strange deviations that can occur when Nature is abandoned in order to follow caprice.

"Where can one see," he said to his old comrade, "more beauty, richness and genius? Nothing, to be sure, is so regular, so beautiful and so cleverly devised, and one cannot distribute ornaments with more elegance and profusion, but shall I tell you what I think? Our Mistress is missing here."

Art's only reply was a sigh.

"I can see clearly," his friend continued, "that resentment and chagrin have played a greater part in this entire work than you have. You're annoyed with our Sovereign and only wanted to make her believe that you can do without her—a vain enterprise; she would laugh at this project and everyone who sees it will take her side, with the result that this beautiful masterpiece will pass, so far as they are concerned, for a bizarre assemblage of parts, which are admirably sculpted, but which compose a monstrous body.

"About two thousand years ago, the idea came to me, as it has come to you, to keep myself aloof; I went to the great Moon then, and arrived first in China. There I invented pointed hats, perpetual boots, even for those who never mounted a horse, and the farthingale for women. At first, the people, loving novelty, pushed those fashions to extravagance. They passed from the extremity of Asia to Europe. There were scarcely more than five hundred thousand people in France then. Do you know what happened? The wind blew off all the hats, or they hung them up behind doors. The booted Infantry was embarrassed by their spurs and kept bumping into things. The farthingale only put great circle of iron round the hems of skirts, narrow but still subject to the greatest inconveniences.

"I take from that the conclusion that neither you nor I are worth anything when we depart from the counsels of our Queen; we're only good to follow her. But would you like me to whisper a secret to you, on your word of honor not to say anything? It's that although she makes us valuable, we're not futile either. I don't always say what I think, but just between us, I've seen her constructing the sulkiest faces imaginable.

There's nothing so gauche for attitude and nothing more ridiculous than those faces. As for the principal characters—which is to say, men and women—for every one she renders perfect, she spoils a thousand.

"That is so true that when we want to make a statue, we're obliged to have recourse to several women: to imitate the contours of the face of one, the waist of another, etc.—which makes it evident that it's infinitely rare for her to present us with a model perfect in all its parts—but shush! You can see the consequence of my sincerity."

"I'm no chatterbox," replied Art, "And with regard to everything you've just said, I'm in absolute agreement."

"Oh well," said Good Taste, "if that's the case, believe me, the shortest follies are the best; go back to your duty. Let's go quite frankly to find our good Mistress; you know, as I do, her mildness and humanity; I guarantee that she'll receive us with the best will in the world. But begin by destroying this beautiful Palace of chimeras."

Art, who knows his own interest better than anyone, followed it on this occasion; he had just invented, very recently, a new kind of firework known as a Bomb; those machines had a terrible activity. He put them in all the parts of the Palace, and with a flick of the wrist, it disappeared like a dream.

Having done that, Art and Good Taste arrived as fast as their wings could carry them at the Temple of Nature.

At first she was a trifle stiff with her former Deserter, but he talked to her so submissively that she seemed touched by it. To finish disarming her, he presented her with a few articles that he had taken care to write while in flight—for he is as ingenious as a Demon—and after having sworn and oath to observe them in their form and tenor, he was gracefully received.

These are the articles:

I swear:

1. Never to take my ambition as far as to imitate my divine mistress.

2. To follow her lessons in all my enterprises.

3. To study her fashions of acting and content myself with aiding her in her operations.

4. No longer to put my mark on anything, in order that everything that comes of my industry will appear to be the Work of our Queen, which she has taken the trouble to finish with particular attention.

5. That nothing will ever emerge from my hands unless furnished with the approval of Good Taste, from whom I want to be inseparable.

In consideration of these clauses, the reconciliation was confirmed and has lasted ever since.

It was at that time that the Palace was built in which he now dwells, very close to that of Nature. He combines with the natural graces everything that skill and genius can invent of the most perfect. We have some idea of it here with regard to the Gardens. Versailles, as far as the Canal, is taken on a small scale from that model. The Tuileries is not far away from the design of a promenade that can be seen in one of his country houses.

I do not know where Nature got those designs; perhaps it was with the help of some Genius, or via the amity of our Sages, but it is certain that they can only have been taken from Mercury, for it is not given to any mortal human to have such noble ideas, so the design has not been followed exactly, and it was impossible to prevent something of the Paltry showing therein.

It is true that it was subsequently recognized, but that was only later. And as one fault attracts another, the barbarity of human Taste created the belief that the faults of harmony and disposition could be covered up by the profusion of ornaments; that is why they are lavished with that surfeit of abundance, which does not abandon the defect of taste.

That is how many excellent pieces are spoiled, firstly by making them too narrow and poorly proportions, and secondly by overwhelming them with conventional or incompatible decorations, following the impulse of Hazard rather than the rules of Genius.

CHAPTER X
The Isle of Fortune

From the Palace of Nature one can see the Isle of Fortune. It is entirely rimmed by rocks that make one tremble; the Sea is almost always stormy in that region, and when the winds are not blowing the calms there are just as dangerous. An eternal fog covers the entire Country and spreads a deep obscurity in a vast plain, which it is necessary to traverse before arriving at the Palace of Fortune. That Palace is built on a high mountain, very steep and surrounded by torrents, bottomless precipices, and rivers that are almost always overflowing.

An infinity of roads lead to the mountain, but they are so narrow and slippery that one has great difficulty staying upright there, and the fog is so dense that unless one gropes one's way, as blind people do, it is almost impossible not to lose one's way. However slightly one deviates, one never fails to stick one's head into one of an infinity of exceedingly muddy cooking-pot, invisible in the fog, which are suspended at about head height. That is what is known on Earth as a *pot-au-noir*. So long as one stays on the path, one does not encounter any of them, but as soon as one moves off it, one runs in to them, to the left, the right, if front and behind, and the least harm that can occur is returning to the path splashed with mud, as at a masquerade. Some people even sustain serious contusions there, and bumps that never heal.

There is nothing very dangerous in all of that, for one does not die of a bloody nose, collecting a few bumps or having one's face blackened, but that mummery has something about it so ridiculous and so unbearable that a great many people are put off by it and go back. As soon as one takes a few steps in the other direction the fog dissipates, the path evens out and the route becomes spacious and facile. On the other hand, that route only leads to mediocrity, repose, a quiet but obscure life, peaceful sleep and leisure, for which humans have an invincible antipathy—although to listen to them, one might think that it was the unique object of their desires.

The Empire of Fortune having has much extent on our Earth as the Earth itself, and not being confined to a corner of our World, as on Mercury, the black spot also extends proportionately, and although we cannot see a real fog, which hides us, there is nevertheless something there, albeit invisible. A kind of Metaphysical obscurity covers it perpetually, and whoever marches confidently with his head held high on the road to Fortune, and sees the door of its Palace open both battens, sometimes encounters a terrible *pot-au-noir*, which breaks his nose and gives him a terrible headache, for the more boldly one strides out on that road, the greater the risk one runs of breaking one's neck.

Our World is full of people who are fully occupied in putting these pots on the end of a stick and presenting them to all those who travel on the Road to Fortune; those people are known as panel-hangers, wire-twisters and trippers. One sees them in every street, at plays, on promenades, in private houses and in one's place of employment, but the most adroit of all live at Court, where they are in their element; they swim there in clear water, and no matter how little one travels on that sea, one never fails to catch a glimpse of those vile fish, worse than sharks and crocodiles.

After we had re-embarked and cleaned off the mud, as is the custom of all those who have run into a *pot-au-noir*,[39] we were amusing ourselves by chatting together, and everyone was relating the most surprising thing he knew about the marvels of Nature, when our Pilot, intervening in the conversation, said:

"You haven't seen anything, Messieurs, since you've never been to a little island that is presently alongside us, and of which it seems that mountains border the horizon. The

---

[39] This transition from the general to the particular at this point is odd, and one cannot help suspecting that some text might be missing here, for whatever reason.

cooking-pots appeared to you as animals in the country we're quitting—and, indeed, they're said to think and reason so long as they function adroitly by hiding in that fog to insult the noses of passers-by—but on the island I'm talking about there are much stranger prodigies. One sees neither animals nor people there; Nature, by virtue of an incomprehensible eccentricity, has only populated it with inanimate entities. The Cooking-Pots there, for example, are really alive and active, as people are elsewhere, and no one is at all surprised to see them marching and reasoning in slippers and nightcaps, nor to encounter mittens and silk stockings running around the streets, going about their business with as much common sense and activity as all the rest of the planet's inhabitants of the Planet. I can speak knowledgably, for it's scarcely three months since I made a voyage there in which I had the honor of meeting the Queen, who is known as the Strong Woman—but it's necessary to have seen the place to know it, since you'd never believe what I could tell you about it.

As neither our business nor our route took us in that direction, and the little we had just heard had given us a great curiosity, we begged the Pilot to be kind enough to tell us what he knew about that strange island. The fellow, whose humor was exceedingly sociable, and who did not lack wit, did not have to be begged to give us that account.

CHAPTER XI
On the Strong Woman

Don't imagine, Messieurs, that the Strong Woman in question is really a woman. She has something like the figure and bearing, but fundamentally, she's nothing but a species half way between a pretty woman and a beast. The last one I saw was tall, of a very regular beauty, well made but all of a piece; her admirably ferocious eyes were very animated; she had the most incarnadine and most shapely mouth in the world, but it was said that she is mute, and the rest of her features were no different. There is something strangely torpid in the entirety of her physiognomy, which makes the arms fall.

Two inseparable Companions of the Strong Woman are Trepidation and Peevishness; she has no other guards but those two individuals of a sort, thanks to their talents, are sufficient to defend her against an army. No matter which of them one perceives first, one lies down, one yawns, one turns over and goes to sleep, The other holds a little magic wand, which she waves at everything she encounters, and that wretched little rod, without causing health to deteriorate, cripples people for twice twenty-four hours, and enfeebles them in such a way that one would think all their limbs were paralyzed. One can see that with such safeguards, the Strong Woman has nothing to fear, so she does not keep any regular troops. Only militias are raised when it is a question of defending the coasts or attacking neighbors, which sometimes happens, as you shall see.

The Strong Woman having succeeded to the Crown, where the heat of the blood inspires audacities and ambitious ideas, she acquired a desire to extend her Empire by the conquest of a small neighboring island which seemed much to her liking; that country is known as Coquetry. It is only a kind of reef of very small extent, but the air there is so sweet and the People so pretty and cheerful that the Strong Woman was dying to take possession of it. That was a manifest injustice, for the rights were well-regulated between the two States and their pretentions were so different that there could not be the slightest reasonable pretext for making war, but one of the Princess' Ministers, whose name was Temperament, a quarrelsome and ambitious individual, persuaded her to undertake the enterprise, which really was the only thing that could content her, of mounting an invasion of the neighboring island, where she imagined that she might find treasures of which she promised herself to make delightful use.

The Strong Woman, having formed that chimerical project, imagined that to succeed in it she needed to combine cunning with force, and to conceal her intention, she put around the rumor that she was going to make a polite visit to the neighboring Queen in order to learn about the mores and customs of the land and see for herself whether she might not be able to find some habit of that brilliant Court that she could establish in her own in order to soften the savage humor of her people.

In order to give more authority to that stratagem, she took troops with her, primarily composed of those of her subjects that were the best known in the neighboring island and who maintained regular commerce therewith. With that in view, the only ones enrolled were English Ribbons of all colors, nonpareils, beauty spots, hairnets, pink Robes, Flowers, Fans, little Cuffs and admirable embroidered Slippers, etc. Of these Soldiers, who would not seem suspect to the enemy, Regiments were formed, and a large Phalanx. All the Officers capable of commanding them were provided, and they were given Ensigns and Flags appropriate for rallying.

After having drilled that Militia for some time in order to discipline them, the Strong Woman had her Troops embark to the sound of Theorbs, German Flutes, Lutes, Harpischords and Violas, which took the place of Trumpets and Drums.

It was at the head of that Army that the Strong Woman landed on the island of Coquetry. First she arranged her troops for battle in two lines, and after that precaution, necessary in enemy territory, she advanced rapidly, believing that she could surprise people who were not expecting an invasion. But the Coquettes, who are alert and difficult to deceive, because they are the ones who deceive others, were not asleep and they had set up a counter-battery so wise to the stratagem of the Strong Woman that they believed themselves to be secure.

Meanwhile, the Queen advanced—but at sunrise on the third day of her march someone came to warn her that the Enemy was in sight. In fact, they soon discovered that the plain was covered with little coquettes, whom were advancing while laughing, dancing to the sound of Basque drums and Castanets, lightly armed with baskets, handbags and assorted shuttles, displaying the most assured countenances in the world.

The two Armies drew closer, and made as if to engage in hand-to-hand combat; the air resounded with the noise of instruments of war, and the echo of the Mountains sent it back even louder and more terrible. The Commandants at the head of the Troops harangued them and said the finest things in the world. The Antipathy that flew between the two Camps breathed implacable Anger into them; barbaric Hatred, foolish Audacity and detestable Rancor were painted on faces; in sum, no one had ever seen at close range so many furious thrusts of fingernails, and thousands of pulled-out hairs. The Sun covered its face in order not to illuminate such crimes; but at the fatal moment when the combat was about to begin, the poor Strong Woman, by virtue of an inexplicable treason, saw all her Troops abandon her, who went to line up with the Enemy.

The Beauty Spots, being the lightest, gave the signal, so to speak, for the defection; the Rouge and the tiny Slippers, which always reasoned obliquely, followed them; the Flowers and the pink Dresses, chilled with fear, lowered their weapons. Only the Fans and the little Cuffs put up any defense, and they only held out briefly. The Coquettes hurled themselves forward with such fury that it was impossible for the poor abandoned Troop to sustain such an abrupt attack.

The only corps that held firm on that occasion was the reserve Phalanx; it sustained the ancient virtue of the nation with some valor. That Troop was composed of baskets of all sorts; the Leaders with springs and garnished with taffeta were at the head, and maintained an entirely martial countenance, awhile the simple Soldiers, although garnished quite simply with yellow cloth, nevertheless testified to considerable boldness and appeared ready to put up a fine defense.

In fact, they were seen falling dead or wounded, covered with honorable wounds all received from the front, but one could say that their defense was more honorable than advantageous to the Strong Woman, for the Coquettes eventually broke through the redoubtable Phalanx and laid low everything that resisted them, breaking cords, smashing whalebone and tearing taffeta; it was a hideous thing to see the frightful ravages they made and the number of prisoners they took.

They left the Queen the liberty to regain her Vessels, for that frolicsome and frivolous People, who only wanted the honor of victory and to profit from the spoils of battle, did not care about pursuing the fugitives.

The Strong Woman, having returned home, was deeply ashamed of that fiasco; she promised herself never to go back, and, finding the Land fortunately depopulated of the treacherous and rebellious subjects who had served her so poorly, she resolved to form a new People more robust than the first.

With that end in view, she invited from the neighboring island what might be called a Population or a colony composed of all sorts of Nations, such as tapestry needles, cardboard cylinders, pieces of canvas, hanks of wool of all colors, marble weights, embroidery frames, one-piece head-dresses, leather slippers, minimal dresses, black wings, etc.

These new Subjects were so greatly multiplied in the island by the power of Fays that nothing else was seen, and really, all that remained of the former inhabitants were a few Romances, such as the *Thousand-and-One Nights*, *Le Virgile travesti*, La *Gigantomachie*, the *Letters of Heloïse and Abelard*, *Le Tableau de l'Amour considéré dans l'état de mar-*

riage, Les Lettres Galantes du Chevalier d'Her***, etc.[40] But
as the faith of those former Peoples was still very suspect, a
distribution was made throughout the land of *Les Méditations
de Buzée, Le Combat Spirituel à cheval qui commande le
Guet*, and *Grandes Heures à la Chancelière*,[41] which circulated incessantly, carried in a beautiful sack of black velvet; they
were the ones that maintained the police and who impose order throughout the isle.

---

[40] *Le Virgile travesti* [Virgil Satirized] (1648-53) is a parody
by Paul Scarron, who also wrote *Le Typhon, ou la
Gigantomachie* (1644*). La Génération de l'homme, ou Tableau de l'amour conjugal humain considéré dans l'état du
marriage* [Human Reproduction; or a Depiction of Conjugal
Human Love Considered in the Condition of Marriage] (1686)
was a pioneering study of sex by the physician Nicolas
Venette. *Lettres Galantes de Monsieur le Chevalier d'Her*
(1691, published anonymously) by Bernard Le Bovier de
Fontenelle offered a satirical picture of the society of the day.
[41] *Les Meditations de Buzée et d'Hayneuve* is a fictitious work
to which one of Nicolas Boileau-Despreaux's satires refers;
the Garnier reprint of the present text substitutes "Cuze" for
"Buzée," but it is an error, not a correction. There are several
books entitled *Le Combat spirituel*, of which the best-known
at the time the present book was published was a translation
by P. Brignon of Lorenzo Scupoli's Italian original, first published in 1633, but none referring to "the horse that commands
the Watch". *Grand Heures à la Chancelière*, another fictitious
title, appears to refer to one of the famous balls at Versailles
hosted by the wife of the Chancellor of France, the Comte de
Pontchartrain, between 1699 and 1714.

CHAPTER XII
On a Picture Seen in the Emperor's Palace

The picture in question is called by a name that comes from the Spanish word *desinganno*, which can only be translated into our language as "disabusement"—which, unfortunately, is not in current use.[42] One can see in that Picture as many as a thousand historical portraits of illustrious men and women who lived on all the Planets of the Vortex.

It is only necessary to touch the names of those that one wants to see, all of which are engraved on the frame; instantly, the person appears, admirably painted at the most brilliant moment of their History—which is to say, on the occasion when they did themselves most honor and demonstrated a higher superiority over the rest of their species. That Picture is the only item that the presently reigning Emperor brought from the Sun.

It has one marvelous property, which is that after having shown the person in all their glory, they are represented again at four different points in life, which is done by means of four lenses, which are shaped in such a way that each one represents things completely different from the way they appear in the Picture.

Optical instruments enable us to obtain in our World, imaginatively, a slight idea of the Picture; for, by means of reflective cylinders and cones, we can see objects quite differently from the simple view that a Painter presents to us. The

---

[42] *Desinganno* does not appear to exist in Spanish, but *disinganno* does in Italian. *Désabusement* [disabusement] was, in fact, added to the Académie's official dictionary of the French language in due course; I have transcribed it directly in order to preserve the intended impression of oddity, although it would usually be translated as "disenchantment" or "disillusionment."

same thing arrives in the Picture, in which the principal figure always remains, but everything accompanying them, including the clothes, is diversified, in accordance with the different roles they played.

In order to make the moving Picture more understandable, I shall describe the last representation that I saw there, which is still very present in my mind.

The Painter depicts a Heroic Warrior on the day of his Triumph, and at the most brilliant moment of that great spectacle. Nothing is lacking in the design of the Conqueror's glory: gold shines, incense fumes, admiration is legible in all eyes, the pomp of his costume and the sublimity of the triumphal chariot seem to offer the Hero to the adoration of the People. In sum, the imagination of the Painter has assembled there all the noble bagatelles and all the serious buffooneries that humans have invented in order to turn heads.

Is one weary of that magnificent representation? The great Marionettes disappear; it is only necessary to take one of the four faceted lenses to see the noble Pantalon in a domestic setting; the arrogance of his Triumph has followed him there. It is in pompous and imperative tones that he demands the complaisance of his children and conjugal tenderness.

A Slave with his back turned to him laughs with his comrade at the misplaced bombast of the Braggart. A wretched Parasite retained by the expectation of supper yawns, without parting his lips, at the twentieth recitation of the latest battle. The Lady of the house lends a distracted ear to the sumptuous detail of the operations of the last campaign, and smiles complaisantly at all the pretty stupidities whispered in her ear by a young Aide-de-Camp who was her illustrious husband's Page. One takes it as read that in the Picture, the words and even the intentions are painted in the faces.

On changing the lens, one perceives the warrior receiving a heap of gold from the hands of his Steward. He examines the coins attentively, calculating their weight and worth, and shows by his countenance that he values the advantage of having looted Nations much more highly than the glory of having defeated them. He complains bitterly about a delay that the humanity of his servants was unable to refuse to the present inability to pay off a Creditor in difficult circumstances but solvent. He avoids the payment of a debt that is equally just and urgent. He pretends not to glimpse the desires of his daughter, who is in love, for fear of being constrained to take a small part in that immense superfluity in order to establish her. A rigid observer of domestic Rules, he cannot accord anything to generosity, or to the pleasures of others. Finally, he locks away his gold, citing the difficulty of the times, and ends the Scene with scarcely-heroic domestic quibbling.

Another lens represents the Hero infatuated; his superb head is submissive to the yoke of a brainless young flirt, who mocks the puerile attentions of the Dictator in a corner of the Picture. A young citizen laughs with her at the anxieties of the Graybeard; one sees that she is assuring the preferred individual that it is not her fault if the General does her the honor of aspiring hopelessly to her conquest, founding his hopes on the simple politeness that she is obliged to show him. On continuing to look, one sees that the girl is not lying, and that the Vanquisher of the Sarmatians[43] is far from becoming hers, for all the objects present themselves successively.

The fourth lens will change the scene: the Conqueror in an armchair, seemingly overwhelmed by dolor; fortune has abandoned him, leaving visible all the weakness that it concealed. That Hero, the terror of Armies, who braved dangers and death, does not have the strength to render himself superior to his disgrace. He turns his head one last time to look at his first Dignities and his former grandeur, and he dies with a shudder. That is what a great man is.

Well, Good God, who, after the contemplation of those human miseries, could still conserve any self-respect, since

---

[43] The Sarmatians were a Scythian tribe to which some Greek writers referred as "woman-ruled." Herodotus accounts for their origin, fancifully, by making them descendants of Amazon woman captured by Scythian men in battle.

even those one believes most pardonable have so many reasons for humiliation? All the Portraits are subject to those disabusive lenses; they are not all similar, because not all humans are ridiculous, avaricious or weak; but many a person who escapes one of these faults falls into another, and almost all people have, during the course of their lives, similar doses of ridicule and impertinence.

The study of that Picture, which is known to everyone, unmasks characters so naively, and makes it so evident how little the most worthy men are really worth, that few people on Mercury have more self-esteem than they merit.

CHAPTER XIII
The Sentiment of the Sages of Mercury Regarding "Bel-Esprit"

It is only too commonplace on Mercury, as on our Earth, to confuse the terms "bel Esprit" and "Homme d'Esprit."[44] The opinion of the Sages, however, is that wit bears no more resemblance to veritable intelligence, superior intelligence, than tinsel does to gold or talc to diamond. A witty man, they say, is one who passes over the truth to grasp the marvelous, who scorns the facile to attempt the impossible, who prefers the agreeable to the useful, the superfluous to the necessary, the brilliant to the solid. He only sees the surface, the envelope of things, only touches the epidermis and only grasps the elixir and the quintessence. He is ignorant of the Sciences and the Arts, only knowing their definition; he knows that Geometry is not Mechanics and that a Painter does not exercise the Art of Statuary, but does not ask anything more.

His ignorance renders him Pyrrhonian,[45] but although he lives without principles and sees nothing as certain, he is nonetheless superstitious, because he is credulous, at the same time as the doubts the most certain verities if they are enveloped by the slightest obscurity or if they are contrary to his

---

[44] It is difficult to reflect this confusion in English because the French *esprit* has a wider spectrum of meanings, embracing spirit, intelligence and wit, than any English term. Thus, although both the cited terms are ambiguous, lending themselves very readily to confusion, the distinction that is being drawn is between superficial cleverness or wit on the one hand, and true intelligence on the other, as reflected in the subsequent decoding.

[45] Pyrrhonism was a school of extreme skepticism named after, but not founded by, the Greek philosopher Pyrrho.

penchants and inclinations. Any examination or effort fatigues him, weighs him down, and he would rather regard the clearest demonstration as a trap set for him than strive to comprehend it. In sum, the wit might become a man of intelligence, if he learned all that he does not know, and if he forgot a large part of what he does know.

A wit only makes use of his memory and his imagination, rarely combining them with a talent for remembrance and that of imagining; as for judgment, one might say that it is excluded from his not, or that he disdains to make use of it.

A person whose memory constitutes all his merit has carefully charged it with all that the ancient and new Poets offer us of harmonious bagatelles; he cites them, and the soporific speechifier is praised; everyone agrees that the man is fundamentally a great mind, a marvelous genius, and does not know why one falls asleep when listening to him.

Another clever person of the same class acquaints himself at an appropriate time with all the anecdotes of the last century and the quips of the old Court; he furnishes himself with them in the morning and pays them out for the rest of the day. He is applauded and admired; the man has seen everything, knows everything; he is a prodigy. The truth is that he knows how to read, that he has riffled through his Collection before going out, that he will entertain you with it for the rest of the year, only to recommence next year in the same order, and he will die convinced that in order to merit the title of a superior intelligence, and incomparable individual, it is sufficient to have a memory and possess an ample repertoire of jolly trivia for the use of the Court and the City.

The latitude of forty-five degrees, the Sages continue, furnishes us with another sort of clever individuals of the second species.[46] Their vivid, sparkling, inflamed imagination

---

[46] Forty-five degrees north is the approximate latitude of Bordeaux, and hence of Gascony, reputed in Paris as a region of colourful, fanciful braggarts, of whom Cyrano de Bergerac became a kind of type specimen.

consumes, so to speak, their memory and gets ahead of their judgment; content to imagine present objects, speeches and facts lightly and feebly, thy compose florid, humorous images, colored like butterfly wings and just as solid. The witticisms off their Compatriots, which they learn in infancy, compose their entire doctrine; their memory goes no further, but does not need to; that Catalogue of Epigrams, combined with the talent of the Nation, enables them to turn to ridicule that which does not merit it. Accuracy of intelligence, acquired knowledge, talents and reasonable sentiments are the favorite subjects of their perpetual irony and their unique resource to please is to parody in burlesque the beautiful, the good and the true everywhere that it is found.

Flee that species of fire follets, who, in truth, do not burn, but who nonetheless fatigue the sight. If what makes the merit of those Clowns can be called wit, what sane man would want to have it? Fortunately, they only have the name, and their Certificates are only signed by the populace.

Feminine Society is no less distributed with a large quantity of a similar worth; they are the successes that our Petty Masters obtain, and they are never refused, so long as they have a passable figure, a certain liberty of attitude, a little physiognomy and talk glibly. Then the greater part of the work is done; the rest consists of showing oneself every day at all the spectacles, of knowing, at least by hearsay, what one can expect of a certain Actress appearing for the first time. One supposes also that he will not have failed to observe that Madame has studied someone through her opera glasses, and what effect that Phenomenon has had on the interested Spectator. He would dishonor himself in society if, on exiting from the première of an Opera, he had neglected to know the name of the Poet and Musician who wrote it. As for his opinion; he has none, but he will repeat to you what is thought on the stairway, for it is in that Academy that he learns to judge Poetry and Music.

In any case, you can judge for yourself: he has the Book in his pocket, he knows the tune and the words of a perfect

Rondeau and a Tambourin that have all the sublimity of the Play, and he sings them passably. People wax enthusiastic, admiring his memory and his voice equally; but if he adds to those prodigies a few couplets from a Vaudeville that no one knows yet, or rhymed calumnies that only appeared yesterday evening, he is fêted, people become ecstatic; he is an adorable man, a marvelous intelligence, a unique individual-one can also add a dyed-in-the-wool *bel Esprit*, who does not lack a modicum of memory and imagination.

CHAPTER XIV
Adventures Dependent on Metamorphosis

Télenis was pretty, very lively and extremely coquettish. Lénidor, greatly piqued by her face and her manner, wanted to have a bit of fun with her, but he would not have wanted for all the Brunettes in the world—for that was all she was—to end the charming relationship that he had with Zélemi, the most amiable young woman in the Empire, and the most accomplished. If one could reproach him for a fault, it was that of being so full of his passion that he could not hide it. Amour was not only on his lips and in his eyes, it shone throughout his person, embellishing it, distributing a thousand graces over his figure and his attitude, causing his indolence and animating his gaiety. In sum, to look at Zélemi was to see Amour in Lénidor's chariot.

Although Lénidor loved the young woman passionately, little Télenis tempted him to infidelity, and whether by virtue of cleverness or pure coquetry, she did everything that one does to people that one would like to put themselves forward—so he put himself forward, and was not turned away. The first week of that affair went at a gallop, and nothing was lacking but the conclusion; according to all the rules of fortification, the position could not hold out for another three days.

But, cries the sage Author of this History, at this point, O human prudence, how limited your sight is! That great vivacity died away almost as soon as it was ignited. Lénidor had suffered like all the others, but he could not divine what it was that stopped him on such a fine road, nor understand why his Rivals had enjoyed a better fate than him. That novelty piqued him; he did not love Télenis, but he did not want to be insulted by her, nor that it could be said that the little minx only ran half the risk; she abstained, however, and that was resolved by destiny.

Lénidor, after having endured all her caprices, all her moods, all her contradictions and affectations, without rhyme or reason, finally complained. At first it was with all the softness of an afflicted lover; she let him speak without even putting on a semblance of listening. One of those about whom he was complaining came in; he was received better than usual, and she was only occupied with him for the rest of the day. Finally he left. Télenis remained tranquil and pensive; she picked up a book; she yawned.

Lénidor did not say a word. He was nevertheless ashamed of attaching himself to a person who seemed to deliver herself so easily to everyone; the lack of success of his efforts did not give him a better opinion of his mistress; he did not know whether he ought to leave her and never see her again or wait a few more days.

He was at that point when she said to him: "What's the matter with you? You're not saying a word; it's surely very churlish to leave me to get bored, like a dog, without unclenching your teeth,"

"If you're bored," he said, "it hasn't been for long, for it seems to me that you've been enjoying yourself in good company all day."

"No—I was dying of boredom. How could I not? Does he even have common sense?"

"But how is it possible, then," said Lénidor, "that you chatted so much with him, that you stood with him at all the windows, that you so often talked in low voices?"

"That was because he was telling me the story of poor ; you can see understand that it couldn't be said loudly in front of everyone who was there."

"What?" Lénidor replied. "It was nothing but that?"

"No, I assure you," said Télenis.

"You're very cruel to make me suffer so much for nothing.

"You? How is that?"

"How is that? Have you forgotten that I love you more than my life, as I've told you, and that I'm in a horrible anxiety?"

"I understand," said Télenis. "You want to know if I love you? No, of course not."

"Obviously."

"That's it, as I say."

"You're very wicked to have made me think so. What pleasure have you obtained from deceiving me? It's an unparalleled perfidy."

"Oh, very well. But what about you—what do you call the buffoonery that you're playing with Zélemi? Is it possible that her beauty, her intelligence and her love are only worthy of your indolence? Begging your pardon, I don't believe it. But as I don't have as many reasons as her to believe the nonsense men talk, I understood that you were seeking to amuse yourself, and I played my part in the amusement. I regard it as a little Comedy we've played, having nothing better to do."

Lénidor spoke more seriously, he became irritated and sulky, he changed his tone, did not forget any of these that were so often persuasive, and charged his discourse with all the vivacity that a violent and urgent passion inspires. He was repaid in kind; he was made to feel ashamed of the infidelity he wanted to commit, and he was threatened that the interested part would be informed.

For himself, he was confused, and would have sworn that such a misfortune had never happened to anyone but him. He had no confidence in Télenis' oath that there was nothing in her heart for him and that she treated all men in the same fashion; he would at least have liked to convict her of lying, in order to quit her with less regret and to tell himself that she was not worth the trouble he had taken over her.

Full of that beautiful imagination, he examined all of Télenis' actions for several days with jealous attention, without finding anything for which he was searching.

He did not doubt that the Coquette, cunning and adroit as she was, must be concealing her true game. In the end, he was beginning to get discouraged, when he perceived that he had the gift of Metamorphosis. He was delighted to have acquired that privilege so appositely.

So, Lénidor changes himself into a butterfly, enters into his Mistress' home, and no longer leaves her. She does not say a word, or take any action, that would give him grounds to reproach her.

That went on for a long time—so long that Zélemi, who hardly ever saw him anymore, made the most touching complaints to him. After swearing a thousand times that he had never loved anyone but her, with the delicacy of a perfect Lover, he revealed the secret of his disparities to her. He confessed the temporary liking that he had had for Télenis and promised not to go back to her again, nor to return to the espionage that had occupied him for such a long time and so inappropriately. (It is necessary to remark that Lénidor carefully kept it hidden from his two Mistresses that he had the gift of Metamorphosis.)

"I want you to continue observing Télenis," Zélemi replied. "It's good that you should finally clarify this enigma of sorts, and know the difference there is between all other women and me."

He could easily have done without that experiment, but he obeyed. Thereafter, he kept Télenis in view; he was always in her house, as a butterfly, or a little mouse, or a fly that settled in her hair, without ever leaving.

Télesis' conduct was consistent: always cheerful, always lively; one might have thought her foolish, but nothing more.

Finally, one day when she was along with one of her female friends who knew her well and was passing over the innumerable lists of her Lovers, Lénidor came to the forefront.

"He's the one I remember most fondly," said Télenis, "but he's so well caught that it would be madness to think about him. I had him for a few days, and if he wasn't a liar, it was only up to me to have more; but how stupid...."

"Why, then," said her friend "did you chase him away discontented? To be sure, you sometimes behave in ways that are so strongly against you that no one anyone could be forgiven for taking you for—I won't mince words—a slut, but you deserve it. It's not enough to be good, or even to be better than others; it's also necessary to appear so, when one takes the trouble."

"Right. Don't I appear so? Ask Lénidor whether he won't tell you that I'm the most virtuous woman in the world. I know from his own lips that he spied on me for a long time, and he surely didn't see anything, because there was nothing to see, and I'm sure that he has as good an opinion of me as of Zélemi."

"By the way," said the Confidante. "Is Zélemi's passion as excessive as people say? Can it really have lasted seven years without the slightest cloud or quarrel? That puzzles me—I don't like things to which I'm not accustomed, and if I were a man, I'd be suspicious of such a great serenity."

"But how can you expect him to be fearful," said Télenis, "when he's free from even the slightest grounds for suspicion?"

"I don't know," replied her friend, "but in Lénidor's place, I wouldn't have such an abandoned confidence. I confess, in sum, that I'd make sure."

Me too, said Lénidor to himself, *but only when I'm entirely sure in your regard.*

He continued his jealous attentions, as fruitlessly as before. He returned to Zélemi and gave her an account of the commission she had given him.

"You've either done badly," said Zélemi, "or you're deceiving me; and for one or other of those reasons, I condemn you to continue the examination for another fortnight."

It was necessary to obey, but he was nevertheless surprised by the proposition. "What," he said, "You don't see me enough; you complain about the slightest dissipations, and you throw a fortnight at me head without my having asked for it? Is there something behind this?"

"Of course not—what could there be?"

"No matter; it's a very small thing; if she's not worth a few more days of attention, they'll soon be over."

It soon was, in fact, for the very next day, he saw a man entering Zélemi's room by a door of whose existence he had never known. He thought at first that it was a game and a coquetry on the part of his Mistress, who wanted to give him the pleasure of a demi-adventure, but he did not remain in doubt for long; the demi-adventure became a very complete one, was followed by a second, and would have gone further if Zélemi had not sent her companions away, because there is nothing so good that one does not want it to end.

Lénidor was in an astonishment, an admiration and a fury that cannot be imagined; he was arranging his discourse, planning to end his Metamorphosis, appear before the eyes of the traitor and heap reproaches upon her—but he did not have time. The door that had just closed opened again and a second Champion came to take the place of the first.

Coming, seeing and conquering were the same thing. No Scene was ever more brilliant or more sustained on one part or the other. It concluded, however, only to be renewed by the arrival of a third Actor.

That one made Lénidor lose patience; be became annoyed by the incomparable volubility of his Queen and left, alarmed by such ardent fire. As he went away he was surprised to encounter near Zélemi's abode one of the Inhabitants of the Crusts of the Sun. He did not imagine that he was going to her house, but as, in a moment of indifference, he was seeking only to amuse himself, he followed the Prisoner of War and was not a little astonished to see him go in where the last one came out.

That vile Complimenter took Zélemi in his arms. Lénidor did not want to see any more. He thought he was finally about to be avenged for his Mistress' perfidy and that she would surely die, but he was quite astonished when he saw that she did not even blink.

It is easily understandable that that was more than enough to cure Lénidor of his passion for Zélemi, so he no longer thought of anything except avenging himself with Télenis for the tragic Scene that he had just endured. With that design he went into her house with the aid of Metamorphosis. He found her alone with her friend; they were amusing herself with some needlework and passing in review everything that they had seen the preceding day; then they combed one another's hair. The conversation turned to him several times; he entered into all comparisons.

"What I'm doing there," said Télenis, "you must find quite ridiculous. We always come back to Lénidor, it's a kind of Rondeau. He has scarcely any more place in my heart than the others, however; you know how fond I am of liberty. I don't want empire over anyone, but if someone gave it to me, I would want him to love me madly. Anyway, I want to escape any slavery; a heart well captured is in eternal subjection; one's belief depends on faith alone; one spends one's life doing someone else's bidding, often obeying painful caprices; the returns never match the cost."

She was at that point when Lénidor suddenly rendered himself visible. They were very surprised, and understood that he had the gift of Metamorphosis. He admitted it, told them the use that he had made of it, recited all their conversations, thanked Télenis very much for the fortunate concern she had for him, and, in order to destroy anything that might diminish that sympathy, gave her a blow-by-blow account of Zélemi's adventure.

Sélima was not overly astonished, but Télenis could not get over it. As we ordinarily judge others by ourselves, we find it difficult to believe what is opposed to our own character.

Lénidor was grateful to Télenis for not even having had the idea of Zélemi's vivacities; his love for the one was augmented as much as his aversion for the other increased. But he feared the torpor of Télenis' heart; he did not take long to tell her what he thought about it. The preference of Sélima, which he knew to be in his interests, further emboldened the manner in which he pressed Télenis in every imaginable fashion to accept the heart of a Lover whom Zélemi had stolen from her. The common Friend added very good arguments to his, and Télenis' natural inclinations provided the best of all.

However, three Orators ordinarily so victorious did not make any progress; freedom of spirit, Télenis' sole Divinity, defended her for a long time—but in the end, it was one against three, and it had to yield, or at least beat a retreat. Télenis did not want ever to be constrained; Sélima assured her that Lénidor was incapable of ever doing anything that might displease her; and he confirmed it with frightful oaths regarding all the engagements that could be obtained from him. Télenis smiled at all that, without making any response; the dispute did not bore her. Finally, unable to resist so many pleas, and, above all, having regard to the recommendation of sympathy, she consented to all that was asked of her.

That evening he went back to Zélemi, whom he found alone, as usual. She made him the most tender reproaches in the world for having gone so long without seeing her; he gave the excuse of the commission she had given him to observe the conduct of Télenis.

"I would not have wanted, for anything in the world," he added, "to have failed to follow her; no one could have been better paid for his trouble than I have been. You would not believe how disgusted I am by it."

He began then to tell her about Télenis everything that he had seen her do, telling her that he had found a means of hiding in her apartment and that he had seen five performances in the same night. As he named those who were reputed to be attached to Télenis, the discourse seemed plausible enough, but as he rendered the essential details of the adventure as Zélemi remember clearly having experience them, she could not admire that strange conformity enough, and what astonished her even more was to see that Télenis had had the same conversations as her. That rendered her serious. She became even more so when she saw that the sequence of the night was positively molded on her own, and the most vivid details, as well as the least important, had a perfect resemblance to it.

"You're not laughing," said Lénidor, who was laughing uproariously at her embarrassment, under the pretext of the humor of the narration.

"No," she said. "I can't laugh at seeing a person like Télenis knowing so little what she's worth and delivering herself with so much infamy to her taste for anyone who comes along; and I'm so surprised to see that there's a woman of that character in the world that I can't get over it. I don't have Télenis' charms, nor her coquetry, nor perhaps her with and gaiety, but at least I know how to love, I know how to be faithful, and if ever you become jealous it will have to be of your shadow, for I only see and only listen to you; my house is an impenetrable retreat and I could not suffer anyone ever preventing me from being always occupied with my Lover."

Indignant at that falsity, Lénidor could not dissimulate any longer; he metamorphosed in front of her. Then, resuming his own form, he said: "You see the facility that I had in observing Télenis. I also made use of it for you, and it was in your room, where I spent last night, that I learned by heart the Scene that I have just described to you in the name of another. You won't deny it; you've seen from the rest of my speech that I've told the truth, since I've repeated it to you, down to the slightest words that were spoken."

Zélemi, who had had a moment to collect herself during that terrible confession, tried to retrench herself in denial.

"Say rather," Lénidor replied, "that you were dreaming at the time, and that the violence of your passion made you mistake for me all those who took the trouble to enter your bedroom."

After finishing that speech in an ironic tone, he left Zélemi's house, never to enter it again as long as he lived, and went to tell Télenis about the conversation he had just had with her. As they were alone, there is every likelihood that she repaid him for the pleasure that his story had given her.

CHAPTER XV
On Simulacra of Calumny

A tradition of more than four thousand years, affirms that it was a long time before the Emperors who reign today, when humans lived in peace on Mercury, governed by equitable Kings full of humanity, that the adventure I am about to narrate occurred.

One night, when the Heavens were more serene than usual, and Venus in full was spreading a light that did not permit regret for the presence of daylight, the sky was suddenly covered, and a thick poisonous vapor covered the entire face of the planet with horrible darkness.

When the obscurity had lasted for some time, an innumerable quantity of red and smoky fires rose up on the limits of the horizon, and that blazing cloud approached the Planet with a frightful din and an incredible rapidity. During the time of its passage a hideous monster composed of a devouring flame divided into an infinity of particles, each of which assumed a fantastic body. Nothing in the world was more frightening than the faces of all those nascent Demons; there were no two that resembled one another in the infinite multitude that inundated the Planet.

A universal terror gripped all hearts; everyone fled; there was no forest dense enough and no cavern deep enough in which to hide.

The Monsters that had fixed their sojourn on Mercury soon perceived that it would be impossible for them to live with the humans, as was their intention, if they did not find the secret of reconciling them to the deformity of their faces, or at least changing their appearance. They recognized by the continuation of the general terror that people would not become accustomed to seeing them in their own form, so they took the resolution to disguise as best they could the defects of their appearance, and to make themselves masks so cheerful and pleasant that everyone would be charmed by them.

That resolution, once made, was soon executed, and with the aid of the secrets of Magic, all their ugliness disappeared. It was not that they actually changed form, but, there being no subtler Enchanters in the world, they found the secret of covering up their deformity so well that it was impossible to recognize them.

A long garment full of decency covered them from head to foot, and a mask replete with mildness and modesty covered their faces. In that state they approached human beings and assure them that they had driven their enemies away, who were the detestable followers of calumny, the hideous monster that had appeared in the blazing cloud.

The People of Mercury, to whom lying and disguise were unknown vices, added faith without any reluctance to the artful words of their new Guests, and were soon going about arm in arm with them. They received in their houses the perfidious enemies that they had detested two days earlier, and, deceived by the false appearance, believed that they had the most faithful and devoted of friends. The Kings followed the example of the People, for it was at the Courts of the great Princes, above all, that they were determined to spend their sojourn, and that was where they made the greatest efforts to establish a solid foothold.

They soon succeeded. They had scarcely been on the Planet for a week than they governed it. Former Servitors were suspect to their Masters. The most solid friends were mistrusted, and the sacred knots of nature gradually relaxed. Fathers feared the perfidy of their children, and the latter the covert traps of their fathers. Husbands hid their views from their wives and wives no longer dared confess their fears or hopes to spouses who loved them. Love itself was devoid of confidence. Someone who had served the Prince well and squandered his days to save those of his Master was lost to his mind and that faithful subject was qualified with the name of a covert enemy.

"As he has served well," said those monsters, "he does not find any recompense worthy of his services; in any case, we know by reliable ways that he is conspiring, that he is making friends, that he is seeking protectors and support. If you knew," they said to the Prince, "what liberties he sometimes takes in censuring your actions, what a sinister interpretation he gives to your most judicious projects, and what speeches...but it would be a crime to repeat them."

On the slightest of suspicions, the most worthy man, the most intimate friend of the Prince—for Princes can have them—was doomed without resource. No attempt was made on his life as yet, but he was distanced from familiarity, and eventually exiled himself, without ever being told what had destroyed him. The very ones who plunged the dagger into his back, stealing his Master's heart, criticized in his presence the misunderstanding and infidelity of the Prince, and offered to serve as mediators between two good friends distanced from one another, they said, by a slight coldness. Then they put on an appearance of employing their offices for a reconciliation to which they blocked all avenues.

"Perhaps, Sire," they said to the Prince, "you have been deceived in his regard. I'm sure that fundamentally, he loves Your Majesty. Calumny is a Hydra with a hundred heads; it infects all Courts. However perfect and godlike Your Majesty might be, perhaps he is not sheltered from the perfidious traits of this world; in all the conservations I have had with a man who is my friend, I have thought that I have seen his innocence laid bare; crime is not capable of the heroic confidence with which he sustains his disgrace; one might think that he does not feel it, and that Your Majesty, in depriving himself of him, is losing more than he is. If Your Majesty returns him to your good graces, I am sure that that will be the means of softening the inflexible soul that adversity revolts, and only appears to be tempted to crime by the desire for vengeance—a passion so natural in all great hearts."

With such darts stepped in aconite or the venom of Cerberus, the Prince was poisoned while feigning to calm him down, and the ruin of the innocent never failed to be the price of such a finely honed calumny.

Then the confidence of the Prince, the spoils of the unfortunates, the important employments and wealth, were the prey of the monsters. Oppressed innocence no longer found any access to the Throne. The most striking merit was persecuted; virtue passed for crime; science and reason were more than sufficient to render the best subjects on the Planet suspect of revolt and sedition.

What was done at Court was practiced with the same artifice and similar success in private houses; there was no longer, if the monsters were believed, any faithful friends, any disinterested domestic, any heir exempt from suspicion, any discreet lover, tender mistress, workman expert in his art or philosopher who knew how to read.

The monsters, linked together by an indissoluble interest, were the only sages, the only enlightened individuals, the only virtuous individuals worthy of recompense; so they invaded everything in order to share in it, with the precaution that the individual who brought a family down would never share in its spoils; it was upon another that the entire price of the injustices he committed would fall, while he would collect in his turn the debris of another fortune that another monster had overturned.

Finally, calumny, the source of all the evils of the Society, governed the Planet absolutely, and I believe that it would have expelled the true inhabitants, as it had already overthrown so many Empires, when the Sovereign who reigns in the Sun perceive the frightful disorder that it had spread throughout Mercury. He attempted several means to remedy the situation; he sent to that favorite Planet Reason, Examination and Verity, charging them to oppose in every possible way the enterprises of calumny.

Reason strove to render suspect the monsters' discourses; Examination sometimes made falsity visible, and Verity, above all, snatched away their masks and laid them bare. Their faces gave rise to horror, but the enemy had acquired such a powerful empire in all hearts with the aid of its associate, un-truth, the self-esteem that it held in pawn, and the flattery or-namented with the finery of amity, that no one any longer had confidence in anyone else. Scarcely had Reason dared to show her face than she was hissed by the people, at Court and in public places, Examination, whom she held by the hand, was declared by and authentic Edict to be a public enemy, and de-mentia went such an extreme that Verity was thrown to the bottom of a well.

Fortunately, those Divinities could not die, but the perse-cution they had to suffer discouraged them to such an extent that they no longer showed themselves anywhere; for Virtues are not proud, as just as a favorable welcome attracts them, jeers frighten them. Only vice knows how to ally impudent effrontery with other horrors.

Things were in that state when the Genius who reigns over the Sun sent one of its inhabitants to Mercury to govern the Planet.

Scarcely had he arrived than he reunited the separated Powers in his own person, as has been said above; then, with a stroke of his supreme power, he unmasked all the monsters and, having rendered them odious in laying them bare, he armed all his subjects, set himself at their head and pursued with overt force the enemies that artifice had rendered invinci-ble for such a long time.

They attempted, in vain, all kinds of ruses to seduce the Emperor's army, to debauch his soldiers and render him odi-ous to the people by publishing in his regard all the horrors that lies and malignity could invent; but, the mask having been removed, the perfidy could not succeed, and it was necessary to revert to combat.

Their defeat was complete; the greater number of the monsters perished on the battlefield, some were put in irons and the rest saved themselves by flight. The last group was scattered through all the Planets, and ours by preference, where they exercise a tyrannical empire of which we can nev-er hope to see the end.

As for those that remained prisoners, the Emperor, who enjoyed the power of Metamorphosis, changed them into bronze statues, after having returned their masks and garments, which hid their defects; but he did not want to take away their lives or their power of movement, so he contented himself with chaining them in iron bonds, which, although as supple as the bodies of those metamorphosians, conserve a solidity that nothing can dissolve or break.

In that state he exhibited them on magnificent stages in the largest squares of all the Cities, and wanted them to continue to live their natural lives there. He also conserved the lives of all the Kings that the monsters had seduced, and condemned them for thirty thousand years to represent every day in Public all the injustices they had committed and all the evils that they had blindly caused their subjects in favor of the monsters.

The monsters, having become bronze statues, but alive and mobile, therefore continue to flatter Kings, Great Men and the Rich, and the latter allow themselves to be intoxicated as they had once been poisoned, but all those tragic plays, admirably performed, always end with the arrival of Reason, Examination and Verity, who discover by an infinity of ingenious ways the artifices and the malignity of Calumny.

Thus, Calumny always retires, covered with shame and overwhelmed by jeers, while the King and the Rich Man, penetrated with repentance for their crimes, suffer all the remorse of their conscience at night; for in the morning, everything is forgotten, and a new stage appears in the theater, on which are represented all the intrigues, al the covert stratagems, all the lies and all the hidden was by which Calumny reaches its ends.

After thirty thousand years, we are assured, the Emperor who reigns then will obtain from the Intelligence that governs the Sun the power to purify the minds of the monsters, and to make them human by forging bodies for them similar to those of the inhabitants of Mercury.

That is what those animated Simulacra are, which are so common on Mercury, and so admirable, since they are the only living and active statues in the Universe.

With regard to those who committed crimes because of the section of the monsters, their punishment ends as soon as they have finished performing all the stories publicly, after having endured the shame and remorse that naturally follow such faults. Then they quit their bronze bodies to take another, like those of the Planet for which they are destined—for they are all exiled, the Emperor still finding some risk in conserving among his people those weak and unenlightened souls, who were unable to distinguish lies from truth during their life, nor their true friends from perfidious enemies.

The Emperor claims that a soul dishonored by stains of that importance retains the stigmata for a long time, and that nothing less than a Great Pilgrimage is required to restore its primal nobility and bring it back to virtue.

CHAPTER XVI
On the Principle of Medicine on Mercury

Although the temperament of the inhabitants of Mercury is the firmest and best in our Vortex, and the purity of the air, seconded by the proximity of the Sun, always maintains them in perfect health, one nevertheless finds physicians on the Planet, where they are necessary at least for the Sages who inhabit it—for they do not all have the philosophical stone, so their health is not unalterable.

The Physicians of Mercury have no peers in all the Planets in our Universe, as one can easily be convinced when one knows how they have simplified their Art and how many frivolous studies and useless items of knowledge they have discarded.

On our Earth a Physician is expected to have all imaginable knowledge in his head; he must know anatomy in depth, although that talent alone demands the study and labor of a skillful man for an entire lifetime. In addition to that he is expected to know the nature of all the liquids composing the mass of the blood; that he familiarizes himself, so to speak, all the paths by which they travel and by which they escape, and the causes that might arrest them in their flow, against the intentions of Nature.

It is necessary for him to know the qualities of all plants, all kinds of wood, bark, leaves, roots, soils, stones, metals, minerals, those of all salts and sulfurs, and necessary that he can foresee with certainly the species of action that all these substances are capable of producing on blood and the humors, in all the different states in which they might be found. That supposes a perfect knowledge of Chemistry, a long and difficult study, for which the entire lifetime of a man is far from sufficient.

The essential aspect of his profession, according to our idea, is to be able to define all diseases, to mark their divisions and to know all their symptoms. He must have present in his memory the names of all drugs, as many simples as composites, and their exact doses

It is necessary, in addition, that he knows all the temperaments in general, and that of each of his patients in particular, because, according to our system of medicine, what suits a bilious individuals harms a phlegmatic, and that which can enrich impoverished blood is capable of rupturing all the channels that contain an overly excited blood.

In sum, it requires so much memory, so much acquired knowledge and so much intelligence to form a good Physician on our world that of one were to encounter one such in a thousand years, one ought not to be surprised to see people raising Altars to him; for moneyed recompenses, praise and acclamations are far beneath such a person, in whom one must imagine something divine.

The Physicians of Mercury are far from any such ambition. As the principles of their Art are simple and not very numerous, its study is easy, and the application of the precepts of the Medicine only requires a very ordinary merit and fairly common knowledge—to such an extent that for a passable gardener, but most of all for a botanist, nothing is easier than to become an excellent Physician.

Thus, it is in the Emperor's flower-beds, in his arbors and his kitchen-gardens that they make their principal studies and obtain, so to speak, their licenses.

Trees, flowers and fruits of every species are cultivated there, principally those that serve for the nourishment of everyone and which produce the universal aliment. It is the only garden on the Planet where those fruits are to be found. For, otherwise, they only grow on the heights, as has previously been seen; but they are cultivated with care in the Kitchen Gardens, for the amusement and instruction of those who devote themselves to the study of Nature.

A Salamander, the Chief of all the world's Botanists, carries out anatomical demonstrations there, and the Analysis of all vegetables.

One learns in those Schools the structure of organic bodies—which, it is said, it is easier to learn from those of trees and plants than those of animals, for the reason that the parts of the former are more sensible and more formed than those of animate bodies. In addition, the liberty to dissect living bodies, at any time, easily allows the observation of the disposition of fibers, their entanglement and the course of the vegetative liquid. One sees there that the abundance or dearth of that Elixir, its thickening or its liquidity, causes the life and health of plants, or their malady and death.

It is in the course of that study that the students of Medicine understand the marvelous artifice of Nature, which, without employing any other principle than a little pure water charged with a few salts and certain sulfurs, produces and nourishes all that vegetates in the soil, for it is from that liquid, which is called the Universal Spirit, that industrious Nature forms the hardest trees and the most delicate herbs, the enamel and the odor of Flowers and aromatic Plants, the taste of fruits and the different forms of all these things, infinitely varied, in spite of the extreme simplicity of the unique principle that composes them all.

The new Botanist having been furnished with this preliminary knowledge, he learns, but in a very general manner, animal anatomy, reserving the infinite detail and exactitude of that Science for Surgeons.

The latter, it is said, having to operate on almost all the parts of the body, need to know exactly the placement, the form and the texture of each, as well that of the parts that cover them and all those that surround them. But for the Physician, it is sufficient to know the usage of situation of the parts, with the incidents that might cause the abundance and dearth of the blood, its thickening or its liquidity.

It is pointed out to them in the course of that study how Nature acts uniformly in the vegetation of Plants and in the nutrition of animals. They see there that the Chyle,[47] the unique principle of blood and the humors, does not differ in any way from the universal spirit that circulates in Plants. Those two liquids, both composed of pure water charged with various salts and different sulfurs, operate all the animal functions with the aid of the circulation of the blood, just as the same substances act in Plants to maintain life and health there, or produce maladies and death.

They also learn the differences in temperaments, which are found between trees as among humans.

In fact, the tree that produces Balm, bitter and sulfurous sap, does not resemble the Cherry tree, whose productions are aqueous and acidic; in the same way, the Vine is not similar to the Chestnut, etc.

These general observations lead them to a very essential preliminary observation, which can be regarded as the principal point of the Medicine; to wit, that the difference of temperament in Plants does not prevent them from all being nourished by the same sap, or all being cured by the same remedies and the same treatment,

In fact, provided that one waters a plant, and labors the ground around it so as to convey the Universal Spirit to its roots, and provided that one protects it from accidents like an excessive frost, which coagulates it, or extreme heat, which can desiccate it, that powerful liquid will do the rest. It is suf-

---

[47] The term chyle is nowadays used in a restrictive sense to apply to a mixture of lymph and fatty acids formed in the small intestine during digestion, of no particular importance, but William Harvey, who discovered the circulation of the blood in the early 17th century, thought that it played a much more important role in bodily circulation; physicians and natural philosophers impressed by the discovery of circulation, as Béthune obviously is, built various fanciful theories around it. In the same way, sulfur was not known in the 17th century to be a chemical element, and the word was used to refer to a class of inorganic substances that was largely chimerical.

ficient for the attention of the gardener that he prune overabundant branches, that he cuts the ones that are marring the plant, and that he sometimes strips the plant of the excess of its flowers and leaves, in order to leave only as much wood as the quantity of Universal Spirit insinuated into the roots, and circulated by them to all its parts, is able to nourish. But whatever temperament a tree might have—I mean, whether it produces balm, acidic liquids or insipid fruits—that small number of remedies and a few others that can be added to them will maintain them all in life and conserve their health.

The reasoning that they make on plants, of the truth of which they are convinced by indubitable experiments, they extend to animals and humans, claiming that the bilious and the phlegmatic, the sanguine and the pituitary, the strong and the weak, the young and the old, all need to be cured by the usage of the same remedy, supported by a regime sagely administered by an intelligent Physician. They sustain that proposition, therefore, which seems at first to be a fanciful idea, but in which some surprising glimmers of light and truth can nevertheless by glimpsed.

All humans, they say, of whatever temperament they might be, are nourished by the same liquid, which is known as Chyle. That liquid is composed of all the aliments and all the beverages that they employ.

So long as that Elixir does not thicken and does not bloat the vessels that contain it, the body enjoys perfect health. It is, therefore, simply a matter of knowing whether the Physician can furnish the means of rendering the blood of animals fluid and able to circulate in their vessels, just as Agriculture teaches us to give aid to trees and plants.

There is no doubt that it can be furnished. Divine Nature, mother of all Beings, has been careful not to refuse us a preservative from so many of the poisons that she spreads over the world—for that is what one may call anything that deflects the salutary action of the blood and leads us gradually to death, by the sad road of infirmities and maladies.

But to assure ourselves of a fact by a simple plausibility, says a Mercurian Physician, let us run though some of the various accidents that are capable of thickening the blood. There are not so great a number as to render that examination difficult, and one may hope that each cause of harm that we offer will naturally offer in its contrary a certain and not at all mysterious Antidote.

Let us suppose, therefore, a robust man enjoying good health. Everyone agrees that the blood and the humors ought to circulate freely, and fulfill all their functions perfectly in a well-organized body.

Now, by a certain principle of Mathematics, all things remain in their natural state unless something disturbs them.

If it happens, therefore, that the health of the man deteriorates, one cannot doubt that the accident in question is caused by some fault that he will have committed against the ordinary fashion of living. Let us suppose that the fault is an overly violent exercise, by virtue of which the blood, deprived of spirits, has become less fluid; is it not true that repose, a judiciously regulated regime and the use of good aliments will restore him to the same state of health that he enjoyed before the excess?

If it is sloth and greed that have coagulated the blood, moderate exercise will render it liquid again.

Indigestion can have the same effect as the two previous causes, but diet alone will repair the damage.

The ravages of acid are easily destroyed by the usage of spirituous bitters, or by the dissolution of salts in an abundant beverage of water, which will carry them out of the body by the ordinary route of excretions. Simple sleep, in a warm bed, will have almost the same effect on its own.

The dearth of nutritive juices is another cause of the coagulation of the blood. Good nourishment in slight abundance will destroy it.

The overly long application of the mind, which fixes all liquids, as well as insomnia, finds a very simple remedy in a little necessary dissipation and peaceful sleep.

The passions that contain dolor, such as sadness, dread, jealousy, regret, aversion, etc., are very powerful coagulants. But the repose of the soul or opposed passions destroy their impressions; that is something to which a Physician ought to pay serious attention, for he will strive in vain to heal the body so long as the soul is sick. The impetuosities of that domestic tyrant can do more harm than all the remedies in the world can cure.

Thus far we have not yet had any need of effective medicaments, and it has been sufficient for us to remove the causes of the harm to find their cure. But if it happens, by misfortune, that those first assistances, which offer themselves of their own accord, have been neglected, and that Nature finds herself overwhelmed, it is then that it is necessary to combine, so to speak, into a single medicament, everything that might oppose the coagulation.

We have just seen that because acids, cold, sloth, indignation, mental labor, overly violent exercise and the dolorous sentiments of the soul cause it, one ought to employ in the remedy, without difficulty, the contrary of all these things, and regulate a regime in a direction appropriate to that idea. These judicious precautions having been taken, it is up to Nature to do the rest, and she undoubtedly will, provided that the length of the illness has not had a deleterious effect on any of the principal organs.

All of that procedure is simple, and there is no question of a large amount of knowledge to fulfill its aims, since they offer themselves of their own accord. Nor is it necessary to employ precious medicaments or mysterious recipes. It seems to us to be as clear as daylight, however, that there is no invalid who cannot be cured by this procedure, since it reliably returns their natural liquidity to the blood and the humor, bring back to health anyone who had health before the unfortunate contagion destroyed it

One could stop at this point without extending this Chapter further, but the Physicians of Mercury support their doctrine with arguments so new, but nevertheless so seductive, that one would be doing a disservice to the members of the Public if one deprived them absolutely of a few of their more general observations.

CHAPTER XVII
The Arguments of the Physicians of Mercury

Those Physicians explain themselves, like ours, on the basis of what we call cold and hot medicaments, but their ideas are not the same. They call hot drugs, including aliments, everything that causes heat and occasions fever, not those that give rise to a temporary perception of heat on the tongue.

In accordance with this idea, they consider that an indigestion that produces a fever, causes great heat, that an abscess produces the same effect, that a migraine warms the head, that a violent and continuous thirst combined with a lack of beverages causes a great interior ardor, and finally, that one can be strongly heated when one makes use of things that produce these maladies; but as they only admit the heat or the cold in the malady that is felt, and not in the medicaments, they do not attribute the slightest effect to pepper, spices and aromatics, however spirituous thy might be, because they do not consider that those drugs can cause the coagulation of the blood, in which the cause of the heat sensed in the malady resides.

The blood, they say—and they understand by that word all the liquid mass that circulates in our body—causes us to feel cold or hot, or the intermediate state, according to whether it is circulating freely or with difficulty; the former state is that of health, the latter that of illness.

It is solely the friction of that liquid against the interior walls of the vessels containing it that causes all the heat in animals, the natural as well as that which is contrary to nature.

When the blood flows freely, the friction it causes is mediocre and the heat caused by that friction is similar in kind—which is to say, mild and moderate; but if the blood has difficulty circulating because its consistency is thicker than usual, its interior friction becomes stronger, and it occasions a greater heat; that happens in the same fashion as the heat we generate in our hands and other parts of the body by rubbing them forcefully.

It is a matter, they say, along with our Physicians, of procuring invariably in the blood the fluidity that is natural to it, in order that these frictions are not stronger at one time than another, so that we will never perceive an uncomfortable heat.

But how can the blood be returned to its natural liquidity, once it has lost it? By composing, in the Chyle, aliments and medicaments contrary to those that cause the thickening of the blood.

It has already been said many times that the action of Nature consists entirely in circulation; it is by that mechanism that she does everything in the Universe.

The sap that circulates in Plants produces them, forming their flowers, their leaves and their fruits, and it is by the circulation that contains the latter that they ripen, become tender, are sweetened, perfumed, etc., and anyone who, for want of reflection, does not know that doctrine, is a blind man unworthy of the name of Physician. What circulation operates in Plants, it also does in animate bodies.

A universal liquid composed of an infinity of different parts separates in our bodies into several liquids of various nature, in accordance with the reservoirs that contain them and the usages for which they are destined. All that operates by circulation, and when it is free and facile, those actions take place easily in accordance with the requirements of Nature; but for the circulation to be free it is necessary that the whole liquid mass circulating in our bodies should have a certain liquidity, in order to flow easily through channels of an infinite smallness, for when it thickens, it can no longer get through.

One of the important functions that the nature of the circulation carries out is that of serving incessantly to crush the circulating liquid in order to increase its mobility and fluidity; for it is easily appreciable that the thinner and finer the particles are that can mingle with the water, the more easily they can pass through pores and narrow conduits with the water that carries them.

Now, it is necessary that all the particles of our aliments are reduced to an extreme fineness in order that Nature can employ them, as much to repair the perpetual depreciation of our substance as to reform the exceedingly fine, delicate and active spirits that serve for all corporeal movements.

These marvelous operations only being carried out by virtue of the ministry of the circulation, it is therefore necessary to render it facile, and, in consequence, to maintain the blood—which is to say, all our liquids—in the fluidity that Nature requires.

It has been said above that the means of maintaining that fluidity is to compose the Chyle of aliments and medicaments contrary to those that thicken our liquids; there is no more to do than make them known.

Experience teaches us that aliments that are difficult to digest—which means those whose mass is solid and impenetrable to digestive leavens—thicken the blood. Such as, for example, almonds, walnuts, all seeds of that nature, those of Melons, Cucumbers, Lemons, Apricots, etc, which are innumerable, all fruits whose flesh is compact and solid, bread whose flour remains in a mass, without rising, and, in consequence everything constituting pastry, which butter renders massive and almost impenetrable to saliva in the mouth and to digestive leaven in the stomach, and finally, all tough meat with long solid fibers; for it is necessary that all our aliments be reduced, so to speak, into a solution, or at least into a kind of very clear jelly, in order for Nature to employ them in bodes for appropriate usages. It is easy to comprehend that she will succeed more easily in refining the particles of render and friable aliments than those that are form, hard or tough.

All the aliments that have just been listed cannot be reduced by the circulation into small enough particles; they interrupt the circulation and prevent the blood from flowing, or at least slow down its flow, in the narrow conduits of our body; and as it is the Nature of blood to thicken in proportion to the slowness of its circulation, it is evident that everything that retards its flow will occasion its thickening.

What aliments do by virtue of their hardness, their solidity and the hard-to-alter size of their particles, certain liquids operate by their own natures, although they possess an almost incredible subtlety. It is thus that wine alcohol—which is to say, strong spirit of wine—thickens the lymph of the blood if it is mixed with it, and the spirit of vitriol congeals the entire mass of blood if a drop is introduced into the artery of a living animal.

We shall see in due course which salts and liquids bring about a contrary effect, but first it is necessary to know that our blood is almost of the same nature as milk; that has been proved by an infinity of very exact experiments, which demonstrate that milk is nothing but very pure Chyle.

It follows from this well-proven theory that everything that can thicken and coagulate milk ought to produce a similar effect on our blood.

Now, all acids coagulate milk, and ought, in consequence, to have the same effect on blood.

But what is an acid? It is nothing other than a solid and non-volatile salt dissolved in water. That salt is fixed and solid, because it has not been worked by Nature, which incessantly tends to render it volatile. But the salt, by a decree of the Sovereign Master, also tends to render it solid.

That combat and that alternative are necessary for the generation, the conservation and the destruction of all things, because fixed salt[48] is inconceivably useful. It is what procures solidity in all things. The Oak, which contains more of it than

---

[48] In the 17th century no one had any idea that what we call common salt was actually the chemical compound sodium chloride, and although it was vaguely understood that there was some sort of relationship between acids and salts, it seemed very unclear; hence, it was possible to believe that there was a kind of general principle of "salt" responsible for organic solidity, as the author suggests here.

other trees of our Europe, is the hardest. It also creates weight; that is why that wood, which contains more salt than any other, is also the heaviest. It also causes hardness, and opposes rotting and all destruction.

That small enlightenment, which comes to us from Mercury, say their Physicians, ought to be and ample subject of meditation for the Physicians of our world. But those of Mercury content themselves with presenting their sagacity, without saying more. They only add that the solid and non-volatile salt, causing solidity, weight and incorruptibility of all things, can also, and must, contrive the thickening of our blood when it is found there contrary to the intention of Nature, which cannot suffer it in animate bodies. That is what experience demonstrates.

In fact, there is not a single grain in all living bodies, and whatever operation that a Chemist might carry out on all the parts of an animal, one only obtains volatile salt; Nature pays great attention to getting rid of the other by means of urines and transpiration, and does so incessantly; for those evacuations are given to us to separate from our blood the overabundance of salt. But when that cleaning is not sufficient—which is to say, when the urines do not flow or one does not drink enough water to dissolve the superabundant salt in our blood—it remains there. Nature cannot volatilize all of it, because she would have too much to do, so what remains thickens the blood and causes all the maladies to which we are subject.

As it is true that the volatile salts are the only ones that enter into the composition of our body, it is also evident that one cannot put too many of them into the Chyle, and, in consequence, that the ordinary usage of aliments charges with balsamic and sulfurous particles ought to be strongly recommended every time one suspects the blood of a patient of being thickened.

All the febrifuges are of this nature, and without having recourse to Quinine, one can easily cure all fevers solely by the use of balsamic and spirituous Plants, provided that one takes as much as those of hot countries in powder as one takes of Quinine in similar circumstance.

The usage of the same Plants cures headaches, retards drunkenness and relieves it, resists scurvy and facilitates the eruption of smallpox. All the peasants of hot countries, where they grow more replete with their virtue, make no use of any other specific, and it is always with such success that they regard all odiferous Plants as a universal remedy and the most precious of the gifts of Nature for conserving the health.

It is true by the general admission of all Physicians, that the maladies that have just been specified have no other cause than the coagulation of the blood; but since the volatile salts deliver us from them, that is a proof of their efficacy in remedies.

A few cups of well-made coffee relieve all the languors, heaviness in the head, involuntary drowsiness, lassitudes and weaknesses that one sometimes feels without their having been occasioned by labor; and that beverage can cure you of an infinity of petty infirmities, which are called vapors, but which can only be attributed to the coagulation of the blood.

It is therefore true that the volatile salts prepared by Nature, or by art, being chosen and wisely adapted in their dosage to the strength of the patient, are infinitely appropriate to dissolve excessively thick blood.

That principle once granted—how can it be denied?—the Physicians of Mercury understand all maladies thereby and extract all cures therefrom.

But, one might say to them, do you not fear that these vegetable spirits, which are inflammable, might ignite the blood? That appear to us, they reply, to be as improbable as it is that oil might ignite in a salad, even though it burns in a lamp.

Following that doctrine, the Philosophers of Mercury call cold everything that we call hot, in the matter of medicaments, and call hot everything that we call cold. For, they say, since sulfurous spirits decoagulate the blood whose coagulation causes our unnatural heat, it is necessary to call the cold, but since lemonade, orgeat, etc. coagulate the blood and occasion feverish ardor, one ought to call those potions hot and inflamed, in spite of the contrary report of touch and taste.

Those Physicians sometimes make it a great merit to belie the report of their senses when reason combats it, and they refer ironically to those who found theories ineptly on the suspect testimony of their sensations, without waiting for the consent of reflective reasoning, as "sublunar spirits."

CHAPTER XVIII
On Bleeding and the Fermentation on the Blood

Among other things, they criticize our usage of bleeding, the necessity of which they do not comprehend in any manner.

Your blood, they say, circulates violently, and by its thickening causes you during fever an intolerable heat. Well, dissolve that unnatural coagulation and then your blood will flow freely, and the feverish ardor will cease; but when someone has extracted six ounces of blood from you, which is nothing in comparison with the twenty or twenty-five pounds that you have, since it is only the fortieth part of it, is there any likelihood that you will be relieved?

Our Physicians allege against that remark, that because the blood is in a violent fermentation, it is necessary to diminish its mass, for fear that it might rupture the conduits that contain it. Well, Messieurs, respond the Mercurians, if the fermentation takes place in the whole mass of the four hundred ounces of blood that we have in the body, how can you reasonably expect that the small portion of six, eight or ten ounces that you have removed will be sufficient to prevent the 390 ounces that remain from rupturing their vessels?

Will you say, like Charlatans, that by opening a vein and diminishing the quantity of blood by one thirty-ninth that you will stop the fermentation? No, you do not say something so puerile, but any nurse and anyone whose work allows them to see milk, coffee or sugar fermenting over the fire will give you the lie, since experience teaches them that when they remove from the pan in which the liquids are fermenting, half or even three-quarters of what they contain, the liquid will still overflow the rim of the vessel.

Your friars say that in fixing air to the blood one stops the fermentation. Fortunately they are subalterns from which such paralogisms do not draw any consequence; but Physicians know full well that giving air to fermenting materials to arrest their agitation is almost the same thing as throwing inflammable materials on to a fire in order to extinguish it, since any solid or liquid only ferments in proportion to its exposure to free air and that suppression of air stops any form of fermentation.

The Physicians of Mercury are not content to assert that by removing blood or giving it air one can arrest its fermentation. If there is any, but sustain that the fermentation of blood is absolutely impossible, and that the idea on which the enormous European theory of bleeding is based is nothing but a chimera, which they claim to destroy by the following arguments.

For a liquid to ferment, three essential conditions are required, without which fermentation is impossible, as experience demonstrates.

Firstly, it is necessary that the liquid is contained in a vessel of which it only occupies a half or a third, in order that a considerable space therein remains empty.

Secondly, that the passage of air is free and in easy communication with the liquid.

Thirdly, that what is to ferment remains at rest

A few examples prove how indispensable these three conditions are in order for fermentation to take place.

If a bottle of strong beer is well corked, the liquid it contained will not ferment and will be conserved for a long time, but as soon as the cork is removed, the beer overflows violently, because it is suspended freely in a space appropriate to free the elasticity of its parts, which the air expands rapidly.

The communication of the air is necessary; it is because that is prevented that the beer does not ferment in the bottle. And if one objects that beer ferments in a vacuum, one will reply that in that state, it is the air contained in the beer that expands by its own natural effort and separates the particles of liquid violently. It is true that in the space, the elasticity of the air does not cause the liquid to ferment, for then the elasticity cannot unwind, but in spite of the space, the beer does not ferment without the communication of air. It is thus that water purged of air freezes without extending its mass, because then it does not ferment; it even hardens without giving evidence of any of the air bubbles that one ordinarily sees in ice, and which cause the extinction of the mass of water.

The liquids that swell up over fire are immediately appeased when they are agitated violently, and the air that is causing the fermentation is forced out.

Oil, into which air insinuates itself with difficulty, and which contains very little of it, heats up over a fire almost without effervescence.

If one continues to knead bread after one has introduced the necessary quantity of leaven, that movement prevents the fermentation and the dough does not rise.

Those three conditions—space, the communication of air and repose are therefore necessary to fermentation. An infinity of further examples could be cited, which would prove the case, but the inhabitants of Mercury are content to show the way, without leading us by the hand along the entire route, and abandon the surplus to the reflections of those who study Nature.

The more one examines those three conditions, without which fermentation cannot take place, the more one is assured that it cannot occur in blood.

Firstly, that liquid is extremely enclosed in its vessels and fills them, to the extent that the vessels react upon it and compress it—which proved that no empty space remains in the vessels.

Secondly, air cannot have any communication with our blood, since it is highly compressed by the elasticity of its own conduits and that of the heart, which fills them at each pulsation with a new quantity of blood, which drives all the other around, eventually bringing them back to the heart. But if one sustains that there is air mixed with our blood, since its passage into the lungs seems to prove, by its alteration and change of color, that it receives it there, that air will not cause fermentation, being in too small a quantity and the space being to full to allow any elasticity to the air, as happens to beer enclosed in a bottle, which does not ferment even though it contains air.

In any case, one cannot say that there is more air in our blood during malady than during health; it is, however, in the former case that Physicians fear fermentation so intensely.

But one last experience proves that air does not occasion the fermentation of blood, since the blood, on the contrary, coagulates and is reduced into a solid mass as soon as it emerges from our vessels and spread out in the open air.

Thirdly, always being in rapid movement, since it passes through the heart approximately thirteen times in an hour, fermentation, which requires repose, cannot take place; but if one says that some fermentations take place in spite of the total movement of the liquid, one gains nothing by that quibble, because, the other conditions necessary to fermentation not being encountered in blood, it will not take place.

In fact, it is not enough for a liquid to be at rest in order to ferment, or that it is capable of fermenting while moving; it is also necessary that it is suspended in the air and not compressed in its vessel. In sum, it is necessary that the three conditions required are all present together, which is not the case with blood.

The Physicians of our world persist: if blood does not ferment, what produces the excessive movement of blood in a fever? What produces the frequency of the pulse, the tension of the arteries and veins, and so many other phenomena that indicate a violent effervescence in the liquids?

The Physicians of Mercury respond to that interrogation with another. Why is it, they say, that the blood circulates more rapidly in sleep than during wakefulness? How does it come about that the movement of the arteries is as violent in the duration of a hard labor as if fever, and why is that same phenomenon renewed every day during our repose, above all if it is ample and animated by joy? How it is, again that a great joy, and, in general, all the movements of an agreeable and keen passion considerably increase the speed of the blood?

Do you want to say, they add, that in all these cases there is a further fermentation of the blood? But if one admits that, it follows that the fermentation of the blood is very advantageous, for everything just listed procures or maintains health. Then the fermentation of the blood would no longer be a harmful phenomenon; on the contrary, the more fermentation there is, the better our health will be—which would be a paralogism, since it cannot ferment. But to destroy the idea of that pretended fermentation, the Physicians of Mercury explain the accidental movements of the blood that have just been listed as follows.

Every acceleration in the natural flow of our blood designates a state of suffering, and indicates that Nature is making a more or less considerable effort, in proportion to the violence that she is imprinting on our liquids.

It has been said above that Nature does not operate anything on the earth, not in its interior, nor even in the whole extent of our atmosphere, except by means of circulation. One can even add that circulation is the veritable Nature, since it is that which executes all the designs of the creator, whether in the generation of individuals, their conservation or their destruction.

That universal movement of circulation tends to no other end that that of crushing liquids, of subtilizing them, of making pure secretions out of impure ones, expelling that which might be harmful and conserving that which might be useful to animate bodies.

In animate bodies in particular, circulation refines liquids, with the design of forming spirits in great enough quantity to provoke and to maintain the general movement of the whole corporeal machine.

The more lively the circulation is, the more it reforms spirits by the effects of trituration and the crushing of overly large particles that can only be subtilized by means of circulation.

It is for that reason that the blood circulates more rapidly during sleep than during wakefulness.

Nature, exhausted of spirits by the labor of the preceding day, presses circulation in order to subtilize the entire mass of liquids and render them apt to refurnish the spirits that were exhausted the day before, and will be necessary for the day to come.

As that operation of Nature is very important, everything collaborates to produce it.

The cessation of all our mental and corporeal functions leaves the spirits the liberty to mingle in the mass of the blood, to render it more fluid and, in consequence, more appropriate to movement.

The warmth of the bed maintains the liquidity of the blood, for experience proves that the slightest cold thickens it, and the situation of our body, which is placed as much as possible in a horizontal direction, further assists the movement of the blood, which finds it much easier to move horizontally, when we are lying down, than vertically, when we are standing up.

Although one cannot say that the body is ill during sleep, one can be sure that it is not in a state of perfect health, since the privation of spirits dissipated during the previous day does not permit it to fulfill its ordinary functions. Thus Nature makes an effort to reestablish its original vigor, and that effort is executed by a greater speed in circulation.

The same thing happens after our meals and during them, if they are long, because then a crude, glutinous and gross chyle mingles with our blood, and it is necessary for that crude portion of the blood to be perfected—which is to say that it is attenuated, crushed, divided and reduced to its smallest particles. But how can Nature carry out that important process? Assuredly, only by means of circulation, and only by augmenting its ordinary speed; for without that, the operation would be too slow, and the state of torpor, weight and drowsiness that is very common after meals would last too long.

One can observe the same occasions to press the circulation in the course of difficult labor.

A large quantity of spirits is dissipated in that exercise, and nature, which incessantly tends to replenish them, in order to furnish a sufficient quantity, hastens the circulation and renders it at least equal to that of fever, as well as the heat that is augmented in proportion to the effort one makes in working, while redness inflames the complexion and the vivacity of the eyes increases, which shine more brightly during fervent exercise than in repose.

One could say the same about the state the body is in during a sudden surge of excessive joy. No one is unaware of the extent to which passions agreeable to the soul cause dissipation; examples are far too common for it to be necessary to cite them. That is why the circulation becomes much more prompt as soon as the soul attains these dissipatory passions, in order that the prompt reproduction of spirits might serve throughout the course of the movement, without which the body would fall into weakness.

One can, therefore, be sure that every time it is necessary to reproduce spirits, to refine liquids, to subtilize their coarse particles, and, in general, to maintain the liquidity of our blood, Nature does everything she can to produce these indispensable effects, without which the animal would perish; and as it is true that Nature only acts by circulation—that she has, so to speak, no other ministry or other instrument of operation—she hastens it or diminishes it in accordance with need. For it often happens that the ordinary circulation is too slow to refine the liquids sufficiently and to form the necessary quantity of spirits by that subtilization. It is then that Nature makes the blood circulate with more force and rapidity.

If one asks by what artifice Nature accelerates the movement of the circulation according to need, with so much accuracy and an anticipation that seems enlightened, one can reply without shame that the mechanism is unknown, and beg those who ask the question to observe that it is not necessary to know the cause of an effect to be sure that it exists, but it is sufficient to be fully assured that it exists to have the right to

213

extract the consequences to which it might lead us demonstratively.

For example, we do not know and will never know by what artifice the heart dilates in order to receive the portion of blood that enters it from the vena cava and pulmonary veins, nor by what force of elasticity, which seems magical, it contracts with sufficient effort to make that quantity of blood enter the arteries, but that ignorance does not prevent us from drawing very accurate consequences regarding the circulation of the blood.

We do not know what light is, or the marvelous artifice by which the reflection of objects is imprinted on our retina, but that ignorance does not prevent us from measuring the incidence and reflection of rays of light as surely as if they were massive and palpable. We know when they separate and at what angle they separate. We reassemble them positively when and where we please, and assure ourselves of the effects that they unfailingly produce, and the kind of hue they produce in accordance with their different inclination with regard to surfaces; and although we do not know the nature of light, which is the principle of optics, we can be sure that that is perhaps the most certain of all the aspects of our knowledge.

For the same reason, it is quite unnecessary for us to know by what art Nature accelerates the movement of circulation according to her needs, and if we were to discover it, it will only be a matter of pure curiosity; it is sufficient to know that she operates that effect infallibly when it is necessary, to know that it is quite natural, and that one need not fear dangerous consequences, as one does frivolously.

For since it never happens that the vessels are ruptured by the violence of the circulation that takes place in a great and long agitation, even though the movement of the pulse is at least as violent in such cases as in a high fever, one ought no longer to fear that accident in fever, since all the cases are equivalent and all the symptoms are similar in the two states. One could say that the beats of the pulse in fever are different from those perceived during hard labor, being hard and almost

214

solid, or concentrated, in fever, whereas one finds them pliant, soft and discovered during the agitation of the body. One says then that because the hardness of the pulse indicates a great solidity in the mass of the blood, one ought to dread that the almost massive liquid might cause damage and rupture vessels because it is not as fluid and supple as it is in the aforementioned violent exercise, and it is principally by reason of the pernicious solidity and hardness of the blood that one aims to diminish its mass.

The Physicians of Mercury do not make any response to that explanation because they claim that, after having proved that the diminution of the mass of the blood does not render it more liquid, bleeding ought to be regarded at least as something indifferent. They content themselves, in order to fortify what they have previously advanced, with proposing a simple experiment that would make their idea regarding the futility of bleeding perfectly clear.

Let a pipe be filled, they say, with some sticky or mucilaginous liquid, and it will be seen that the liquid does not flow any more easily if the pipe is half emptied than it did when it was full. The reason for that is that the difficult flow of the liquid in the pipe only results from the adhesion of the liquid to the sides of the container, and that it attaches itself equally whether the pipe is full or half empty. But if instead of emptying the pipe partly in order to assist the liquid to flow one merely rendered it more fluid, either by heating it, if it is meat jelly, or by adding pure water, if it is a sticky mucilage, it will be seen to flow without difficulty, and it will not be necessary to diminish its mass.

The same thing would happen to our blood, if one set out to liquefy it instead of removing it from our veins.

But what, one might say, is the art of liquefying our blood when one finds it coagulated? There is only one, reply the Physicians of Mercury, and that is to liberate it from whatever is coagulating it—and circulation, the unique mechanism of Nature, will do the rest.

One single Entity in Nature is the unique principle of all coagulation. It produces the solidity of metals, the hardness off marbles and that of precious stones; it is that alone which, in vegetables, renders plants compact and which, in animal bodies, causes mucilage and the thickening of liquids. Salt produces all these effects, as has already been said.

It enters into the composition of everything that nature produces, but it becomes sensible above all, and almost visible, in all our aliments, since it composes all their different savors as well as their odor. For the sulfur to which one attributes perfume is nothing but a volatilized salt. If anyone wants to doubt this explanation it would be easy to heap up demonstrative proofs, but the Physicians of Mercury, supposing that one can regard that verity as a demonstrated principle, do not bother to prove it, and continue thus.

Since salt is the sole cause of the coagulation of our blood, and that it is also necessary by virtue of the requirement of Nature, for our blood to be incessantly impregnated with and, so to speak, intoxicated by salt in a state of perfect health, it is evident that it is only to an excess of salt that the coagulation of our blood occurs, in the same way that a well-proportioned mixture brings about health.

The excess of salt congeals or liquids; nothing, therefore, is simpler than to destroy it, since it dissolves with an admirable facility in water and water insinuates itself without any difficulty into the narrowest conduits of our vessels, and then passes by virtue of a foresight of sage Nature, laden with overabundant salt, into the excretory vessels, to be evacuated by the urines and insensible transpiration.

Those Physicians have observed a thousand times that in a state of malady, whatever it might be, urines are infinitely more salty[49] than in health, as is the sweat by means of which insensible transpiration operates.

---

[49] Author's note: "One can examine the saltiness of urines either by the urines, by their weight, or by various mixtures of a few liquids, etc."

On these indications, they instruct their patients to drink water, in order to thin their blood and procure in consequence the fluidity of that liquid. They then indicate a salutary diet to their patients, in order that the digestive leavens can dissolve the little nourishment that they take in spite of their weakness. For those enlightened Physicians are well aware that the grossness of ill-digested aliments collaborates with the excessive saltiness of the blood in its thickening. Always aiming at the same objective, they prescribe the nature of the aliments that their patient ought to use, not being unaware that those which are difficult to digest in the ordinary run of affairs will be even less digestible, because of the weakness of all the digestive liquids and the slowness of the action of the stomach and arteries, almost all relaxed during long illnesses.

Given these few precepts founded on experience and reason, the Physicians of Mercury are sure that one can leave our arteries and urines full of blood in complete safety, and regard as a chimerical procedure the futile Plethora that makes s much noise in our Schools.

What would one think, they say, of a Fountain-builder who sees that the water in a basin is overflowing, because it cannot flow away through a blocked discharge pipe, if he used a bucket to empty the water out of the basin in order to prevent it from spreading out over the flower-beds? Would one not say to him: "Clean the water in your basin, which is covered with mucilaginous weed that is blocking the discharge pipe, and then allow the water to flow, for, the discharge being greater than the jet of the fountain, as much water will escape via that conduit as the jet can supply."

The same mechanics ought to be observed in the animate body. The veins that bring back the blood are more ample and have more capacity than the arteries that fill them. Thus, the engorgement of the vessels will be impossible as long as the liquid is sufficiently fluid to flow freely; but it will be no more able to do so even if one extracts it to the last drop.

CHAPTER XVII
Fermentation Continued

After having denied the fermentation of the blood and having proved in their fashion the futility of bleeding, our Doctors of Mercury establish the different states of the blood in health and malady, and the clarify, before anything else, one suspect idea that can lead us into very great paralogisms.

Without knowing why, they say, we call that which co-agulates milk a "ferment," in the same way as that which ferments dough and causes bread to rise, although the two things produce quite different, and even opposed, effects, for the former, which is put in milk, coagulates and diminishes the mass by hardening it, whereas the leaven that one mixes with dough inflates and extends its mass, and softens it by rarefying it.

From that error of nomenclature a false maxim follows, which is very important because of the vicious consequences to which it leads us.

Milk, it is said, is of the same nature as blood, as everyone is forced to admit. But if milk can be fermented, perhaps blood can be too—and then, losing sight of the idea of the pressure that coagulates and thickens the milk, to follow that of the leaven that extends and, so to speak, diffuses the dough, the conclusion is drawn that since blood can be fermented its mass can be extended, it can be diffused, and, in consequence, sometimes occupy more volume than it had. To avoid scorn, however, and draw an accurate conclusion, it is necessary to say:

Milk is thickened and rendered solid by the effect of pressure, so anything that is of a similar nature to that acid, which is improperly called a ferment, will have the same effect on blood as on milk—which is to say, coagulate it, thicken it, and render it massive and not fluid—and as we know of nothing in Nature[50] that can ferment milk in the manner that the leaven ferments dough—which is to say, by extending its mass and loosening its particles—there is every appearance that nothing can have that effect on blood, and that, in consequence, blood is only susceptible to coagulation, and not fermentation, any more than milk is capable of fermentation.

Since it is, therefore, quite certain that neither acids not alkalis, no matter how violent they are, can ferment milk by extending its mass, but that any acid can coagulate and thicken it, one ought not to believe that any acid of alkali can ferment blood by extending its mass, but only that acids can coagulate or thicken it.

With regard to alkalis, they redden milk, as Boherave explains, if one boils them together, apparently by virtue of the mechanism that naturally white chyle is changed into red blood by means of the circulation that causes heat and produces in the liquid of or body very nearly the same species of circulation that the heat of fire occasions in the milk. But the operation that reddens milk while it circulates on the fire does not prevent it from coagulating, as the same Author notes; with the consequence that one can conjecture with reason, supported by experience, that nothing can ferment blood by extending its mass, since nothing can have that effect on milk.

However, an infinity of things can coagulate blood, since they coagulate milk, and even the powerful alkali that reddens

---

[50] Author's note: "Which Boherave has proved by very decisive experiments, so that all good German, English and Italian physicians, and even those in Paris, who have not made their fortune following, to the detriment of their patients, the innumerable paralogisms of their School, eventually renounce them, because they have no need of them, and, to acquit their conscience, clearly admit the truth and head toward their old age following in the footsteps of Nature." By "Boherave" he means the Dutch physician Herman Boerhaave (1668-1738), the great pioneer of physiology. He was appointed professor of botany and medicine at Leiden in 1709.

milk boiling over a fire coagulates it in part, which is almost what sublunar Physicians improperly call the dissolution of blood. For it is not in the least dissolved, since, on the contrary, it is clotted in flakes and floats thus, separated from the lymph, with the result that that state of the blood, the most mortal of all, ought to be reckoned as an excessive coagulation instead of being called dissolution; for one naturally understands by the word "dissolution" fluidity and liquidity, which is quite different from fixation and coagulation. But we often link two incompatible ideas solely by a conformity of terms, which results in errors as palpable as a child would make who believed that he could eat an item of furniture because he had heard it said that it was in very good taste.

The error of the fermentation of blood is not only established by the confusion of ideas that the word "ferment" contains, badly explained and understood in too vague a manner; it also derives from a false consequence that is drawn from the nature of blood, in relation to the artifice that Nature employs in fabricating it.

Blood, it is said, is only produced by chyle, but chyle is only formed by fermentation. Thus, blood must be capable of fermentation.

That is as if one constructed the following argument: spirit of wine is only produced from wine, but wine is only formed by fermentation, so wine spirit must itself be capable of fermenting blood—which is false, since, on the contrary, as has been said, it coagulates milk and blood.

To destroy fundamentally the prejudice that is born of the fabrication of chyle, it is necessary to repeat briefly the manner in which it is elaborated by Nature.

Our aliments are initially fermented lightly in the mouth by saliva; the leaven of the stomach impregnates them, and then ferments and dissolves them when they have fallen into it. On leaving the stomach, softened, and with their breakdown commenced, bile probably gives them a new fashion, which refines then further in the intestines, and the pancreatic juice that is mixed in with them, along with the other liquids, finishes attenuating, dividing and fermenting them throughout the length of the route that they follow in the intestines and all the time they spend there; but when they are sufficiently subtilized and crushed to enter into the milky veins, they are no longer fermenting, for the aliments have become chyle, and, carried into the reservoir of Pecquet[51] to fall from there into the heart, have taken on the quality of milk, which, as said above, does not ferment either with acids or alkalis.

In the state, however, the chyle has acquired, like milk, an extreme facility of coagulation. In fact, all acids coagulate it totally and alkalis coagulate it partially—which is to say, in flakes—composing little masses that separate from the Lymph and acquire a volume too considerable to follow it into the narrow and tortuous conduits of the circulation, which causes death momentarily.

One observes that the fermentation of our aliments, which is necessary to form them into chyle, is always executed in accordance with the general laws of fermentation.

Firstly, they mingle very easily in the mouth with air, they enjoy a convenient space, and they then fall into the stomach, which is only ever filed to a certain point in its capacity, under pain of indigestion, stomach aches and vomiting. The first intestine conserves the aliments in a sufficient repose, for the little movement they receive there has only been instituted by Nature in order to make the fermenting juices slow more easily throughout the mass of our aliments and is further combined with a condition very useful to fermentation, which finished bringing into play all those that we have already observed, that of the warmth of the place, which Nature has very sagely instituted—for everyone knows that fermentations and digestions are only ever executed perfectly when the fermenting juices are excited and activated by a suitable warmth.

---

[51] The "reservoir of Pecquet" or *receptaculum chyli*, an important lymph vessel which receives chyle from the intestine, was discovered by the anatomist Jean Pequet (1622-1674)

After that long explanation of all the doctrines of fermentations and coagulations, the Physicians of Mercury having proved that our blood cannot be fermented, conclude that bleeding, which is only prescribed on the false idea of the fermentation of our blood, can only be a chimerical remedy, since its necessity has only been established by pure sophistry.

But in order to leave nothing doubtful in regard to that question, which my Sage has judged very important, he adds a discourse on fever, which he has already explained on the basis of fermentation.

The symptoms of fever, he says, are yawns, heaviness in all the body parts, a general chill, slight partial convulsions and a strong convulsion spread throughout the body, which causes a universal tremor. Those are the preparations for the approaching fit, and one cannot doubt that all these indications are visible proofs of the coagulation of the blood.

When the bout of fever begins all the symptoms of frisson cease and one begins to feel a mediocre heat, which increases steadily until the fit achieves its full strength.

Then the pulse beats more rapidly and the pulsation become unequal because the thickened blood is flowing unevenly and with difficulty. The pulse feels harder, because the blood filling the arteries is more solid in consistency than it ought to be. Thirst is augmented because the thickened blood does not permit freely the filtration of the lymph that ought to moisten the membranes with which the mouth, esophagus and stomach are lined internally. The head becomes heavy, because it is reforming few spirits from that mass of thickened blood, and the innumerable small vessels of the head are too swollen by the continual arrival of a liquid forcefully pushed by the large vessels but too viscous to flow easily in the small ones. Reverie almost always accompanies feverish sleep, which is not astonishing in view of the derangement that the pressure of arterioles and muscles causes in the brain; the headache derives from the same cause.

They explain the augmentation of rapidity that affects the circulation in this way. The blood, they say, was doubtless considerably thickened during the frisson, but when that coagulation reaches its peak and the animal does not die, it is necessary that the coagulation ceases. That happens in accordance with the following mechanism.

The first drop of coagulated blood that arrives in the heart warms up, extending and augmenting it volume there, from which it follows that it drives with more force the blood it displaces into the pulmonary artery. The second does the same, and so on, with the result that the whole mass of blood then occupies slightly more volume, and, having more fluidity, is forced to circulate more rapidly. In addition, Nature, which comes to the aid of the mass of sticky and viscous blood, in order to subtilize it, acts in that important circumstance by the same means and following the same intentions that engaged her to prefer the movement of circulation when the occasion for violent exercise has reproduced many spirits in refining the mass of blood.

No one seeks, as has already been said, to explain the mechanism by which Nature acts in that occurrence; perhaps it would be futile even to attempt it, as it would be to try to explain how the mere sight of a disgusting object can make us vomit, or by what mechanism a soul surprised and violently consternated by mental dolor sometimes causes instant death.

It is sufficient for a Physician to know that Nature never fails to do a certain thing in a certain circumstance—as, for example, she always augments the rapidity of circulation when it is a matter of breaking up and subtilizing the whole mass of the blood—and to be sure, by virtue of innumerable experiments, of the operation of Nature, to have the right to affirm, that it is she who is operating, by efficacious but unknown means, the new movement that the blood adopts during the fit of fever.

It is even admitted that the blood occupies more space throughout the habitude of the body when it has been repeatedly attenuated, broken down and reheated in the heart, that it does not do so during the frisson, when it is cooled and more condensed.

That augmentation of volume doubtless assists Nature to render the circulation more prompt.

But, say the Physicians, that extension of the volume of our blood is a true fermentation. That is admitted, for it is certain that every time a liquid comes to cool it, it loses volume, and recovers it when it is reheated; but that extension has its limits, and they are very narrow.

For if one wants to put clear water in a cubic vessel two feet long in every dimension, to a height of twenty-three inches, one will see that the water in question after being warmed, which is very similar to the state of our blood during the frisson, until that same water has acquired the heat that our blood obtains during fever, that the water will only be elevated in its basin by a fifth of an inch, or two at the most which is less than a hundred and thirty-eightieth part of its total volume. Thus, that almost inconsiderable augmentation can be discounted, inasmuch as the blood had lost a little of its volume during the frisson, and that which it acquires by feverish heat only brings it back to something approximating its natural state.

That does not permit us to dread that that slight augmentation will rupture the containing vessels; one has only to remember what they are capable of sustaining, even very considerably, when the coagulation of the blood causes them to be filed much more than Nature requires.

If anyone wants to say that, because the blood contains a large number of balsamic, oily, fatty and volatile particles, it must be more subject to inflation by heat and other liquids, the response will make the observation that oil, fats, balms and sulfurous and bituminous substances in general boil over a fire without fermentation, and that blood ought not to do so any more than them, for that reason.

Thus, all the great apparatus of frivolous reasons that establishes bleeding, collapses at the feet of the Physicians of Mercury, unless one wants to admit to them that bleeding can be useful, when the disorder of the sentiments of our soul and a very vivid passion occasions a violent movement of circula-

224

tion, or when hard labor and long exercise sometimes cause our blood to circulate more rapidly than in a powerful fever, which absolutely frightens common sense.

My Sage finished that long Treatise by representing how advantageous it would be to reduce Medicine to the simple principles that compose it on Mercury, but afterwards making this reflection on the character of sublunar spirits.

"Those people," he says, "are such natural enemies of simple verities that they could never imagine that a benefit as precious as that of health might depend on the facile and not very numerous principles that are adopted on Mercury. The insensate taste of our species for the difficult and the false marvelous always leads them to seek expensive, rare and complicated remedies. One can even affirm that they would rather have recourse to philters and magical characters and words than cure by the usage of the unmysterious remedies that good Physics recommends.

"In fact," he adds, "it is neither the truth nor reason that we seek, and it is not to those who inform us in clear and simple terms that we want to listen. But if a Charlatan presents himself, if he comes from far away, if he is authorized by mere hearsay, who praises himself, who suborns some of the weak but accredited brains who start fashions, be will be followed, and people will solicit the favor of dying by his hand; if he adds to his prestiges that of exposing his doctrine in harmonious speech, saying incredible things and affirming impossible feats, the foremost places will be at his disposition, and the Court will soon augment the seduction of the City with the example of its credulity."

SF & FANTASY

Adolphe Alhaiza. *Cybele*
Alphonse Allais. *The Adventures of Captain Cap*
Henri Allorge. *The Great Cataclysm*
Guy d'Armen. *Doc Ardan: The City of Gold and Lepers*
G.-J. Arnaud. *The Ice Company*
Charles Asselineau. *The Double Life*
Henri Austruy. *The Eupantophone; The Olotelepan; The Petitpaon Era*
Barillet-Lagargousse. *The Final War*
Cyprien Bérard. *The Vampire Lord Ruthwen*
S. Henry Berthoud. *Martyrs of Science*
Aloysius Bertrand. *Gaspard de la Nuit*
Richard Bessière. *The Gardens of the Apocalypse; The Masters of Silence*
Albert Bleunard. *Ever SMalher*
Félix Bodin. *The Novel of the Future*
Louis Boussenard. *Monsieur Synthesis*
Alphonse Brown. *City of Glass; The Conquest of the Air*
Émile Calvet. *In a Thousand Years*
André Caroff. *The Terror of Madame Atomos; Miss Atomos; The Return of Madame Atomos; The Mistake of Madame Atomos; The Monsters of Madame Atomos; The Revenge of Madame Atomos; The Resurrection of Madame Atomos; The Mark of Madame Atomos; The Spheres of Madame Atomos; The Wrath of Madame Atomos* (w/M. & Sylvie Stéphan)
Félicien Champsaur. *The Human Arrow; Ouha, King of the Apes; Pharaoh's Wife; Homo-Deus; Nora, The Ape-Woman*
Didier de Chousy. *Ignis*
Jules Clarétie. *Obsession*
Michel Corday. *The Eternal Flame*
André Couvreur. *The Necessary Evil; Caresco, Superman; The Exploits of Professor Tornada* (3 vols.)
Captain Danrit. *Undersea Odyssey*
C. I. Defontenay. *Star (Psi Cassiopeia)*
Charles Derennes. *The People of the Pole*
Georges Dodds (anthologist). *The Missing Link*
Charles Dodeman. *The Silent Bomb*
Harry Dickson. *The Heir of Dracula; Harry Dickson vs. The Spider*

Jules Dornay. *Lord Ruthven Begins*
Alfred Driou. *The Adventures of a Parisian Aeronaut*
Sâr Dubnotal *vs. Jack the Ripper*
Odette Dulac. *The War of the Sexes*
Alexandre Dumas. *The Return of Lord Ruthven*
Renée Dunan. *Baal; The Ultimate Pleasure*
J.-C. Dunyach. *The Night Orchid; The Thieves of Silence*
Henri Duvernois. *The Man Who Found Himself*
Achille Eyraud. *Voyage to Venus*
Henri Falk. *The Age of Lead*
Paul Féval. *Anne of the Isles; Knightshade; Revenants; Vampire City; The Vampire Countess; The Wandering Jew's Daughter*
Paul Féval, *fils. Felifax, the Tiger-Man*
Charles de Fieux. *Lamékis*
Louis Forest. *Someone is Stealing Children in Paris*
Arnould Galopin. *Doctor Omega; Doctor Omega and the Shadowmen* (anthology)
Judith Gautier. *Isoline and the Serpent-Flower*
H. Gayar. *The Marvelous Adventures of Serge Myrandhal on Mars*
G.L. Gick. *Harry Dickson and the Werewolf of Rutherford Grange*
Delphine de Girardin. *Balzac's Cane*
Léon Gozlan. *The Vampire of the Val-de-Grâce*
Jules Gros. *The Fossil Man*
Edmond Haraucourt. *Illusions of Immortality; Daah, the First Human*
Nathalie Henneberg. *The Green Gods*
Eugène Hennebert. *The Enchanted City*
V. Hugo, P. Foucher & P. Meurice. *The Hunchback of Notre-Dame*
Romain d'Huissier. *Hexagon: Dark Matter*
Jules Janin. *The Magnetized Corpse*
Michel Jeury. *Chronolysis*
Gustave Kahn. *The Tale of Gold and Silence*
Gérard Klein. *The Mote in Time's Eye*
Fernand Kolney. *Love in 5000 Years*
Paul Lacroix. *Danse Macabre*
Louis-Guillaume de La Follie. *The Unpretentious Philosopher*
Jean de La Hire. *Enter the Nyctalope; The Nyctalope on Mars; The Nyctalope vs. Lucifer; The Nyctalope Steps In; Night of the Nyctalope; Return of the Nyctalope; The Fiery Wheel*
Etienne-Léon de Lamothe-Langon. *The Virgin Vampire*
André Laurie. *Spiridon*
Gabriel de Lautrec. *The Vengeance of the Oval Portrait*

Alain le Drimeur. *The Future City*

Georges Le Faure & Henri de Graffigny. *The Extraordinary Adventures of a Russian Scientist Across the Solar System* (2 vols.)

Gustave Le Rouge. *The Mysterious Doctor Cornelius* (3 vols.); *The Vampires of Mars; The Dominion of the World* (w/Gustave Guitton) (4 vols.)

Jules Lermina. *Mysteryville; Panic in Paris; To-Ho and the Gold Destroyers; The Secret of Zippeliu; The Battle of Strasbourg*

André Lichtenberger. *The Centaurs; The Children of the Crab*

Listonai. *The Philosophical Voyager*

Jean-Marc & Randy Lofficier. *Edgar Allan Poe on Mars; The Katrina Protocol; Pacifica; Robonocchio; Return of the Nyctalope;* (anthologists) *Tales of the Shadowmen 1-11; The Vampire Almanac* (2 vols.)

Xavier Mauméjean. *The League of Heroes*

Joseph Méry. *The Tower of Destiny*

Hippolyte Mettais. *The Year 5865; Paris Before the Deluge*

Louise Michel. *The Human Microbes; The New World*

Tony Moilin. *Paris in the Year 2000*

José Moselli. *Illa's End*

John-Antoine Nau. *Enemy Force*

Marie Nizet. *Captain Vampire*

C. Nodier, A. Beraud & Toussaint-Merle. *Frankenstein*

Henri de Parville. *An Inhabitant of the Planet Mars*

Gaston de Pawlowski. *Journey to the Land of the 4th Dimension*

Georges Pellerin. *The World in 2000 Years*

Ernest Pérochon. *The Frenetic People*

Pierre Pelot. *The Child Who Walked on the Sky*

J. Polidori, C. Nodier, E. Scribe. *Lord Ruthven the Vampire*

P.-A. Ponson du Terrail. *The Vampire and the Devil's Son; The Immortal Woman*

Georges Price. *The Missing Men of the Sirius*

Edgar Quinet. *Ahasuerus; The Enchanter Merlin*

Henri de Régnier. *A Surfeit of Mirrors*

Maurice Renard. *The Blue Peril; Doctor Lerne; The Doctored Man; A Man Among the Microbes; The Master of Light*

Jean Richepin. *The Wing; The Crazy Corner*

Albert Robida. *The Adventures of Saturnin Farandoul; The Clock of the Centuries; Chalet in the Sky; The Electric Life*

J.-H. Rosny Aîné. *Helgvor of the Blue River; The Givreuse Enigma; The Mysterious Force; The Navigators of Space; Vamireh; The World of the Variants; The Young Vampire*
Marcel Rouff. *Journey to the Inverted World*
Léonie Rouzade. *The World Turned Upside Down*
Han Ryner. *The Superhumans; The Human Ant*
Pierre de Selenes: *An Unknown World*
Angelo de Sorr. *The Vampires of London*
Brian Stableford. *The New Faust at the Tragicomique;The Empire of the Necromancers (The Shadow of Frankenstein; Frankenstein and the Vampire Countess; Frankenstein in London); Sherlock Holmes & The Vampires of Eternity; The Stones of Camelot; The Wayward Muse.* (anthologist) *News from the Moon; The Germans on Venus; The Supreme Progress; The World Above the World; Nemoville; Investigations of the Future; The Conqueror of Death; The Revolt of the Machines; The Man With the Blue Face*
Jacques Spitz. *The Eye of Purgatory*
Kurt Steiner. *Ortog*
Eugène Thébault. *Radio-Terror*
C.-F. Tiphaigne de La Roche. *Amilec*
Simon Tyssot de Patot. *The Strange Voyages of Jacques Massé and Pierre de Mésange*
Louis Ulbach. *Prince Bonifacio*
Théo Varlet. *The Golden Rock. The Xenobiotic Invasion; The Castaways of Eros; Timeslip Troopers* (w/André Blandin); *The Martian Epic* (w/Octave Joncquel)
Pierre Véron. *The Merchants of Health*
Paul Vibert. *The Mysterious Fluid*
Villiers de l'Isle-Adam. *The Scaffold; The Vampire Soul*
Gaston de Wailly. *The Murderer of the World*
Philippe Ward. *Artahe ; The Song of Montségur* (w/Sylvie Miller) *Manhattan Ghost* (w/Mickael Laguerre)

MYSTERIES & THRILLERS

M. Allain & P. Souvestre. *The Daughter of Fantômas*
A. Anicet-Bourgeois, Lucien Dabril. *Rocambole*
A. Bernède. *Belphegor*; *Judex* (w/Louis Feuillade); *The Return of Judex* (w/Louis Feuillade); *The Shadow of Judex*
A. Bisson & G. Livet. *Nick Carter vs. Fantômas*

V. Darlay & H. de Gorsse. *Arsène Lupin vs. Sherlock Holmes: The Stage Play*

Séamas Duffy. *Sherlock Holmes in Paris*

Paul Féval. *Gentlemen of the Night; John Devil; The Black Coats ('Salem Street; The Invisible Weapon; The Parisian Jungle; The Companions of the Treasure; Heart of Steel; The Cadet Gang; The Sword-Swallower)*

Émile Gaboriau. *Monsieur Lecoq*

Goron & Émile Gautier. *Spawn of the Penitentiary*

Paul d'Ivoi. *Around the World on Five Sous* (w/Henri Chabrillat)

Rick Lai. *Shadows of the Opera: Retribution in Blood; Sisters of the Shadows: The Curse of Cagliostro*

Steve Leadley. *Sherlock Holmes: The Circle of Blood*

Maurice Leblanc. *Arsène Lupin vs. Countess Cagliostro; Arsène Lupin vs. Sherlock Holmes (The Blonde Phantom; The Hollow Needle); The Many Faces of Arsène Lupin; The Island of the Thirty Coffins*

Gaston Leroux. *Chéri-Bibi; The Phantom of the Opera; Rouletabille & the Mystery of the Yellow Room; Rouletabille at Krupp's*

Richard Marsh. *The Complete Adventures of Judith Lee*

William Patrick Maynard. *The Terror of Fu Manchu; The Destiny of Fu Manchu*

Frank J. Morlock. *Sherlock Holmes: The Grand Horizontals; Sherlock Holmes vs Jack the Ripper*

Jean Petithuguenin. *The Adventures of Ethel King*

Antonin Reschal. *The Adventures of Miss Boston*

P. de Wattyne & Y. Walter. *Sherlock Holmes vs. Fantômas*

David White. *Fantômas in America*

Pierre Yrondy. *The Adventures of Thérèse Arnaud*

Victor Margueritte. *The Bacheloress; The Companion; The Couple*

SCREENPLAYS

Mike Baron. *The Iron Triangle*

Emma Bull & Will Shetterly. *Nightspeeder; War for the Oaks*

Gerry Conway & Roy Thomas. *Doc Dynamo*

Steve Englehart. *Majorca*

James Hudnall. *The Devastator*

Jean-Marc & Randy Lofficier. *Royal Flush*

J.-M. & R. Lofficier & Marc Agapit. *Despair*

J.-M. & R. Lofficier & Joël Houssin. *City*
Andrew Paquette. *Peripheral Vision*
Robert L. Robinson, Jr. *Judex*
R. Thomas, J. Hendler & L. Sprague de Camp. *Rivers of Time*

NON-FICTION

Stephen R. Bissette. *Blur 1-5. Green Mountain Cinema 1; Teen Angels*
Win Scott Eckert. *Crossovers* (2 vols.)
Jean-Marc & Randy Lofficier. *Shadowmen* (2 vols.)
Randy Lofficier. *Over Here*

ART BOOKS

Jean-Pierre Normand. *Science Fiction Illustrations*
Raven Okeefe. *Raven's L'il Critters; Rave's Faves*
Randy Lofficier & Raven Okeefe. *If Your Possum Go Daylight...*
Daniele Serra. *Illusions*
Randy Lofficier. *Over Here*

HEXAGON COMICS

Franco Frescura & Luciano Bernasconi. *Wampus*
Franco Frescura & Giorgio Trevisan. *CLASH*
L. Bernasconi, J.-M. Lofficier & Juan Roncagliolo. *Phenix*
Claude Legrand, J.-M. Lofficier & L. Bernasconi. *Kabur*
Franco Oneta. *Zembla*
L. Buffolente, Lofficier & J.-J. Dzialowski. *Strangers: Homicron*
Danilo Grossi. *Strangers: Jaydee*
Claude Legrand & Luciano Bernasconi. *Strangers: Starlock*
Thierry Mornet & Juan Roncagliolo. *Guardian of the Republic*
J.-M. Lofficier & others. *Strangers 0: Omens & Origins*
J.-M. Lofficier, M. Garcia, F. Blanco & J. Pima. *Strangers 1: Strangers in a Strange Land*